The

MW01152207

By Jeffery Russell

Dramatis Fae

Serril: A wood elf who would like to apologize to linguists for his section title.

"Moles on a spit!" Gammi said as he handed Durham a skewer. Durham had his mouth half open before the words caught up to his brain.

"Ermmm...what?"

"Classic dwarven dish. Very traditional," the dwarf said. His bald head gleamed under the noon sun and his beard seemed to have acquired as many ingredients as the lunch. "Stuffed 'em with diced-up wormies, just like me Elder used to," he whispered theatrically at a volume precisely calculated to make sure everyone heard. "That's me secret ingredient. Don't tell!"

"My lips are sealed," Durham said. He gave the moles another look and closed his mouth tightly to demonstrate.

There was a sound from across the knoll that resembled a coughing goat. Durham realized it was what passed for Thud's notion of laughter.

"Not what ye was expecting for lunch, eh?" Thud said.

"Well, I..." He glanced helplessly at Ruby, hoping for some help. She was a scribe and had more experience with dwarves than the six hours that Durham had acquired. He'd assumed that, as a fellow human, she would make an effort to be some sort of cultural ambassador to help him survive past lunch. Ruby's current interpretation of being helpful seemed to be a silent smirk. She was perched on a stump in the shade of the oak that crowned the hill, scribbling in her journal as usual. Probably making note of the dwarven secret recipe for worm-stuffed moles on a spit, complete with sketches and charts. She also, he noticed, had bread and cheese—two things conspicuously absent among what the dwarves were eating. They'd been told meals would be provided but Ruby, apparently, had been wise enough to be skeptical. With age came wisdom, the saying went. Based on that, Ruby had an enormous quantity of it. The impression could be belied by the half dozen feathers she had sticking out of the gray bun of her hair. Durham had initially thought she was one of those people that dressed to try to look like one of the fae but eventually he'd realized they were extra quills.

Thud made his way through the scattered groups of dwarves and plopped down on the grass next to him. Somehow he made the action grandiose. The dwarf always seemed to move and act as if he were standing on a stage. He looked the part, with a curled waxed mustache, crisp black kilt and colorful layers of shirts and vest beneath a long black coat with tails. Thud reached out and took the skewer from Durham's unresisting grasp, navigated it past his mustache and happily sank his teeth into it.

"It's like this, lad," he said, wiping mole juice off of his chin with his sleeve. "What's yer favorite food?"

Durham paused, having not expected a direct question after an explanatory lead-in.

"Well, sausage, I guess. And cheese," he added, casting a longing glance toward Ruby's wedge. She scooted the cheese closer to herself without looking up from her journal.

Thud nodded.

"Aye, aye. Fine choices I'm sure." He chewed his mole thoughtfully. "Cheese, where you takes liquid from a cow lady's business parts, mix it with a bit o' juices from a baby cow's fourth stomach and then let it grow all fuzzy-moldy for a few years, eh?"

"I suppose..." Durham said, not having really thought about how cheese was made before.

"And sausage," Thud continued, "where you takes all the bits with the tubes and orifices and grinds 'em up together. Then you takes an intestine, squeeze the turds out of it and stuffs the ground-up tubey bits in."

Durham actually had seen sausage made once but had heretofore successfully repressed the memory.

"Have you ever had a bananer?" Thud asked

"Banana," Ruby corrected. Thud ignored her.

Durham shook his head, figuring that since he had no idea what Thud was talking about that 'no' was a pretty safe answer.

"Fruit from down in Akama. S'like a yeller boomeroo, kinda, except round and sometimes it's red or green."

Durham mentally fished through that sentence for a bit.

"Boomeroo?" he decided on, response-wise.

"Kangarang?" Thud muttered to himself. "Don't recollect exactly. Looks like a crescent moon. Comes back at ya when you throws it."

"The moon? Or the banana?"

Thud narrowed his eyes at him as if speculating on his intelligence.

"Boomerang," Ruby said. Thud ignored her.

"No matter," he went on. "Me point is that you never ate one so it can't be your favorite food, now, can it?"

"No!" Durham said, happy to finally have an answer he was

sure of.

"Your favorite food is sausage and cheese. Why?"

"They...they taste good?"

"So do bananers but they ain't your favorite. Why ain't you never had one?"

"Well, I don't live in Akama, I guess."

"Precisely!" Thud beamed at him as if an important point had been made. He frowned after a second or two as it became obvious that Durham had missed whatever that point had been.

"I'm trying to explain cuisine to you, lad. Work with me here." There was an edge of exasperation in his voice. "You have cows and pigs where you're from, eh?"

"Yes."

"So you have sausage and cheese. You don't have nanner trees though so you ain't had one o' those. Where you live determines your cuisine, is me point."

"Right." Durham felt like he'd finally caught up to at least part of the conversation.

"Now, where do dwarves live?"

"In the Hammerfell Mountains, in Kheldurn." Durham answered. Several of the other dwarves promptly adopted slightly misty-eyed expressions.

"Yes! Literally IN the bleeding mountain." Thud said, jabbing enthusiastically with his finger, presumably in the direction of Kheldurn. "Think we has cows or pigs or nanner trees down there?"

"No?" Durham guessed.

"What we has is moles and worms and shroomies. Fungis and lichens. Wiggly white fish, bats and bugs." He waved his skewered mole demonstratively, much of which he'd somehow managed to consume through the conversation. "So this right here? Fine example of dwarven cuisine, this is."

"Obliged!" Gammi called out. He was under the great oak, chopping more worms.

"Some o' the things I've eaten across the world...well, make ya right happy for a mole on a stick," Thud said.

"You must travel a lot," Durham quickly commented, hoping to change the subject before Thud could launch into a discourse on things he'd eaten in foreign lands.

"Ah, yeh," Thud said, taking the bait. "Comes with the job, don't it?"

"I thought this was a one-time thing."

"Well, no. That's why we was hired. Experience, see. Your king didn't tell ya much, did he?"

"Erm, no." That was one way of putting it, Durham thought. Not only had he not yet ascertained the purpose or destination of the expedition he hadn't even been aware that the king had anything to do with it. Just a message from an assistant vizier, delivered via scrawny pageboy. 'Report courtyard, tomorrow, dawn. Accompany dwarven expedition. Assume several weeks. Food provided. Bring a hat." He hadn't realized that the expedition was comprised of dwarves rather than being a human expedition to visit the dwarves until he'd arrived in the courtyard and seen them all, grubby and brown, beards bristling, bustling around in their pleated black kilts with their oxbear teams hitched to elaborate wagons. Plus Ruby, of course, who, while human, wasn't much larger than the dwarves but managed to stand out by wearing a robe the same color as her name. The Athenaeum always managed to have a scribe on hand whenever anything interesting seemed like it might happen. Durham avoided scribes, figuring that "interesting" was not a word that was necessarily synonymous with "pleasant". He hadn't given the specifics of the message much thought, choosing instead to be stunned that he'd gotten the message at all. It had been a glimmer of hope, a chance.

"So, you do this sort of thing often?" Durham asked, trying

to be vague regarding how little he knew about what exactly they were, in fact, doing.

"It's our job, lad. We're The Dungeoneers!" Thud proclaimed. He gave his chest a thump. "Need something recovered from down deep in some rotten hole? We're the lads to get it for ya."

"What sort of things?"

"Artifacts, man, artifacts! See, no king worth his pointy hat wants some blasted relic laying around where any pig farmer can stumble in, pick it up and, say, overthrow the kingdom. Not good for stability. Take our last job, over in Iskae. The Horn of Ganadahn. Blow into the thing and anything for about a mile in front of ya gets blasted flat. You think the king of Iskae wanted that in anyone's hands other than his? Not by a long shot."

"So...you're adventurers?"

Thud snorted. "Hells, no. Can't abide adventure. 'Adventure' is a word people use to put a shine on lack of preparation and surviving through dumb luck. We're professionals and that means we leave the adventure out of it."

"So, we're headed to somewhere dangerous, then, to recover some powerful magic thing?"

Thud squinted at him for a bit, the question of Durham's

intelligence apparently still unresolved. Even Ruby stopped writing long enough to spare an incredulous look. Thud reached into his breast pocket and pulled out one of the 'cigar' things that he seemed to always have in his mouth whenever he wasn't putting moles into it. As best Durham could tell it was bits of dried leaves rolled up in a larger dry leaf that the dwarf would then light on fire and put in his mouth. This was naturally followed by sporadic coughing and smoke seeping out of his head. Durham hadn't managed to determine the purpose of this yet but had decided it must be of great benefit in order to put up with a head full of smoke.

Thud pulled a branch from the fire and pressed the glowing tip to his cigar, puffing at it until blue smoke began seeping from the corners of his mouth. He blew out a long stream then scratched thoughtfully at his tangle of beard. He had long fingers for a dwarf, adorned with silver rings.

"We're heading to the Crypt of Alaham to recover the Mace of Guffin. Figured you'd be more in the know, what with being the Vault Keeper and all..." he said.

Durham's stomach fell as a few pieces clicked together in his head.

"I'm...I'm not the Vault Keeper. That would be Dorham. We

get mixed up on occasion. I'm just Durham the guard."

Thud let out a low, smoky whistle. Then he grinned.

"Well, looks like you're in for a bit o' adventure then, eh?"

-2-

Durham had started the morning with a helmet that smelled of onions. It wasn't an uncommon problem, as many of the night shift guards used the helmets as soup bowls and, particularly if it was an end of the shift meal, weren't especially diligent about rinsing them out afterward. Finishing a shift with a gob of porridge glued into your hair or an errant pea or two behind your ears was just part of the price you paid for being a guard. The other part of the price was the two copper thumbs a day helmet rental fee and one more for a truncheon. Technically both articles of equipment were optional. Reality, however, was otherwise inclined. Without the stick no one took your orders very seriously. Without the official guard helmet you were just a guy with a stick and there were plenty enough of those to go around already. Then there was the thumb a day meal fee, another to put in the dented milk can that sat next to the coffee urn and three more for a bunk in the barracks. Their pay was a silver talon a day but the paymaster didn't even carry talons as far as Durham knew. He just showed up with a sack of copper thumbs, deducted your expenses and gave you your change, minus an additional thumb for administrative expenses.

Durham had been punctual, as always, when he arrived at the caravan. It was a lesson his adopted father had driven in to him. If you aren't where you're supposed to be then the things that are supposed to happen to you are going to happen to someone else, he'd always said.

In Durham's experience, many of those things were of the sort that he'd have rather happened to someone else but he was still in the habit of punctuality. In this instance he was in agreement with his father. This was an opportunity, the first he'd had in years, and he had no intention of sleeping through it. He'd spent far more time in a dead-end guard posting than he was comfortable admitting to himself and now, at last, he had a chance to show his worth.

The castle courtyard was already bustling at sunrise with activity of the sort that the nobility expected to have done before they awakened and carried out by the sort of people who didn't have much say in the amount of sleep they got. Woodsmoke hung low in the still dawn air and maids with yokes of steaming water skillfully pinwheeled their way through a stream of scullions rolling ale casks and barrels of potatoes and onions through the puddles and mud. The caravan he was to accompany had been pretty obvious in the midst of the bustle but the dwarves had rather surprised him. It was about four times as many dwarves as the sum total he'd seen in his life. He'd approached the wagons tentatively.

"What's your business, sir?" a dwarf asked as he neared. He had little round spectacles, a long narrow beard with a mustache and a large green turban with a blue jewel at the front. He was carrying a scroll nailed to a board, allowing him to write on it as he strutted around. It lent him an air of administrative authority as effectively as a stick and a helmet provided guard authority.

"Durham reporting for duty, sir. I've received orders to accompany the caravan."

"Right then," the dwarf said. He squinted at the scroll, muttering. "Durham…quantity: one." He made a check-mark. "I'm Nibbly. Welcome to the company." He gestured toward the wagons. "On ya go." He began yelling orders at other dwarves, apparently of the opinion that Durham had received sufficient instruction.

The wagons were unlike any Durham had seen before. Or, rather, they were like different types of wagons he'd seen but combined in a strange hybridization. Each was unique, seemingly designed for specialized purposes and then further customized by whichever dwarves were associated with it. Some were of wood, some of metal. Several had multiple levels, complete with balconies and cupolas. Smokestacks on a few, spikes on others, some open, some enclosed, some plain, some brightly painted in blues and greens and yellows like nomad wagons. A woman sat on one of them. She wore a wide cone hat, a deep red robe and the black cassock that marked her as a scribe. It was one of the more ordinary looking wagons, full of grain sacks, but with a row of trunks and bins ringing the exterior. The scribe was alternating between casting an appraising eye at what was being loaded onto the wagons and writing in a journal, likely recording her observations. Durham had once seen a stall at a street festival selling dolls with heads made from dried apples. The woman on the wagon would have fit right in amongst them, raisin eyes in a wrinkled apple head. Durham climbed up next to her.

"Racist," she said.

"Sorry?"

"Ten wagons to choose from and you pick the only one that has a human on it. Racist."

"I...uh...I don't speak Kheldurn," Durham fumbled.

She grinned at him. "Just bumping your quill. I'm Ruby." She offered a wizened hand for Durham to shake.

"Durham."

"Sitting next to a dwarf is not without its own hazards and I tend to avoid it as well. In any case, no one who isn't a dwarf speaks Kheldurn and they go to great effort to keep it that way. Allows them to speak freely amongst themselves anywhere they go. One of the more serious crimes among the dwarves is teaching Kheldurn to a non-dwarf." She started writing in her journal again, as if making note of this. "Regardless, they all speak Karthorian like you do. Or at least something that occasionally resembles it. You'll have no problem speaking with them. It's unlikely that they'll speak Kheldurn where you can hear them."

"They have a unique accent," Durham said.

"Yes. Dwarves are quite good at mimicking human accents and, when they learn a new word, learn the accent of whomever taught them the word at the same time. These particular dwarves have been all over the world and learned to speak in a hundred different cities. They consider all pronunciations equally valid and switch between them at whim." Ruby pointed at a spectacularly rotund dwarf, possibly the first person Durham had ever seen who was actually wider than he was tall. "Gong there, for instance, managed this morning to say the word 'lollygagging' with a different accent on each individual syllable. Truly a remarkable feat. Gong is the head of the Vanguard team. First group into the danger spots. The dwarf over there in the top hat is Thud. He's the head of the company." Durham looked where she was pointing. Even without the top hat Thud would have been easy to spot. He strode through the courtyard alternating between calling out instructions in a booming voice and roaring with laughter at brief snatches of conversation with those he passed, his long black coat swirling. The other dwarves seemed to orbit around him.

"Those seem unusual names for dwarves," Durham said.

"Expert on dwarven names, now are you?" Ruby arched an eyebrow. "Many are earned names. Dwarves are quite taken with giving themselves new names as tributes to notable deeds. Or sometimes because they just like the sound of them. Gong took his name from a sound he managed to produce from a troll's head, so I'm told."

"Thud too?"

"Short for Thaddeus. Seems he's not fond of his full name."

"Ginny!" Thud yelled from across the courtyard, waving at a nearby dwarf laden with tool-chests.

Based on the name, Durham half expected Ginny to be female but Ginny sported a trim pointy beard and a neat mustache.

"Reporting, sir!" Ginny said, in a female octave.

Durham shot a questioning look at Ruby.

"Dwarves are sequential hermaphroditic parthenogens," Ruby said, anticipating his question.

"What?"

"They can change back and forth from male to female and are capable of fertilizing themselves to make more dwarves. They exhibit what we regard as male characteristics, typically, but some favor a more feminine approach."

Durham sat with his mouth hanging open. Ruby poked him in the tongue with her quill feather making him gag and sputter.

"So, Ginny is, what, short for Regina? Virginia?"

"I rather think it's long for 'Gin'," Ruby answered. "She's head of hazard team and Thud's second."

"So, the changing sex thing. How does that work? Does it

take a while or is it the sort of thing that might happen in the middle of a conversation?"

"Hard to say," Ruby said. "Does she need to clear her throat or did she just become a male? Is he just pausing for thought or did he just impregnate himself mid-sentence?" She shrugged. "Dwarf physiology isn't really my field."

"Is there an easy way to tell?"

"Which sex a dwarf is at the moment? Not that I'm aware of but I haven't managed to think of a situation where it would matter, either, so I've not dwelt on it much. Now, if you'll excuse me, I have a great deal to make note of in my journal." With that she went back to writing. Durham took the hint and moved to the next wagon in line. It was full of metal boxes and weapons wrapped in oilcloth which turned out to not be quite as comfortable to sit on as the sacks of grain. It also had what appeared to be a fully functional smithy crammed onto the back of it.

He felt that he'd completely fumbled the conversation with Ruby which didn't come as a surprise as it was the first conversation he'd had in seven months. It was an experiment he'd devised. When one's job consisted of standing in one place for a long period of time, one tended to have time to do a bit of speculating. It had occurred to him that, as a guard, the majority of his daily interactions with people consisted of the same few phrases uttered over and over, everyone mindlessly following a script that allowed them to avoid any actual interaction.

He'd narrowed it down to thirteen words and phrases and had determined to see how long he could get away with using them exclusively. 'Yes' and 'No' were the obvious ones, though he freely allowed variations such as 'Yes, sir,' or 'No, ma'am', figuring that the content of the message remained the same. Likewise with 'Halt' and 'Stop'. 'Hello, how are you', 'I'm fine' and 'Have a nice day' were his power phrases. Those three alone managed to do over half of the daily work. 'Move along' was a good one to use if the other person showed any inclination to say something that would require a response not on the list. 'One of those, please' served well for buying anything and 'Thank you' was enough to conclude those interactions. 'I don't know, ask him' was a suitable response to most questions, both answering and diverting the questioner to whichever random bystander Durham had indicated. Phrase eleven was a bit of a wild card, allowing him to state whatever amount someone had to pay to enter the city. This one was particularly important as padded fees were the majority of any city guard's income. City entrance fees, taxes collected, bribes, merchant incentives and stolen property recovery. No one joined the city guard to become rich —the main appeal for most of the guards was being given a big stick. The one slightly enviable aspect of Durham's posting was that it afforded a steady income from the regular flow of sheep coming through the gate. One copper thumb per head in entrance tax, one copper per dozen as a "counting fee". The twelfth was another wild card, being the interrogatives: who, what, when, where, how and why. Durham's thirteenth phrase was the least used in conversation but was the phrase Durham used more than the other twelve combined.

"Bugger it."

As with any experiment, ideally one learns something from the results. The success of Durham's conversational study had taught him two things. First was that he led a spectacularly uninteresting life. Second was that he was a spectacularly uninteresting person.

ɛɛɛ

There is a distinct evolutionary advantage to being fuzzy, as much of the mammal kingdom had discovered, particularly when you wanted a human to scratch your back. The dwarven evolutionary tree had embraced this concept wholeheartedly only to discover that once you started talking and expressing opinions a human's desire to scratch your back became directly inverse to how fuzzy it was.

From his new perch on the armory wagon, Durham was attempting to determine just how many dwarves there were. He was finding it difficult as the majority of them seemed comprised entirely of leather and hair and all of them were strutting about, constantly disappearing and reappearing from behind different wagons or weaving amongst the shaggy oxbears as they were harnessed. He had more luck once he turned his attention to the wagons. Most of them were loaded already, piled high and tarped in a manner that didn't leave much space for passengers. The bench on the front of each wagon had room for two which, with ten wagons, indicated between ten and twenty dwarves.

"Oi! You there!"

Durham looked down to see a dwarf, which wasn't too much of a surprise, given the circumstances. Apart from his kilt the dwarf wore only a leather harness, displaying a physique like an early draft from a sculptor that worked with meat and hair.

The morning was chilly and Durham had to consciously avoid staring at the dwarf's nipples.

"You riding with me?" the dwarf asked.

"Is that okay? Is this your wagon?"

"Aye to both o' your questions." The dwarf thrust his hand up. "I'm Clink."

Durham had to lean to a precarious angle in order to complete the handshake.

"Durham."

"Watch yer butt back there. Lotsa pointy bits. A deep shaft better than some of the other wagons, however. Least you ain't riding with the chickens."

"I'll manage," Durham said, carefully leaning his official guard stick in a place where it would be easy to get to. He was surprised that he was going to get to ride in the wagons at all. Caravan guards typically had to walk alongside doing their best to exude menace. The realization came to him that there were no other caravan guards in evidence. There were a few guards on the wall above the courtyard gate, leaning on the parapet and watching but obviously on post. Come to think of it, the dwarves didn't look much in the need of guarding.

"I get to take me rest for a bit now," Clink said as he climbed up and positioned himself on the wagon bench. "Advantage of having a two ale bladder, I s'pose. Up before everyone else so I got me work done early." He gestured at the oxbears. "These are the ladies that'll get us where we're going. That's Left Butt on the right and Right Butt on the left. I was standing in front of the wagon when I named 'em so the names made a bit more sense at the time, even though I was looking at their heads."

Durham considered that. "You could switch them, maybe."

"That'd just confuse the poor dears. See, Right Butt don't see so good out of her right eye. She hears Left Butt on that side and it spooks her just enough to keep her moving. When she's nervous she flicks her tail back and forth. It gives Left Butt a tickle now and then and that spooks her just enough to keep her moving. If I swapped 'em around we'd never get anywhere."

"I meant maybe you could switch their names."

"Last thing we needs is two oxbears having an identity crisis. They don't mind if you call 'em Arby and Elbe, though, if that makes peace with your propriety."

Durham nodded, as if this was somehow valuable information. "I'm surprised you didn't call them Left Ass and Right Ass."

Clink shook his head. "Too obvious. I feel that the

avoidance o' the overt pun adds an element o' mystery lending depth an' obscurity to the name's humor."

"Arby and Elbe it is, then," said Durham.

Another dwarf arrived at the wagon and clambered up. He had a tiny face, wizened and dark, almost lost in a large black hood and was holding an apple in his mouth to leave his hands free.

Clink waved his hand. "This is Cardamon. Cardamon, Durham."

"Mmmph," Cardamon said, shaking Durham's hand. His hand was tiny and felt like soft leather. Cardamon sat, tugged his hood over his eyes, propped his legs on the foot board and began snoring, apple still in his mouth.

"Cardamon ain't much for talking until around noon or so," Clink said.

Durham saw that most of the other dwarves were aboard their wagons as well. The few still on the ground began directing the procession with elaborate arm gestures as the caravan slowly began to move forward.

"Forward Butts!" Clink called and with a lurch and a creak their wagon took its place in line. They moved through the gate, rumbled across the drawbridge and into the cobbled streets of

Karthor. It was early enough that traffic was still light—mostly street merchants lugging their wares to their stalls. They stopped and stared as the dwarves passed, some even cheering and waving. Dwarves weren't a common site in Karthor. Most of the residents had never even seen one outside of a traveling circus and were perhaps assuming that that's precisely what their caravan was. The dwarves returned the waves cheerfully. Durham basked in the bit of reflected glory, imagining that their audience was envious of his being part of the procession. He even tried a wave or two before realizing that no one was paying him the slightest bit of attention.

He sank back against the side of the wagon, deciding to try and get comfortable instead. The roads around Karthor were well patrolled and it would be at least mid-afternoon before they reached anywhere that would potentially require a caravan guard. They passed through the dawn gate. The air was cool and crisp, the horizon over distant farm-clad hills tinged pink with the fading remnants of the sunrise. Smooth roads and oat fields as far as the eye could see.

He had to appropriate a new ride after lunch. Cardamon was now driving the wagon he'd spent the morning on and Clink was in back working the smithy. Durham wasn't sure what Clink was actually doing but it involved a lot of sparks and loud hammering. He'd guessed that he'd be able to find a more comfortable ride than the 'hard, metal, spiky things' wagon and had selected one that was loaded mostly with barrels. His new driver had given him an amiable nod then turned his attention back to his oxbears. They were still rolling their way through farm fields and thatch-roofed villages and the ruts of the track were still reasonably smooth. He'd managed to swipe a few eggs from the chicken coops on the ninth wagon to make up for the lack of lunch. Eggs, apparently, weren't a traditional part of dwarven cuisine and Goin, the animal wrangler, had seemed skeptical that Durham intended to eat them.

"Never quite got the taste for 'em meself," Goin said. "Like snot when they ain't cooked and rubbery when they is."

"You don't keep the chickens for the eggs?" Durham asked.

"Well, no. We use the eggs to make more chickens," Goin said. He paused thoughtfully. "Well, the chickens do, at least. I try to stay out of the particulars."

"Do you eat the chickens?"

"Sometimes," Goin shrugged. "When we run low on frogs. Taste almost like frog, chickens do. Mostly we use 'em to find traps in the dungeons. Generally not much left worth eating after they find one. 'Less you want to scrape their bits out from between spikes crusted up with gods know what or who else."

Durham had chosen that as his cue to bow out of the conversation to try to figure out how to cook his eggs on the back of a moving cart. He'd settled for holding a torch under a fry pan which produced something unlikely to sway Goin's opinion on eggs.

The Crypt of Alaham, Thud had named it. Seeking the Mace of Guffin. Ruby had silently handed him a journal from her satchel as they'd packed up after lunch. Trying to read it while bouncing along in the back of the wagon was making his eggs sit poorly.

"Alaham, Sorc./Nec., 3rd Karthorian Dynasty, 314-358. First noted in region of Tanahael, 350, became council member of city-state of Tanahael 5 years later. Accused of necromancy by one Lord Wingen of the Tanahael council. Responded by assassinating entire council and reanimating their corpses to declare him king. Reign renowned and feared for cruelty and execution spectacles (ref Scr. Wick III Vol XVII). Purportedly achieved lich status and enslaved 'dozens of dead', 358. Tanahael later destroyed, purportedly via livestock reanimation (citation needed). Alaham believed responsible. Mausoleum located one league N Tanahael crossroads. Month of Moons, 873; Report re: Radish Wilson, farmer, claiming active undead presence in vicinity of ruins of Tanahael. As of this writing considered to be actively dangerous location. Avoid."

He had to sound each word out. Reading skills weren't a notable requirement for city guard duty.

Durham leaned forward toward the two dwarves riding on the front of the cart in hopes of making it clear that he was talking to them. He'd not gotten their names and had so far been frustrated in his hopes of either of them referring to each other by name in order for him to learn them.

"I've got a question, if you don't mind. I'm Durham, by the way."

"Dadger Ben, acquisitions team and public relations," the dwarf driving the cart said. He had a wispy white beard and a bald head capped with faded blue tattoos. "Call me Dadger." He jabbed at his partner. "This here's Giblets. He's our geologist. If he don't know something about stones then it ain't worth knowin'. Pleased ter meet ya." Giblets gave a backwards wave without looking back. Giblets' beard was trimmed close to his chin and he seemed to be missing an eye. It was hard to tell as he kept that side of his face screwed into a perpetual squint that obscured whatever might or might not be there. He'd spent the ride so far rocking back and forth on the bench mumbling a barely audible but relentlessly constant stream of what sounded like gibberish. He made Durham slightly nervous.

"Now, what's yer question?" Dadger asked.

"What's a lich?" Durham asked.

His question was greeted with several seconds of puzzled silence.

"Yer mean like wot a puppy does?" Dadger finally asked.

"No, like this Alaham fellow."

"Ah, a lich! Ya say the last part like the beginning of 'chicken'."

"Chicken lich," Giblets mumbled. "Now 'at'd be somethin'." He spoke like his mouth was full of marbles. Durham was perplexed that he now found himself in his second chicken conversation of the afternoon and wondered if this was the sort of thing that a soothsayer would consider an omen.

"A lich is an undead type thingy," Dadger said. "Wizard

hides his life somewhere outsides his body, like in a vase or a jewel or somethin' then keeps strutting around in the dead body. Makes 'em tough to kill as you have to find 'n' break whatever it is they hid their life in."

"In a prophylactery, it's called." Giblets said.

Ruby began having a loud coughing fit in the wagon in front of them.

"Or transport 'em," the other dwarf added. "Prob'ly the easiest way rather than playin' at hide 'n' go seeksies."

"Transport them?" Durham asked.

"Yeh, they gots to stay kinda close to their thingmajig or their body just keels right over. 'Course their life is still bottled up somewhere and if they get lucky and get close enough again, well, then you're right back where ya started.

"How did he destroy a town with..." Durham looked at the journal again. "...livestock reanimation?"

"Well," Dadger said, sucking at his mustache. "I imagine having yer dinner come back to life in yer stomach and expressing its displeasure might be the gist of it. Along with the bones from all your prior dinners knocking around the place. I'm hypothesizing though."

"And the mace?"

"What about it?"

"What is it? What gives it artifact status?"

Dadger shrugged.

"Don't really know. In facts, our employers tends to keeps things like that pretty close to the vest, if ya know what I'm saying, lest we be tempted to keep it, I s'poses. We tends to find out anyway. Thud will give us the inside whisper afore we go in after it. He considers it a matter o' safety, regardless of what our employers might think."

"An artifact, though," Durham said. "I imagine that they tend to be worth quite a bit..."

"Don't go thinkin' like that. We gets paid well for our services and successful jobs leads to more jobs down the road. Plus, we gets to keep anything else we finds and you'll gets yer fair share." He puffed his diminutive chest out. "Dangerous artifacts removed, treasure obtained, dangerous places made safe. That's the Dungeoneers, lad. That's what buys our moles 'n' ale."

"So this mace is with this necromancer lich?"

"Aye, seems he was known fer carryin' it. Locked away in his crypt, somewheres. Ruin the size of Tanahael is bound to attract adventurer types and if they recover the mace, well, who knows what they'd do, eh? So we're gonna get it first 'n' yer king can lock it up nice 'n' tight in his vaults."

"So, people can actually do this? Necromancy?" he asked.

"Don't figger it comes easy, lad, but yeh, fella with a bit o' talent in the sorcery department and a cracked nog gets the notion and next thing ya know yer ancestors is walkin' 'round the town."

"But...why? What use do walking dead people have?"

"Slaves, maybe? The sort that don't rebel or need feedin'. Secrets that were lost. Key to immortality of sorts, if'n ya don't mind not takin' yer own meat along with ya. Armies, too. Surely you know the Daemonwars, no? The skeletal army the Hermits raised to turn the tide?"

"Yes, but...I guess I thought that was mostly myth. Or just not possible anymore. That kind of magic is gone, isn't it?"

"Well, not so much gone as controlled by The Hermits, mainly so's we don't have more Daemonwars. But, believes me, 'controlled' and 'eliminated' 's two diff'rent things. Meanin' no offense but you're a city lad, ain't ya? Once you're out in the wilds, out near the fae mounds and the daemon hollows, well, magic is a bit thicker, if'n ya get my meaning. I don't reckon this Alaham fellow is powerful enough that he has an army, on account of his not being one of the Hermits, but there's bound to be a couple dozen at least."

"So you're seriously expecting walking skeletons in this place?"

"More concerned with the sword-swingin' skellies, frankly."

"How do they even move with no muscle?"

"Well, that's the magic part, ain't it? Thinks of 'em more as poppets where you can't see the sticks an' strings. Can't really say much more than that, as I ain't too learned on the subject of neckermancy. I expect we'll get briefed on that too. Thud likes to be thorough"

-4-

They camped that night on the lee side of a grassy bluff near where a stream burbled its way across the road. The dwarves were slightly more formal with their dinner arrangements than they had been with lunch, producing eight small stumps from one of the wagons, setting them out in pairs and laying boards across them to form benches. They sat five abreast and laid another board across their knees to form a table. Durham's knees were too tall to fit under the board and the clay bowls were too hot to hold so he ended up sitting on a wet log and using his helmet as a soup bowl. The meal was stew which Gammi had let bubble away all afternoon over a coal box in the back of the cook wagon. It was thick, brown and lumpy and tasted good but Durham made a point of not asking what was in it for fear of finding out. The sun wandered behind a low range of hills to the West as they ate and a few pixies began flitting around at the edge of the firelight. Goin caught a couple of them in nets and popped them into fairy lanterns. The lanterns were spherical in shape, a design Durham hadn't seen before. Goin hung the lanterns from poles and gave each pixie a bit of cake. They glowed with blue light, bright and happy. The dwarves produced decks of cards and began playing a game that Durham found hard to follow. Dwarven decks had the usual suits of mugs, coins, swords and wands but had two additional suits as well, chains and stones, which made dwarven card games excessively complex.

Thud sidled up next him as he watched. He was puffing on one of his cigars and his rings glittered in the faelight.

"Much for cards?" he asked.

Durham shrugged. "Not often. The guards usually play dice

instead." The truth was that most of the guards in Karthor were a bit on the mentally thick side and found the rules of most card games a bit too much to manage. Durham had always felt that the strategy in dice had more randomness than he was willing to put money on. Consequently, he didn't play much of anything.

Thud settled onto the bench next to him with a flourish of coat arranging. "Being a guard a family sorta thing? Was your father a guard?"

Durham shrugged again. "Not sure. Never knew my father."

Every conversation in the camp instantly ceased. Thud recoiled back from him. Durham felt a surge of panic. Had he violated some sort of obscure dwarven rule of etiquette?

"No father? And your mother?" There was a note of urgency in Thud's voice. Of fear, even a tinge of anger.

"Didn't know her either. I was apprenticed from an orphanage to a carpet weaver. I wasn't much good at it, though."

"Dammit, lad, we're going into a dungeon after an artifact. Why didn't you tell me you was an orphan?"

"I didn't...uh..."

"Know of any prophecies concerning you? Got any strange birthmarks at all? Weird dreams? Peculiar old men acting grandfatherly? Unusual pets or trinkets?"

Durham sat with his mouth hanging open.

"No?" he finally managed. He thought for a moment. "I had a cat that used to puke in my boots but I thought that sort of thing was typical as far as cats went."

Thud was pacing back and forth, furiously puffing at his cigar. "The whole reason kingdoms hire us is to keep artifacts out of the hands of people like you," he said. "Ain't you never listened to a bard before? Every story that begins with an orphan ends with a destiny. And there's always an artifact along the way. Deliberately putting the two together is like throwing coals at a powder barrel. If we wasn't a day out of Karthor I'd be of half a mind to send you walking back."

"Sorry," Durham said, lamely. He wasn't quite sure what he was apologizing for. His parentage, or lack thereof, hadn't been something that he'd felt he'd had much say on.

"Well, can't be helped now," Thud said. "Orphan, here through unusual circumstance, menial background. Don't look good." He shook his head. "No good at all. Least we got a scribe here in case some history is about to happen."

Ruby certainly had her journal out, which wasn't, however, particularly unusual. She was sitting on the far side of the fire, quill dancing across the page.

"Damned if that didn't turn this from just another week on the job into a potential adventure," Thud went on. "We'll have to lay in some extra precautions." He clasped Durham on the shoulder. "Nothing against you, lad, ain't your doin' but you did just mightily complicate things. Whether you're meant to be here or not you still gets to do the job, eh? You're here representing our employer. In some small ways that makes you our boss, but mostly it means that you'll be along with us every step of the way inside the dungeon. Once we're on site you think of yerself as me shadow, got it? Someone's gonna expect you to be able to make an accounting of things when ya git back, so we wants to make sure you actually do get back as well as have something to give an accounting of. You stick with me like lichen on stone so I can keep an eye on ya. That way if any kind o' destiny pops up might be I can at least steer it clear o' me team."

Dwarves, it turned out, were difficult to sleep next to. Durham lay on his bedroll beneath one of the wagons, contemplating the wooden slats above him. Clink and Cardamon slept near him, in hammocks strung between the axles, inhaling through their anterior ends with great gargling honks and then exhaling from their posterior ends with equally disturbing sounds. To make matters worse they were out of sync with each other. He'd tried jamming tufts of grass into his ears and nostrils but this turned out to not even slightly improve his chances of sleeping.

Yesterday a guard, today an under-qualified expedition escort with possible prophetic complications. Next up a dungeon full of death and horror. He suspected that even if the dwarves were the most pleasant of sleeping companions he wouldn't be resting any easier. Thud had made it clear that sitting on the wagons and waiting while the dungeon was explored wasn't going to be an available option. Not that Durham would have wanted to do so. Even if I'm not supposed to be here this is still an opportunity to prove myself. His guard posting was the bottom rung of a tall career ladder and he'd been stuck there for years. Just because he now found himself on a different ladder didn't mean that he couldn't climb it. Surely returning from a dungeon expedition would be worth something in the guard promotion department, wouldn't it? The trick is managing to return, ideally in and with the same number of pieces. Thud had also made it clear that Durham would be next to him the whole way and it wasn't in Thud's best interests to get killed which offered a small sliver of solace. He pictured himself alongside Thud, kneeling before the King, presenting the mace.

"Who is this fine young guard," the King would say.

"Private Durham, sir."

"A mere private?"

"He saved the expedition, your Highness," Thud rested his hand on Durham's shoulder.

"We must recognize this mighty achievement."

And then the sound of the royal sword being drawn, the taps, one on the right shoulder, one on the left.

"Rise, Sir Dorham."

"Durham, your Highness."

"Er...Durham. Of course."

At some point the darkness of the underside of the wagon turned into the darkness of the inside of his eyelids. Dawn came along about five minutes later.

Late morning saw them leaving the area under Karthor's influence and entering into the long wild stretch that lay between Karthor and Iskae. Fir trees grew thick to either side of the track, towering overhead, slicing the sky into a gray ribbon of watery light. It was a damp morning, less of a rain, more of a mist with a surly attitude. Durham rode on the second wagon with Ruby, Gong and Nibbly, the dwarf who had checked him in the prior morning. The back half of the wagon was enclosed into a compartment like a carriage, the front half stacked with empty barrels. Ruby was inside the compartment. The wagon sagged slightly toward the front right corner where Gong was sitting, methodically shelling and eating hazelnuts. His melonesque physique was clad in partial plate mail and the front right wheel creaked on every bump in the road. Nibbly was squeezed to the side of the bench to allow Gong ample room but didn't seem to mind. He was whistling cheerfully, his turban bobbing back and forth to the tune. Durham sat atop the wagon's compartment which gave him a good view over the lead wagon of the road ahead. The front wagon was Thud and Ginny's, nomad style, a bright green and blue home on wheels that looked fresh from a circus. It matched Thud perfectly. The shadows grew thick around them as they moved between the trees and the wagon train began lighting up with fairy lanterns which mainly served to turn the gloom blue. Thud clambered into view atop the front wagon and made a complicated series of hand gestures. Nibbly reached under his bench and pulled out a crossbow.

"Is that what those hand gestures meant?" Durham asked.

"I've no idear wot them hand gestures meant but typically they all boils down to 'get yer crossbows out,'" Nibbly said.

Gong sighed with a noise like a pipe organ in need of a wash.

"I do know what them hand signals mean and would be more than happy to correct you but, in this case, you're actually right." He cracked a final hazelnut, popped it in his mouth then pulled his own crossbow from under the bench. It was quite a bit larger than Nibbly's and bristled with accessories, the cup-holder being the only one that Durham was able to readily identify.

"I don't have a crossbow," Durham said. "Just my truncheon."

"You thought you was escortin' a caravan and you left without a crossbow?" Gong asked. He was working a lever on the side of his that ratcheted the string into the cocked position.

"It's recommended gear for caravan duty but I couldn't afford the rental fee."

"Well, if anything gets past Madame K'chunk here I'll be sure to refer 'em to you." He slotted a bolt the size of a baguette.

"Here, take mine," Nibbly said, handing it back. "I ain't

much in the crossbow department. Me eyes ain't so good for much more than ten foot or so. Besides, I got a spare." He pulled a much smaller crossbow out from under his kilt.

Nibbly's crossbow was smaller and lighter than the ones Durham was used to but seemed to almost vibrate with constrained energy. It didn't look to have ever been fired before. The string was still coated with beeswax.

Thud hopped off the front wagon and stood alongside the road until they caught up to him. He grabbed onto the side of the wagon and hung there as they rolled on.

"What d'yer know about this area?" he asked Durham. "Bandit problems? Any fae?"

"I think there are supposed to be some forest elves out here," Durham said after a moment's thought. It was his first opportunity to be of any use and he didn't want to flub it. "They're peaceable enough as long as you follow the usual elf rules. No bandits, on account of that. No fae mounds that I've heard of, at least not close to the road. The East road doesn't see much travel, as there's nothing really out here to travel to. Nothing for a long ways, at least. I suppose that the big stretch of nothing is where Tanahael was?"

Ruby appeared from the compartment behind them. She

squinted at him. "What did you learn growing up about Tanahael?" Ruby asked. She had her journal out and quill poised.

"Just that it was the name of a kingdom that used to be to the East. And that it was haunted. I expect you have a better idea of its history than I do."

"Well, yes," Ruby said, "but we like to hear local accounts of regional history in case there is a detail mentioned that we'd not heard before. Sometimes the smallest detail can open up an entire new scope of understanding of a piece of history."

"Did I add much?"

"Not a thing."

"You even knew about the elves?"

"The Nallach Fae. Peaceful, deciduous. Omnivores, but not of sapients."

Thud gave a satisfied nod. "Wood elves likely means we won't run into much in the way o' beastie problems either."

"Aren't dwarves a type of elf?" Durham asked. He seemed to recall having heard that once.

"Just as fair warning that's the type of question that could garner you a punch in the nose, depending on who you're asking," Thud said. He cast a sidelong glance at Gong, who looked ready to punch Durham in the nose. "But yeah. Lot of dwarves don't like to admit it but we're part of the fae too." He got a look in his eyes that Durham was coming to recognize as Thud warming to a topic. "See, the place you're born determines what type o' fae you are. Meaning your environment. Dwarves is the fae o' the mountains. Wood elves is forests, obviously. Then you got yer merfolk, yer harpies, trolls and whatnot. We all basically get crossed with our environment, or some with types of creatures. Pixies is the bug fae, goblins the rodents. But us bein' related don't exactly mean we see eye to eye on much. We has as much common ground in our thinkin' as you humans do with monkeys. Forest elves is concerned with keeping the forest protected as if you cut down too many trees then you ain't got a forest. Dwarves, on the other hand, ain't too worried about a mountain going anywhere. We dig down in and pull out all the shiny bits. The forest elves see that as being exploitative, whereas we see them as being basically useless. Fortunately we don't cross paths too often being as there ain't too much in the way o' forests under the mountains."

Durham looked at the deep shadows between the mossy trees suspiciously. "Do you think they'll cause us any problems because you're dwarves?"

"Naw. They're watching us, most certain, but as long as we don't go lopping trees down we should be fine. Don't bother looking too much. If they don't want to be seen then you're not likely to spot one. Wood elves is all barky looking with leafy hair. If they sit still they just look like a shrubbery."

"What about the mounds? What type of fae are they?"

"Them's the fae of magic and they're right bastards. You see one o' them you put a crossbow bolt between their eyes and start running."

"A crossbow will kill one?"

"Nope. But the bolt in their head might catch on a tree branch or something and slow them down for a second or two."

"What do they look like?"

"Depends on who's doing the looking. They usually look like someone you desire. Someone you'd want to follow, accept an invitation from. And then you're not seen again for a decade or two or ne'er seen again at all, depending on if they make you a guest at their feast or the main course. Every century or so they has an extra big feast and they sends out the Wild Hunt. And they ain't huntin' for deer. They'll clean out a whole village if they come across one."

Thud finished his cigar and made as if to flick it off into the woods but then thought better of it. He ground it out on the side of the wagon and stuck the butt in his pocket. "No need to go antagonizing them," he said. "I got to finish making me rounds of the other wagons. Don't go shooting them crossbows at anything less'n I tells you too." He hopped off of the wagon, waiting by the side of the road for the next one. Durham looked out at the trees, at the bushes moving softly in the breeze, his fingers sweating against the crossbow's stock.

♫♫♫

It was late when they heard the crashing noise from the left side of the road. Something big, moving amongst the trees, just out of sight. The trees bent around it, creaking, snapping back into place behind it with drunken swaying and swirls of leaves. The dwarves reacted so quickly and precisely it almost looked choreographed. They leapt from the wagons, crossbows in hand, rolling underneath and taking cover behind the wheels. Durham followed after with slightly less grace, crawling beneath the wagon next to Nibbly. Gong had taken cover on the far side rather than trying to fit beneath the wagon. The noise came again, closer, followed by a great snorting noise. A stand of alder saplings parted like a crackling curtain and a massive beast stepped into view.

It was a moose. Durham had seen the head of one on the wall in an inn once but, without the rest of the body it had looked more comical than intimidating. The head certainly hadn't given the correct impression of just how large the full package was. It was nearly seven feet tall at the shoulders and half as wide, a great slab of shaggy muscle balanced on spindly looking legs. Its antlers jutted out from the sides of its head like giant spiked wings, framing a nose that looked large enough to fit a saddle to. It stopped at the sight of the row of wagons and oxbears, its tiny eyes glaring. It made a long high pitched noise of sheer hate, somewhere between a trumpet and a scream, following it with a low bellow that made Durham very much wish to visit the jakes. The wagon above them creaked and slid a bit as the oxbears considered beating a hasty retreat.

"Oi!" came a yell from just in front of the wagon. Thud was there. He had a lit torch in one hand and was waving his arms back and forth. "Clink! Load The Diplomat! I'll try and keep it occupied!"

Thud had the beast's attention. Unfortunately, Thud was about four feet away from Durham. The moose made a chuffing noise and pawed at the dirt with a hoof. Thud darted behind the wagon, placing it between them. The moose snorted, lowered its head and leapt forward with a shocking burst of speed.

There was an immense splintering noise and the wagon was suddenly no longer over Durham's head. He was still in shade, however. The moose was now standing directly over him. He glanced over his shoulder. The wagon was on its side, its wall staved in where the moose had hit it. Nibbly and Gong were crawling away from it, caked with mud. The oxbears were in a tangle in front of the wagon, rolling around awkwardly trying to regain their feet. He couldn't see Ruby. She'd been inside. Thud ran past them, still waving the torch, trying to turn the moose's attention away from the oxbears and the wagons. The moose turned to follow and Durham scrambled out from under it, trying to avoid getting stepped on. He found himself in a position directly behind it, loaded crossbow in hand. The arse end of the beast was only slightly more attractive than the front had been. He took aim at the obvious bullseye, so to speak, and fired.

The moose leapt in to the air with a bray, legs splayed out, managing to hunch its butt forward at the same time. It landed and came about in a shuffle of legs. Durham now found himself facing the front of a moose with an unloaded crossbow in hand. It looked to have very rapidly come to the conclusion that he was the responsible party, largely due to him being the only target available. Durham crawled backwards on his elbows as quickly as he could. There was a scattered sound of more crossbows firing and the moose danced and roared. Then came a loud chonk noise from the end of the wagon train and a bolt the size of an oar hit the moose in the head. It was a glancing blow, the massive bolt deflecting high and spinning off into the trees but it was enough to stagger the moose. It swayed on its feet and shook its head. Durham looked back to see Clink on one of the rear wagons standing at the trigger of a ballista, a crossbow the size of a rowboat. The Diplomat.

Another bugling call came from the woods. The moose turned to look, possibly glad to have an excuse to leave off. The call came again and it trumpeted back, jogging back into the trees, disappearing as suddenly as it had arrived.

"More mooses?" Nibbly said from under the wreckage of the wagon, eyes widening.

"Moose." Durham said.

"Where?" Nibbly raised his crossbow.

"No, the plural of moose is moose."

Nibbly considered this. "Not mooses? Or meese? How do you know when yer talkin' 'bout more than one if the words is the same?"

"Figure one might as well be a dozen."

"Stands ter reason, that."

Gong appeared at Durham's side and extended his hand to help him up which turned out to be more symbolic than helpful due to their height difference. Thud had stuck his torch in the ground and was helping Nibbly to his feet. Nibbly's turban was in a sad and crumpled state and he set about rewinding it. Ruby's head emerged from the hole in the side of the wagon, blinking owlishly as if she'd just woken up. Other dwarves began appearing from beneath their various wagons. Several dwarves clustered around the damaged wagon, poking at it and making 'hmmm' noises.

Durham glanced up the road in the direction that the moose had gone and did a double-take. There was a shrubbery in the middle of the road. He was pretty sure that it hadn't been there before. The shrubbery started walking toward them and Durham's eyes made a confused reevaluation of it, resolving it into a mobile thing with legs and arms rather than a bush. It looked like an ambulatory clump of wisteria vines, wrist-thick branches twining around each other in a humanoid shape. The dwarves had fallen silent, watching the newcomer approach. It stopped about ten yards away from the front wagon and waited. Thud gave a nod and Dadger straightened his kilt and walked forward to meet it. Ruby fell in behind him and Durham jogged forward to catch up, figuring that if the thing wasn't intent on killing them right away he'd at least like to get a good look at it.

The elf was about four feet tall, putting it on eye-level for the taller dwarves. Hanging moss draped its branches, giving the illusion of clothing. Its head and face were a thick knot of thin green tendrils, large pupil-less eyes of amber and a tangle of ivy leaves in place of hair. As a whole it looked like something Durham might expect to find in the hedge of an overly zealous gardener. It held a curled ram horn in its hands which Durham suspected had been the source of the call from the woods that had drawn the moose away.

Dadger gave a respectful bow of his head. "Light and water to you, brother."

The elf nodded back. "Stone and ale," it responded. "I am called Serril. Did thy company bear injury?" His voice was like a trickle of water, full of drips and splashes.

"Nothing a little spit and dirt won't take care of," Dadger

said. "That was you that pulled that thing's attention away from us? My thanks."

The elf gave a small nod of acknowledgment. "Whither goest thou in yon forest glade?"

"Erm…" Dadger said.

"He wants to know what we're doing here," Ruby translated.

"Ah. Just traveling through," Dadger said. "Forsooth," he added.

"Pray, state thy purpose, be it errand foul or mission blessed, lest we for injury claim redress."

"Bloody hells," said Dadger. "Never had a headache come on quite this fast before."

"He wants to know what we're up to," said Ruby. "Your answer is going to determine whether or not he's mad about us hurting the moose."

"Mad that we we hurt the moose? Damned thing bashed in a wagon, near crushed three of us and wanted to mate with the oxbears!"

"I would remind you," Ruby said. "That there are a remarkably large number of bushes visible from here."

Dadger cast a wary eye at the forest.

"We're on our way to the ruins of Tanahael," he answered.

The elf's eyes widened. "Shadows hang over thee! A darker and more wretched place is not to be found 'ere week's journey. Seek ye thy doom?"

"He says…" Ruby began.

"Yeah, caught the gist o' that one," Dadger said. "We…uh… goest forthwith to Tanahael to…erm… banisheth shadow and… er…bugger it. We're gonna clean the place up and put the lich in its second grave."

Serril considered this then leaned to the side to peer around them at the wagons and the rest of the dwarves. The vines of his face wriggled into a new expression that was distinctly skeptical.

"I fear thy skill and number be sorely lacking, for a lich offers perils a moose doth not."

"I'll take your concerns under advisement. We're a little more prepared for delving underground to root out a lich than we are for moose surprise."

The elf shrugged. "I'll not stop thee in thy determined doom."

"Well, that's good, then. You know where Tanahael is? If you can give us directions it'll save us some wanderin' around."

"Reach forest's end, then three leagues beyond. Look to the side for a climbing, winding path of stone. Thy wagons will have an ill-time of it."

"Well, we'll worry about that when we get there. Thanks for the directions. Erm, sorry about yer moose."

Serril gave a dismissive wave. "Ill-tempered beast. We'll set its hurts aright."

There was a loud crash behind them. They turned to see that the other dwarves had managed to tip the overturned wagon back onto its wheels. Clink was still manning The Diplomat. He'd reloaded it and had it pointed at the woods where the moose had disappeared, watching suspiciously.

Serril walked past them, moving confidently through the dwarves' midst as if they presented not even the slightest concern. He approached the broken wagon and reached out to the splintered boards, pulling them back into place with his hands. He began stroking them, singing softly as his fingers traced across their surface. There was a crackling noise and a few small popping sounds. The elf stepped back with a satisfied nod and Durham saw that the wagon was fixed. Not in the way a carpenter would have done it. The boards seem to have actually grown back together, tinged with green as if the wood were alive and unseasoned.

"How did he..." Durham began.

"Fae magic," Ruby said. "Some of the dwarves can do similar things with stone. Cardamon over there is one, think Giblets might be another. Mend cracks, smooth it, even push their hand through it. Haven't you ever noticed how the city walls of Karthor look like a solid sheet of stone? Dwarven-made."

"I always thought they'd just plastered it over with cob or something."

"Pray," the elf said, turning away from the wagon. "Accept our hospitality and join us for repast and refreshment."

Durham heard a hiss of breath from Nibbly. There was a glint of panic in his eyes.

Dadger scratched at his beard, considering. "Yer offer is a great honor but, meanin' no disrespect, we'll have to decline. We can't leave the wagons unattended and I don't want to have to make some of the lads wait here while the rest of us enjoys yer company. Also, we just ate and we're full to burstin'."

Nibbly sighed with relief.

"Then we'll not hinder thy journey," the elf said. "And if luck smiles upon thee, no moose haunts Tanahael."

Dadger's cheeks reddened. He looked like he was of half a mind to say something and half a mind telling the first half to keep its mouth shut.

"We shall drink to thy fortune," Serril went on. "Peace in Tanahael shall be welcomed with open arms." He nodded a farewell, turned and stepped back into the forest, disappearing from view as quickly as the moose had.

"Nicely done, lad," Thud said to Dadger, clapping him on the shoulder. "You're worth every thumb o' yer pay savin' me from havin' to talk to elves."

Gong muttered under his breath as they reloaded the wagon and harnessed the oxbears, neither of which looked entirely convinced that the moose was gone. On the plus side, there was no hesitation on their part when the order was given to move.

"What's the problem with eating with wood elves?" Durham asked as they got under way again. "Are they like the fae mound feasts?"

"No, they has their own hazards," Nibbly said. "Plate of leaves, twigs and berries for the food but the worst part is after. That's when they start recitin' poetry for ya." He shuddered. "S'all gibberish words with dots and 'postrophes and they can go fer hours on end. S'all 'bout elves meetin' and romancin' then one of 'em dies nobly and the other one pines away for fifty or so stanzas. If you're truly cursed some other elf plays the music to go along with. Elvish music sounds like someone blowing on a set o' wind-chimes with a flute."

♪♪♪

They reached the edge of the forest several hours later and the caravan slowed to a halt again. Serril and two other elves stood in the road ahead. They watched in silence as Dadger Ben walked forward to meet them. After a minute, the elves each handed him something then vanished into the trees.

"What was that all about?" Durham asked.

"Elvish gift giving ceremony," Nibbly said. "They likes giving presents when you leaves their lands."

"Nice of them," Durham said.

Nibbly snickered. He stood and cupped his hand to his mouth.

"Oi! Ben! What'd we get?"

Dadger stood and called back. "A box o' dirt, a clump o' hair and a sack o' pancakes!"

Nibbly arched an eyebrow at Durham. "And that's elves for ya."

The sun was low in the sky when they reached a river and the road turned South to follow it upstream. The water was deep and clear, frothing white as it streamed over tumbled boulders. They hadn't gone far when Durham became aware of a faint roaring sound ahead. It grew louder as they approached, drowning out the rushing noise of the river. There was a thick mist in the air and Durham could see tiny rainbows where red sunbeams broke through the trees. The riverbank rose as they went, taking the road with it until the river itself was well below them.

The waterfall, when they reached it, was a white torrent thundering from the mouth of a great stone face carved into the cliff nearly a quarter mile above. The face was cracked, eyes rimmed with moss. The base of the falls was a great swirl of mist beneath them.

The road ascended one side of the falls, steep and narrow, zig-zagging its way to the top. The wagon train rolled to a stop and Gong trotted forward to confer with Thud. They had their heads together for a minute, gesticulating. It looked as if they were having to shout in each other's ears to be heard. Gong was pointing back alongside of the road. Durham looked and realized that there was a break in the trees, indicating that there had once been a road there, leading away from the river. A pair of dwarves trotted into the break, returning shortly to wave the wagons in. It took a few minutes of merriment to turn the wagons around. The break continued in a tree-lined swath, the road it had once been overgrown with thick grass but not enough to impede the wagons. Two hundred yards in it widened into a clearing, dim with shadow. They were just far enough from the falls to reduce their volume to background noise, more soothing than deafening.

A sagging farmhouse sat at the end of a small patch of onions, faint yellow light flickering between the gaps in its shutters, giving the drifts of mist a wan tinge. It had a thatch-bonnet roof, tall and narrow, the hay gray with age and green with moss. The hut looked like a great shaggy beast in the fading light, about to lumber off.

"Circle the wagons up and make full camp," Thud called. "We ain't taking the wagons up that trail until we have a full day to do it and have a chance to scout up top."

"Not too bad," Nibbly said, looking the site over as he maneuvered their wagon into its place in the ring. He glanced back at Durham. "Some of the places we've made base camp…" he widened his eyes and shook his head. "Hey," he said to Cardamon as he passed by toting a bundle of gear. "Remember that camp in the swamp?"

Cardamon grunted. "Had stuff growin' 'tween me toes for a month after that."

"Nice spot, this one," Nibbly said. "Fresh water close by, plenty of shade…"

"River of death to fall into in the middle of the night when you're having a pee," Cardamon added. "Probably a damn plague of pixies once night falls, this close to the water. We'll have to put the nets and blinds up."

"We like to see both sides of things," Nibbly said. "Keeps us prepared for all eventualities."

"Except mooses," Cardamon said. "Was expecting a bear."

A man appeared in the doorway of the farmhouse. He wore a green cloak with a silver clasp and shiny black boots. He made his way down the slope to them, a pitchfork casually resting on his shoulder as if he'd been forking hay in his dining room. His face was browned and lined like dried beef and bore the sort of expression one might expect upon finding ten wagons, twenty dwarves and a pair of humans in one's onion field.

"Oi there!" Dadger bellowed, stealing the initiative. He strode out to meet the farmer. "Might ye be Farmer Radish Wilson?"

"Yuh," the farmer responded, his expression adopting a faint touch of curiosity and a healthy slap of suspicion.

"Got yerself an active tomb hereabouts somewhere, eh?"

The farmer nodded slowly.

"Mebbe. Who's askin'?

"Word of your discovery has reached your king and he was so concerned fer the wellbein' a' you and yours that he sent us out to make sure that tomb ain't going to be a danger to nobody."

Ruby, standing next to Durham, made a small 'hunh' noise in her throat.

"Nicely done," she murmured.

The farmer's expression had softened.

"The king you say? Sent you to me farm to protect me?"

"Aye, that he did!" Dadger answered. "Dadger Ben is the name, and this fine lot here is The Dungeoneers." He gestured back at them without looking, safe in the assumption that they'd not wandered off to far. "We'll have that hole sealed up tight before you know it."

"There sure is a lot o' you," Farmer Radish said. He shifted back and forth and licked his lips.

"Dungeoneering is a tricky business," Dadger said. "We like to be thorough. I expect you see people come through here often on their way to Tanahael? Adventurers and such?"

"Used ta. Not so much anymore. Place is picked clean. All that's left is the bones walkin' 'round and ain't much draw there I reckon. Them sort ain't much fer bravin' danger less'n there's a pile o' gold at the end of it." He spat. "Bastards used to come through, go through all me drawers and steal whatever they fancied, dig up me onions and off they go without so much as a 'by your leave.'"

"Why is your moniker Radish if your agricultural commodity is onions?"

The question came from a very small dwarf with a patchy mottled beard and goggles whom Durham had heard referred to as Mungo. He'd wandered up unseen and now stood at Dadger's elbow. Gnome, actually, Durham realized, now that he was getting a closer look. Mungo was a gnome. Disguised as a dwarf. The blatantly false beard was a giveaway. It appeared that Mungo had crafted it himself out of hair collected from a wide assortment of cats and then glued it to his face. Dadger hrmphed at the interruption.

"Used to grow radishes," Radish Wilson answered. "Switched to onions. Didn't want to change my name to 'Onion'. Stupid name, that."

Mungo nodded sagely.

Dadger opened his mouth to regain control of the conversation.

"Do the onions trade better?" Durham interrupted.

"No, but they seems ta grow a bit better 'round here so there's more of 'em."

"Mungo, have you shown Durham your new project yet?" Dadger asked in the polite sort of way that threatens murder.

The gnome looked up at Durham, eyes huge behind his goggle lenses, disturbing grin on his face. Gnome mouths are wide and their facial expressions tended to wrap well around the sides of their head. Mungo had gamely crafted his false mustache to fit, causing it to extend almost to his ears like a horizontal sideburn. He grabbed Durham's hand and began pulling him away.

"Please pardon my associate's enthusiasm," Dadger said as they left, "I wanted to ask about camping the wagons…" his voice was soon lost among the bustle of the camp preparations as Mungo pulled Durham toward his wagon. The gnome was speaking, whether to himself or to Durham was unclear. A rapid mumble of words that sounded like a question and answer session.

Mungo's wagon had the look of an argument between a dozen cabinet-makers. The interior, when he swung the rear door open, was astonishing. Every inch of space was in use and labeled as such. The hammers and spikes strapped there, the ropes hanging there. The bin of chalk amid the drawers of twine. Pickaxes and shovels, ten foot poles, mirrors and tongs. Everything seemed to fold out and open into more things that unlatched and spun.

The gnome squinted at him, an alarming effect through the magnified goggles.

"Did you win the scooter race?" he asked.

"Sorry?"

"I observe that one of your boot soles is more worn than the other, indicating that you are a scooter rider. The presence of dried herbivore dung on the sides of your boots suggest an agricultural environment. Riding a scooter in an agricultural environment suggests a race at a harvest festival of some sort. Elemental!"

"I came in third," Durham said after contemplating

alternative responses.

"My powers of observation are finely honed," the gnome said. Mungo tugged at a small lever and what seemed a rack of leather punches folded down into a workbench and with a few quick darts of his hands among cupboards and drawers he had a collection of parts and tools arrayed in front of him. He selected a brass tube and with a snap of his wrist it extended into a gnome-sized spyglass. He held it out.

"Hold the lens in the smaller aperture to your eye and observe."

Durham braced himself. That the gnome had modified the spyglass in some way was a safe assumption and, while it was unlikely that it would be a spring-loaded spike modification, it was certainly possible that it might be a spyglass designed to helpfully moisten your eye for you or shine a light in it to help you see better. Consequently he was surprised to discover that he was looking at a patch of the onion field behind the farmhouse, except closer.

"Keep looking and maintain your normal demeanor," the gnome said in a whisper from his elbow.

Durham tried to do so, everything he did suddenly feeling unnatural.

"As you are an officer of the law I feel I must confide in you," the gnome said. He leaned past Durham, poking his head out the back of the wagon, eyes darting. He hopped up on the work table, allowing him to lean in close to Durham's ear. "I'm not actually a dwarf. I'm a gnome disguised as a dwarf."

His beard tickled Durham's ear and Durham sneezed. He was allergic to cats.

"Don't tell the dwarves" Mungo whispered. "They mustn't know."

"But why?"

"What do you see?" Mungo said, his voice suddenly louder as Gammi strode past them with a yoke of pots sloshing with water.

"Onions."

"And with your alternate eye?"

Durham switched the spyglass to his other eye.

"Onions."

"Not the eye utilizing the telescope, the other eye."

"The inside of my eyelid?"

"Precisely!" Mungo said.

"Why are you disguised as a dwarf?" Durham asked, trying to bring the discussion back to a topic he felt was slightly more interesting. Gammi had reached the cookwagon and was happily adding things to his pots of water.

"I'm undercover. Agent Mungo of the Universal Export Company."

"You work for an export company?"

"No." He rolled his eyes. "We don't call it the 'Gnomish Intelligence Agency' because then, obviously, everyone would know. I'm informing you out of professional courtesy so we don't inadvertently interfere with our respective operations."

"I'm not sure that I have an operation. I'm not even here as a guard."

"Yes, putting you right among the company leadership. Excellently done. I may have opportunities to utilize your assistance." He'd taken the spyglass away and now produced a pair of spyglasses attached to each other with an array of folding brass pins and dials.

"What exactly is your, erm, operation?" Durham asked.

"Classified. Apologies. Now, look through these."

Durham looked. It was still a close up view of the onion field but now bored both eyes instead of one.

"Much better viewing, yes? I call them duoculars but that's just a working title. Clink wants me to call them a 'telescoop' with little dots in the Os so that they resemble eyes. Ginny said that would make them look like boobs though."

"Maybe spyglasses?" Durham said.

Mungo frowned at him. "We may have different notions of the definition of the word 'undercover."

"I'm almost certain we do. Why would you think that I would help you against the dwarves?"

"Against the dwarves? Oh, no, no. On the contrary. Their success is paramount. I assure you our operations have no cross-purpose."

"So why is it a secret?"

"Protocols! I wouldn't expect you to be familiar with them. Espionage stuff, you know."

"Do the farmer's boots strike you as odd?" Durham asked. He was looking through the duoculars at Dadger Ben and Farmer Radish. They were still deep in discussion. He handed the duoculars back to Mungo.

The gnome looked and frowned. "Mondalinian leather."

"Shiny, expensive boots. On a farm. Brand new boots."

"Farmers must get new boots sometimes, yes?"

"New cloak too. Clasp looks silver. But, according to the farmer, nothing unusual about the local onion trade. Sometime in the last week or two he spent a fair bit of money."

"Ah!" the gnome said, "You suspect him of something! A murder perhaps?"

"What? No! I'm just trying to make it fit together in my head and it doesn't yet."

Mungo gave a sage nod. "Your powers of observation are excellent! Keep me apprised of the progress of your investigation."

Durham left the wagon, wondering why the gnome intelligence agency would have a spy amongst a dungeon crew. Was he spying on the dwarves or something else? Was one of the dwarves dangerous in some way?

♪♪♪

The other dwarves had circled the wagons, squared the horses and triangled the tents. Gammi was puffing mightily at a stack of smoldering sticks that wasn't quite a fire yet. There was a vertical metal pole in the center of the prospective fire, rods sticking out from it tree-like, pots of water hanging from them. Gammi paused, catching Durham's eye.

"I sees you met Mungo," he said. There was a twinkle in his

eye.

"Yes," Durham said. "Ummm…interesting fellow."

"Lad's cracked as a stone pick. Thinks he's a dwarf. We plays along with it 'cause he's damned good at making useful little gizmos. Best just play along with it. He gets right ornery otherwise."

"Noted." Durham mentally debated telling him about the 'Universal Export Company' but decided that would be a conversation best had with Thud, if, indeed, it was a conversation he should have at all.

"If'n ya wants somethin' other than mole for meal ya might wants ta go thump one o' them chickens on the nog," Gammi advised.

"An excellent suggestion," Ruby said as she walked up and began inspecting the contents of Gammi's pots. She gave Durham an expectant look that made it clear she intended to take no part in plucking or cleaning the chicken but every intention of taking several parts of the chicken once it was edible.

Durham cast a slightly helpless glance toward the chicken wagon.

"I've never…uh…"

Ruby sighed.

"You're a guard. Surely you know how to hit something over the head with a stick."

"Well, yes, but usually only if they have it coming."

"Pretend it asked you for a copper for some soup."

Durham made his way to the chicken wagon and stood there, doing his best to look lost. It was a trick that had served him well over the years.

"Oy?" Goin said, when he'd spotted him.

"I'm supposed to have a chicken for dinner," Durham said.

"Ah," Goin said, arching an eyebrow. "Well, they likes corn quite a bit, with some water, though I doubt they'd turn down a spot o' ale if'n ye offered. Which one ya fancy, then?"

"To eat. To eat for dinner."

"Aye, lad," Goin grinned. "Jest havin' ya on a bit. Here, I'll get ya this fat lump 'ere." He reached into a cage and with one deft motion removed a chicken and made a little twisty motion on its neck with his hand. There was a distinct snap and the chicken went limp.

Well, that solved one problem, Durham thought.

"What do I...?"

"Ya pulls out all of its feathers, lops off the head and feet, then ya reaches up its bum and pulls out all the wriggly bits. Save them bits, though. Good fer soups and such."

"Reach up its bum?" Durham repeated, his brain having paused at that part.

"Aye," Goin said. "Think of it as a character building experience. If ye don't mind me sayin' so lad, you could use a bit more character. Yer a bit drab amidst this wondrous company o' fine dwarves. No better place to start lookin' than up a chicken's arse."

♪♪♪

Durham was still picking a stray feather or two out of his teeth after dinner when Thud stepped up to the fire and made a twirly 'gather around' motion with his cigar. It left a flat ring of smoke that floated in the air in front of him.

"All right lads, here's what we're up against," Thud said. The orange light flickered on him, drawing long shadows on his features. "Whatever's left o' Tanahael is up top them cliffs. Tomorrow we're going to scout up there and decide if we're going to take the wagons up or leave 'em down here. This ain't exactly a hidden ruin and it ain't particularly far from civilized parts so I expect adventurers been crawling over this place for centuries. Like as not the place has been played out for a long time. Nevertheless, our benefactor is of the belief that there's still an artifact here, in Alaham's crypt. As best we know, that crypt ain't been discovered yet or, if it has, it either ain't been opened or no one's managed to plunder it. That tells us it's either well hidden, well secured, not easily accessible or extremely dangerous.

"Alaham was a necromancer in his day, and also the king o' these parts. So we can surmise that he had the resources to make his crypt to his liking. He's had a lotta years that he's likely been occupyin' hisself with orderin' dead things around to improve on the place. Ain't gonna make many guesses until we sees the place and gets a feel for it but I'm expecting it's gonna be a damned sight more than a hall and a coupla burial chambers. We can also expect the usual sorts of necromancy like wot we saw in Mondalin last summer. Skellingtons, walkin' corpsies, so on and so on.

"The scribes say seems Alaham turned hisself into a lich. He's going to look like a skelly with his meat dried on him and is gonna be able to likely lay down some pretty tough magic as he's had a few hunnert years o' practice. Now liches work by a necromancer putting his soul somwhere's outside his body. In some sort of container, typically. You can't kill the lich unless you find and destroy that container. Bein' as such, liches usually put quite a lot of thought into hiding and protecting their phylactery, as they calls it. We don't know what it looks like but Ruby tells me that liches tend towards bein' a bit full o' themselves so it's probably shiny. Think it has to be of a certain quality to even be used as a phylactery thingy so it ain't likely to just be some clay pot in a corner."

Nibbly raised his hand. "Are you telling us we need to break any valuable looking containers?" His voice quavered slightly.

"Gods no," Thud said. "Part o' the process is them sticking their heart in there while it's still beating. So check fancy containers for anything that looks like a big, nasty thumping prune."

"Technically," Ruby said, "any part of them that is still living will suffice. The heart is traditional but, as long as they do it quickly, they could conceivably perform the ritual with any body part."

"Valuable point," Thud said. "So, check fancy containers for anything shrivelly. I 'spect your first clue will be something trying to kill you afore you can check."

The faint breeze shifted and sent a swirl of campfire smoke into Thud's face. He coughed and flapped his hands at it before going on.

"Now, our ray of hope here is that Farmer Radish seen undead 'round here. With all the adventurers been through the place, active undead tells us that there's still somethin' here that's raising them, otherwise they'd a been cleared out long ago. A necromancer lich would be a pretty damn good candidate for that. And if there ain't no lich then there's something else responsible so don't miss the silver fer seekin' the gold.

"We're after an artifact called the Mace of Guffin. Story goes that it imbues the bearer with necromantic power so it ain't too much of a stretch to figger why Alaham mighta had it and be wanting to hang on to it. Black haft with a head that gives off little green magic wispys and whatnot. Like green steam, kinda. I recommend that you avoid breathing that in should you come across the thing. Don't know what it might do to ya but I ain't aiming to find out. It's also s'posed to pack one helluva wallop should you get hit with it so's if ya sees something comin' at ya with a wispy mace try and avoid getting hit by the thing lest you get knocked through a wall.

"The city ruins themselves is likely clear of anything readily portable. That don't mean there ain't stuff to be found there, of course, if you're savvy like we is. Keep an eye out for good stonework or statuary and if you find something, doc it. Just last month Rasp got a nice little sack o' gold for a nekkid lady statue he documented in Barmay. Sittin' in some lord's garden now."

There was a chorus of congratulatory proclamations aimed at an inscrutable looking dwarf with a long, narrow white beard and lines of script tattooed across his face. Durham hadn't gotten close enough to read them yet and wasn't of a mind to. Rasp bowed slightly in acknowledgment.

"As for tomorrow, scouting team will be me, Ruby, Nibbly, Giblets, Mungo and the full vanguard team. Vanguard might wanna get an early start. That trail up looks mighty fierce and I ain't helping roll Gong to the top of it."

Gong snorted.

"Rest o' yous rest up tomorrow, see to the gear and supplies. Ginny'll be minding the camp. Questions?"

There weren't any, though Durham had several dozen that he decided to refrain from asking in front of an audience for fear of looking like an idiot. Everyone knew quite a lot more about what was going on than he did and making them all wait while things were explained to him didn't seem like the best way garner to good will.

"Unlikely that there's going to be an undead presence this far from the city but I want a full watch posted tonight jest in case," Thud called out as the dwarves began drifting away from the fire. "No tellin' how far a skelly might take it in its skullbones to wander. We're pulling outta here at sunrise which means you scouts need to be up and hopping afore then. I'll send Gammi around banging a spoon on a fry pan by means of early warning.

"You heard the dwarf," Gong bellowed. "Quit with yer mumbling. Clink and Rasp got first watch. I'll take second watch with Keezix and then Max and Grottimus gets to be the early worms."

Durham stood for a time, looking at the night sky. The cliff loomed over the tops of the trees. He could see the stone face at the top of the falls, the water streaming from its mouth and eyes a silver cascade in the moonlight. Tanahael and the Crypt of Alaham awaited.

Durham awakened to Thud's bristly face looming over him.

"Make with the vertical, lad! Ye just have time for breakfast afore we head up the trail."

"I'm on the scouting team?" Durham asked. His mouth tasted like stale feathers.

"Yer me shadow, remember? You coming goes without saying." He paused. "Until jest now when I said it, at least." Ruby stood just behind him, a heavy walking stick in hand. Durham had been under the notion that Thud's shadow proclamation had been for Durham's safety. This was being challenged by the fact that he now found himself with the morning agenda of walking toward the haunted ruins of a city rather than toward a creek with a bucket.

Gammi was making his way around the camp with a steaming pot, ladling its contents out as he went. He reached Durham and stopped, arching an eyebrow.

"How many legs did it have?" Durham asked.

"More'n four."

"Think I'll have to pass," Durham said. His stomach gave an unhappy growl.

"Got them pancakes too, what the elves gave us."

"Any butter or jam to go with them?"

"Got some grub paste…"

Durham frowned.

Gammi rubbed his bare head thoughtfully. "Well, the elves usually put tree sap on 'em but they didn't give us none. Lotsa trees around though." He paused only briefly before catching the gist of Durham's expression and continuing. "Or I got a bit of honey if that'll work for you."

Durham brightened up.

"Honey and pancakes? I can work with that."

Gammi winked. "I'll be back 'round directly.

He returned a few minutes later carrying a honey bucket, the sack of pancakes slung over his shoulder. He also, curiously, had donned a long coat of chainmail that hung down to his knees.

"Still might be some bees, bark and bears in the honey. Ain't been filtered. Probably fits right in with Elvish cooking though." He set the bucket down and dropped the sack with a fluffy thump. "Got a surprise for you, too."

Durham's arm hairs twitched.

"Oh?"

Gammi reached into the sack and pulled out a limp stack of pancakes. He plopped them down onto Durham's plate, gave Durham a grin then turned and sat down on them.

Durham's mouth was hanging open as if it had intended to say something to prevent his pancakes from being sat upon but had been too stupefied by the notion that a dwarf was sitting on his pancakes to actually express anything. Gammi stood back up and gestured grandly at the somewhat flatter stack. The pancakes had lines criss-crossing them from the chainmail and were concave with the curve of dwarven buttocks.

"We calls 'em waffles. Holds the grub paste better. Honey too, most likely. A great advancement in pancake technology."

"Why do you call them that?"

"It's what Thud yelled the first time Gong accidentally sat on his pancakes."

🐾🐾🐾

The trail had once been a road. Ancient wagon ruts were still visible along much of it, eroded from their new life as run-off ditches for rain. Foliage encroached from the sides, narrowing the route to the width of the local wildlife. They saw tracks in the numerous patches of mud as they ascended—deer and goats, primarily, occasionally a bear track. The waterfall was only occasionally visible but its roar was constant, limiting any conversation to yelling in ears and hand gestures. Thud was in the lead, a walking stick in each hand making it seem he was skiing up the hill. Durham followed with Ruby just behind him. She had a broad cone-shaped straw hat and two walking sticks as well which made Durham suspect that he was missing out on something with his single walking stick. He'd rescued it from the firewood as they'd left camp. Giblets followed Ruby, with Nibbly taking up the rear.

Mungo had hiked up with the vanguard team—they'd left about twenty minutes before Durham's group. Durham had spotted a few of the trail marks that they'd left but didn't know what they meant. He didn't envy them. The trail was irritatingly steep and they, apart from Mungo, had all been in full armor. The morning air was cool but the sun was out, it's heat adding up with each step until he had sweat stinging his eyes. An occasional mist-laden breeze provided a few seconds of relief but those were much less common than the clouds of insects arriving for breakfast.

They reached the top of the falls about an hour after they'd left camp. The great stone face looked down on them, adorning the front of an old cyclopean dam across the top of the falls. Durham wondered if the face was a likeness of Alaham or if it predated him. Behind the dam was a long narrow lake in a steep forested valley. The sound of the falls faded and the air filled with the scent of pine as the road they followed continued up the side of the mountain. It wasn't long before they came to the vanguard team resting at a vantage point that offered a broad view of the valley below.

Tanahael lay below them.

It was far larger than Durham had expected. He knew that it was the ruin of a city but had expected a few scattered broken buildings and wells, not a ruin that was still as extensive as an actual city. It filled the valley, a tumbled ocean of stone. Nature had reclaimed much of it. The trees were thick enough to be a forest in parts and the streets were choked with bushes. Vines climbed dark gray walls and ferns adorned the rooftops. A dozen or so towers still stood tall enough to rise above the trees, their tops broken and jagged against the sky.

Thud made a loud 'gurmph' noise in his throat. "Well ain't that a sight." He unshouldered his pack and fished around in it, finally producing a pair of Mungo's duoculars.

"One o' Mungo's thingjiggys," he said to Durham. "First one he made was just two spyglasses stuck into some goggles. Looked like a right tit wearing it and they liked looking off every which way." He raised the duoculars to his eyes and fiddled for a minute with the knobs and gears.

"Ah, there we go," he said. "Hmmm." He lowered the duoculars. "Not sure what I was expecting ta see. Everything just looks the same but closer." He pointed down the hill. "We'll scout about today then hole up 'til nightfall. Gonna stay the night to see if things take a turn after dark. Signal the base camp, eh?"

Mungo produced a tube from his pack and set it up on a small tripod. He pulled out a paper-wrapped ball the size of a plum and Thud handed him his cigar. Mungo touched it to a cord on the side of the ball which ignited in a shower of sparks then dropped it in the tube. There was a deep thump noise and a trail of smoke into the sky, now a brilliant flare of white, a falling star in day.

ꙮꙮꙮ

They spent the better part of the day exploring the city. Weed infested broken plazas of upturned stones overlooked by the hollow windows of the shells of buildings. Birds flickered between trees that grew up amid toppled walls. The air was thick and lazy with sun, cicadas buzzing from the bushes. They entertained themselves by speculating on what different parts of the ruin had been. Mansions and houses, markets, wineries and mills, guard houses that looked much the same as what Durham was used to, complete with comparable levels of hygiene. What they didn't see was any sign of a threat. Periodically Thud would point out old fire pits.

"Adventurers been here," he said. "Them fires are far newer than the ruin and we ain't seen anything that could be carted off for a profit. Figger we should keep an eye out for anything that looks like it might have been a temple. If we're trying to find a crypt then seems it'd be close by."

"Can't imagine that it hasn't been found and looted also," Gong said. "Place this big ain't exactly a secret. I'd warrant every adventurer within a thousand leagues has been through here."

"Yeh, well the mace ain't been found, though," Thud said. "And the king thinks it's still here somewhere so we'll find the tomb and clear it out. If it ain't there then we'll scour this city 'til we're sure that it ain't here anywhere."

"Couldn't one of the adventurer groups have found it and taken it?" Durham asked.

"Unlikely," Ruby said. "The mace is not a subtle artifact.

Unless they stuck it in a box and forgot about it then it would have been noticed. Believe me when I tell you that you don't want it to be anywhere other than locked in a box deep underground."

"Isn't that precisely where we think it is?"

"Yes," Ruby said. "The difference being that the king feels that it should be his box deep under his ground."

***

They found a wide street lined with temples late in the afternoon. A row of pillars ran the length of the street, marble entryways to what had once been grand buildings to each side. Statues of the Gods stood before each temple, some broken, some fallen, all of them green with moss. The largest temple lorded over the others at the end of the street. Gravestones were visible behind it. The interior was built in the shape of a pointed arch, the peak of the ceiling high overhead. Many of the stones had fallen in and thick curtains of ivy hung down, glowing green in the dusty shafts of sunlight. The floor was a mix of broken and tumbled stones amid thick patches of mud and rotted plants. Like the rest of the city, the temple had been stripped of anything that might have been of value save for the huge rune on the wall behind the altar. There were some things, apparently, that even adventurers were wise enough not to try and steal and it seemed that the Rune of Grimm was on the list. Durham and Ruby lowered their gaze and shielded their eyes with their hands, the traditionally appropriate response to Grimm's rune. Gazing upon the rune was said to draw the god's attention and Grimm was the sort that folks liked to escape the notice of.

"God o' the dead, ain't he?" Thud asked, eying the rune appraisingly.

"God of death, god of bone, god of justice, god of balance," Ruby recited. "Among other things, of course. He's one of the three gray gods and graveyards often have his altar. Usually it's just a shrine in the corner of the graveyard. I wonder if Alaham had this built? I can see how a necromancer might find appeal in Grimm."

"Well, can't see that there'd be a huge market for a twelve foot tall granite rune and it'd be tough getting that onto one of the wagons," Thud said. "We'll doc it and leave it be."

"What do you mean by 'doc it'?" Durham asked.

"We write down a description and location. Sends that off to be cataloged at Kheldurn. When dwarves is hired to build something that needs some kinda monuments they can look at the list to see if it's been tagged somewheres. If so then they can send out a team to recover it rather than makin' a new one. Big market in old statuary. Rich folk types likes 'em in their gardens. Gonna take us a week to tag all the statues in this graveyard. They kept the stonecarvers busy in this city."

The graveyard beyond the temple was far larger than Durham had realized. Large enough to qualify as a necropolis. The monuments clustered thickly together—stones and statues, crypts and mausoleums, spreading left and right along the wall of the valley as far as the eye could see. A cliff rose at the back of the cemetery, several hundred yards away. The overgrowth here was thick, the trees taller and greener, a fact which Durham's brain shied away from thinking too much about.

"Empty," Giblets said, or at least something that approximated the word 'empty'.

"Sorry?" asked Ruby.

"All dem graves sunk, see? Nuttin' in em." He pointed at a row of depressions in the ground.

"Are you suggesting that someone dug all of the bodies up?"

"Naw. Neckermancer, eh? 'Speck dem bodies dug demselves up. Less shovelin' that way."

Gong trotted down the steps into the graveyard and poked his head in the nearest crypt. He looked back at them and shook his head.

"Empty."

Thud whistled. "There must be, wot? Thousand or so graves here?"

"More than that," Ruby said. "This is the only graveyard we've seen and likely served the entire city. Tanahael was a city of ten thousand people. That works out to around forty thousand dead per century. The city stood for at least six centuries." She fell silent, letting them do the math in their heads.

"Ain't that many graves here, though," Gong said.

"Once the yard is full, you bury the new ones on top," Ruby said. "Notice how the ground here is higher than all of the area surrounding it? The graves were probably stacked many layers deep. It wouldn't surprise me if they also had catacombs somewhere."

Durham was suddenly glad to still be on the temple steps.

"Can't say all dem graves empty," Giblets said. "Can't see 'em all."

"Unlikely," Ruby said. "I don't know how many undead Alaham can maintain but it's going to be a number in the dozens rather than the hundreds or thousands. He's probably been raiding this graveyard for bodies for centuries. Even with that there's going to be a lot of undisturbed graves out here."

"Tanahael fell before the Gods of the humans went to their sleep" one of the vanguard said. He pulled his helmet off. It was Rasp. He was close enough now that Durham could see that the lines of script tattooed across his face looked like some sort of religious text. "Time was the temples here would have kept this ground hallowed. Kept the dead at their rest. The power of the Hermits is not great enough to keep light in all of the shadowed places."

"The dwarves have different Gods, don't they?" Durham asked. "Are they asleep too?"

"Aye, we do, and no, they ain't" Rasp said. "But they're like dwarves in their ways, preferring to sit in chambers of stone, feasting and drinking, digging deep within the earth and crafting wondrous things from the metals they find."

"Then they sell those wondrous things to others," Nibbly said. "Those people then hire dwarves to build dungeons to protect their wondrous things. Then others hire us to go into those dungeons and recover those wondrous things to be locked away, creating a continuing market for new wondrous things.

And thus the great wheel of the dwarven economy turns."

Rasp frowned at him.

Ruby pointed straight ahead at a large ivied mausoleum that lay near the center of the necropolis. It was connected to the temple by a narrow strip of grass empty of headstones but with scattered cobblestones evident as if it had once been a paved path. "The catacombs are likely in there, based on ease of access."

They made their way to the building Ruby had indicated, Durham taking great care to stay on the path. He'd always avoided the graveyards in the city, easy to do as there was an aura of stench around them strong enough to be noticeable even over the city's pervasive odors. He'd once seen gravediggers scurrying out after a heavy rainstorm to rebury the bits that had surfaced through the mud and that had been enough to put him off of chancing a repeat visit.

The tombs they passed gaped dark and empty, capstones pried loose or broken.

A wrought-iron gate lay on the ground near the mausoleum entrance, half dissolved into rust. The thin shaft of light from the open doorway showed a floor strewn with shards of pottery, walls lined with broken urns and, at the chamber's center, a narrow flight of steps leading down into darkness.

"Ain't sure catacombs is where Alaham would put his tomb."
Thud said. "Most likely place for adventurers to have been
through also. Dark hole in a graveyard, they'd be like fairies to
cake."

Giblets made a milky gargling noise in his throat, spat, then
gave a jerk of his head. Not at the graveyard, but at the cliff face
of the valley wall, rising ahead of them. "Speck dasit," he said.

The trees had obscured their view. The valley wall lay at the
back of the graveyard, a ragged cliff rising high overhead. There
were tombs there, carved into the face of the cliff, curtained with
ferns and ivy. Dozens of large rectangular openings in the stone
offering glimpses of pillars in their shadowy recesses. A larger
circular opening lay at the center of them all, just above the
valley floor, its edges carved in a frieze of runes. Within, a great
doorway stood beneath an ornate pediment.

Ruby borrowed Thud's duoculars and gave the tomb a closer
look. She lowered them and nodded. "The runes are the
egotistical chest pounding you'd expect but they do confirm that
it's Alaham that's in there."

"Or," Thud said, "it's where he wanted folks to think he is. In
either case, that's where we're going to start tomorrow morning.

Mungo, go signal the others to start prepping the wagons to come up. Rest of us will set up camp in one of the temples out by the entrance."

"Avare," Ruby said. "Travelers fall into his domain."

"Avare it is," Thud said. "Hope he don't mind dwarves."

✦✦✦

They were not the first to camp there. The fragmented scraps of what remained of the temple's original furnishings had been shoved to the sides of the room and the floor was stained with soot beneath a gaping hole in one corner of the roof. The fallen stones had even been arranged in a semi-circle around the campfire's remnants. The Rune of the Wanderer was carved into the wall above a stone slab altar, cracked and mossy from past rains. One wall was tumbled outward, a few ambitious stones remaining as a suggestion but enough of the temple's structure remained to give the illusion that it was shelter. They soon had a fire flickering in the corner, shadows dancing on the weathered walls. Durham leaned against one of the stones and munched on one of his remaining pancakes. He had no honey for it but, on the other hand, the pancake had the bonus of not having been through Gammi's waffle upgrade. Ruby had already curled up on her blanket and was snoring with a sound like a giggling duck. Thud and Nibbly had their cards out with Mungo advising both players to the point where he was playing the game against himself with the dwarves serving merely as a means of moving the cards around. Giblets watched, rocking back and forth occasionally and laughing at inappropriate times. He had a piece of stone in his hand that he would suck on from time to time then study speculatively, as if gleaning information from it. Gong and the five dwarves of the Vanguard had spread around the perimeter of the room and were settling in to sleep, save Rasp, the one posted to first watch. He sat in the temple doorway, out of the firelight, mace on his shoulder.

Thud eventually gave up on the cards, leaving Mungo and Nibbly to sort out who ended up with the pot. He wandered over and sat down next to Durham with the sound that was his namesake. He fished around in the vest beneath his coat until he produced a hammered steel flask.

"My apologies for the last time we tried having this talk," he said. "I likes to get to know folk I'm traveling with but got thrown a bit by the whole orphan thing. This line of work breeds caution in some unusual type ways. Ain't your fault though, even if it does turn out to be a problem."

"Do you really think that I might be part of some kind of prophecy?" Durham arched an eyebrow.

"Nope. Meaning no offense but I don't actually hold much with prophecies. Seems to me they're all a bit vague and then gets twisted about later to fit what happened. Or some bard's clumsy idea of foreshadowing when he's telling a story. So maybe you'll be one after we're done but you ain't one yet, if you get me meaning." He sipped from his flask and made a noise Durham couldn't quite categorize.

"Now," Thud said, "'bout your guardin' duties. How long ya been doin' that?"

Durham thought for a moment.

"Three years?"

"And how's that been for ya?"

Durham shrugged. "All right, I guess."

"What they gotcha guardin'?"

"Usually I guard the postern gate."

"That's a ponce word for the back door, ain't it?"

"More like a side door, really. At least this one. It's where they bring the livestock in and out."

"Mmm. See a lot o' action there, do ya?"

"Well...no. Mostly it involves searching flocks of sheep."

Thud regarded him silently for a moment.

"We made some dramatically different career choices to bring us to the same place," he said.

"I was never really aware of having made any choices, other than joining the guards in the first place"

"You gotta make the choices exist in the first place to get the ones ya want. If you just grab the ones that wander by ya end up on the postern gate." He sucked on his cigar contemplatively. "So, wot you're tellin' me is that you maybe ain't used that club a yers all that much."

"Well..."

"Sheep uprisings maybe? Contraband hidden in the wool?"

Durham gave Thud a narrow look, beginning to suspect that he was being made fun of.

"You gots any other sorta skills what might be useful in a dungeoneering type environment?" Thud asked.

"Like what? Lockpicking? Healing?"

"Nah, like 'sperience with machinery or engineering, mebbe. Architecture, botany, stuff like that. We got a healer and lockpicking ain't nearly as useful as you might think."

"Don't dungeons have locked-up chests full of gold?"

"Naw. They're deep down in a dungeon, see? What's the point of lockin' 'em? A five-bit lock ain't gonna stop anyone that crawled through spike traps and goblin dens to get to it. Happens sometimes but they can be sorted out pretty quick with a hammer and a prybar."

Durham thought for a bit.

"I can pluck a chicken. Sort of. Still learning."

Thud dug a finger in his ear and thoughtfully inspected the results for a moment, puffing away on his cigar. He took a swallow from his flask and handed it to Durham.

"What got ya into bein' a guard in the first place?" Thud asked.

Durham took a swallow from the flask and felt the paint peel off of the interior of his entire gastrointestinal tract.

"I liked figuring things out," Durham said after several minutes of coughing. "I had this idea that in the city guard I'd do things like solve who killed the man in Lancedboil Lane, for example, or who robbed the bakery. That sort of thing. Didn't work out that way, though. Instead I'm the sheep gate guard."

"So you actually wanted to be a thieftaker?"

Durham stared at the fire for several seconds then took another swig from the flask. His face made several complicated contortions and one of his legs developed a spastic twitch. Thud took the flask away from him.

"I got caught in an alley once when I was a kid. Street kids—older than me. One had a knife. I didn't have anything—the orphanage wasn't big on walking-around money. They decided they were going to settle for my clothes instead. They had me down and were pulling at me, the knife at my throat. Suddenly, behind them, this gleaming giant in blinding silver. Least that was how it looked at the time. Sun on armor. Captain of the city watch. He kicked the kid with the knife so hard it flipped him end over end. The other three were off like cats. That's what I wanted to be. Captain of the guard."

"Three years gaurdin' a sheep gate though?" Thud asked. "Ain't there no promotion type opportunities in yer city guard?"

"My first day on duty I walked into the patrol house I'd been assigned to. There was a shepherd there, complaining to the lieutenant about sheep thieves."

Thud rubbed his nose. "Sheep thieves? That a problem of significance?"

"You'd be surprised," Durham said. "So he sends me to follow the shepherd back to the gate he's complaining about and take up guard post. My one and only assignment. For the first year at the end of each month when I'd show up for my pay he'd squint at me and say, 'Who the blazes are you?"

"Private Durham."

"Durham? Aren't you the Keeper of the Vaults?"

"No, sir, that's Chancellor Dorham."

"What's your post?"

"Anterior postern side gate, sir."

"Ah, didn't know we had a post there. Good to know, good to know. Good idea that. Anything to report?

"No, sir.

"Good, good. Any relation to Chancellor Dorham?

"Not that I'm aware of sir."

"Excellent! Otherwise I'd have to find someone with less experience to take that gate."

Durham shrugged. "Then they would hand me my pay and off I went back to counting sheep."

"An' ye never requested a new post?" Thud asked.

"A few times around the end of that first year," Durham said. "He always answered that he'd keep an ear out and let me know if he heard of anything and gave me one of those 'surprised interest' expressions like it was the first time the subject had been mentioned. But no, it was my second year when I really sunk my chances."

"Made a mistake, did ye?"

"No," Durham said. "I solved a sheep murder."

Thud blew a smoke ring and took a pull on the flask, mulling that over.

"Thinks ya might needs ta elaborate a bit on that, lad."

And so Durham told him. He told him of the strange ritualistic circumstances surrounding the discovery of the murdered sheep. He told him of the singular one-legged seamstress, the cryptic cipher tattoo and the secret fishmonger identity of the mysterious rogue, Harengs. He spoke of part of the evidence being eaten and another part being knitted into a lumpy sweater. And at last the reveal, when all of the seemingly disparate parts came together to show that it had been the victim's sister Bluebell all along. By the time he was done, Mungo, Nibbly and Giblets had joined Thud in his audience.

"The watch captain read my report," Durham said, as he neared the tale's end. "Laughed until he had tears running down his face then sentenced Bluebell to execution by way of being the main dish at the City Watch potluck. He at least remembers me now. Every time he sees me he asks if I have any new baaaffling cases and starts laughing again."

"And so you been stuck there ever since, eh?" Thud asked.

Durham nodded. "I've been thinking of a career change."

"For how long?"

Durham shrugged. "I have a plan all worked out. These sorts of things take time."

"That they do," Thud said. "Gots something ya needs ta do, an' ya figgers out what ya needs to do to make it happen and then ya has yer plan, eh?"

Durham nodded, looking pleased with himself.

"'First thing tomorrow morning I'm gonna starts fixing this,' you says to yerself," Thud went on. "Next thing ya know twenty years o' tomorrows has gone by and yer still watching the sheep gate."

Durham stopped nodding, in spite of the fact that Thud's second comment had been more prescient than the first.

His lower regions informed him that the Dwarven spirits had arrived at their debarkation station and he took the opportunity to excuse himself and step outside. The eye-moon was low in the sky, half-lidded but bright, tinging the ruins with rusty light. People always referred to it as 'the red moon' but Durham had always thought it looked more orange. He stepped behind the broken wall of what looked to have been a smithy which, as far as desecrating a ruin went, seemed a relatively safer choice than the back of the temple. He could hear the dwarves' distant chatter off to his right—they seemed to be telling stories about livestock. Which meant that the noise he'd just heard to his left wasn't a dwarf.

He slowly turned his head.

Ten yards away was a huge horned skeletal bull, glimmering red in the moonlight. More alarmingly, it was in a full speed charge straight at him, head lowered, horns pointing.

Durham shrieked and ran.

After a few steps it occurred to him that he had not, in fact, bothered to stop peeing before running, nor done up his pants and that both of these factors were about to turn into serious logistics issues.

There is a part of the brain that, ordinarily, doesn't do too much other than watch and wait. The monkey brain, the bit that exists primarily for those moments when things are suddenly happening too quickly for the conscious brain to deal with; moments when destiny is suddenly approaching at high speed. And then it takes over. Its job is to make decisions and to make them instantly. It does this largely by circumventing the entire thinking process, taking no time to assess the consequences of its decisions or the likelihood of them leading to long-term success, merely choosing what seems the best option for staying alive for another second or two. It was this part of Durham's brain that had shrieked and started him running. Now, with the new problems presented, it made another rapid decision.

Durham spun around and ran backwards.

It's understandable how this might have been a decision that could have briefly seemed like a good idea—he was no longer sprinting full speed into his urine stream while still moving away from the thing rushing at him. Spinning around, however, revealed that it was moving toward him at an appreciably faster rate than he was moving away from it and was, in fact, right behind him. Or now, rather, in front of him. That was when his still unbuttoned pants lost their battle with gravity and dropped around his ankles. Running backwards is difficult at the best of times. This was not the best of times.

Durham landed flat on his back and felt his insides abruptly deflate. The thing skidded to a halt over his prostrate prostate, elongated skull face dripping.

The monkey brain again chose shrieking as the best available option on its menu, perhaps because it was the one decision it had made already that hadn't failed horribly. What actually came out of Durham's mouth was a noise more like an asthmatic getting punched in the stomach.

The first shriek had actually done its job, however. The great cracking noise of the bull's skull shattering into pieces was almost simultaneous with the heavy thunk sound of a trio of crossbows. It collapsed on top of Durham, a pile of rattling and clonking bones. He gasped desperately to get air back in his lungs and, mercifully, finally finished peeing. A circle of bearded faces, or faced beards perhaps, looked down on him.

"You alive down there?"

Durham gulped and nodded then went back to wheezing.

Thud gave a great shout of laughter and slapped his hands on his thighs.

"Damndest thing I ever saw," he said. "Big skelly lugger comes runnin' at ya and ya turns aboot and pees in its face."

Gong and Nibbly were doubled over and shaking.

"Aye, 'eres mud in yer eye, eh?" Gong said.

"Spray and pray!" Nibbly shouted.

"Might wanna tuck them fam'ly jools away 'fore someone makes cufflinks out of 'em," Thud said.

Durham struggled to tug his pants back up while Thud began kicking bones off of him.

"Well, seems you may 'ave solved the mystery of the haunted ruins," he said. "That cow musta been wandering around out here for near six hunnerd years now. This'll make a fine tale for ya in the future to follow up that sheep murder story with."

"Think ye may have just gotten yer earned name, lad," Gong said. "Blamed if I can figger what it should be, though."

"Hmmm", Thud said. "Incowtinent?"

"No ring to that, is there?" Nibbly said. "Don't exactly roll off the tongue."

"Peacock?" Gong offered.

"Too vulgar sounding," Thud said.

Nibbly's face broke into a grin. "Calf!"

"Calf?"

"Aye, cuz it's a 'wee cow'."

🐾🐾🐾

"I can't help but notice that all o' the actual dangers we've encountered on this trip 'ave been livestock," Nibbly said. They'd moved back in by the fire, most bustling about with their bedrolls.

"I don't believe moose would fall in the 'livestock' category,"

Ruby said. The commotion had woken her up and she was sitting cross-legged on her blanket, sipping at a cup of her ruby colored tea. "'Large edible herbivore' is the closest category they'd have in common."

"Are you attempting to suggest some sort of synchronicity?" Mungo asked. He'd strung his blanket into a tent using a complicated array of ropes tied to various anchor points throughout the room.

"No, can't say that I am as I don't know what that is," Nibbly said. "But I'm going to be keepin' an eye on the chickens."

"Ye gots more important things to look at," Thud said. "Goin's the one on chicken-watch. You should express yer concerns to him though. I'm sure he'll appreciate the tip. Make sure I'm there for that."

"Are we sure this is the right place?" Durham asked. It was early the next afternoon. They stood at the rim of the opening in the cliff face. Pillars carved from the living rock were to each side, a tall stone door slab before them. It was inlaid with a swirling pattern of silver, lines whorled around socketed indentations. The wagons were twenty yards behind them, stretched in a line back towards the avenue of temples. They'd started the ascent at dawn but had taken nearly four hours to reach the top and then another two hours to navigate the ruins of the city. Dwarves were bustling up and down the wagon line now with arm-loads of gear. Some donned armor, some were assembling large pieces of equipment, others were shoveling dirt into wooden barrels.

Thud gave a great, bubbly sort of sniff, the sort you feel slide down the back of your throat.

"Well," Thud said. "Ruby says it's Alaham's. Could be true, could be a trap. Gotta start somewhere though."

"It's his," Ruby said, squinting at the runes. "That's his sigil up top. There's some sort of puzzle lock on the door. Looks like the indentations are meant to have something placed in them in order to open it." She was making a rapid sketch in her notebook of the runes and lock. "Various colors of gems, seems to be, color determined by solving..."

Thud chortled. "Well, that's why ain't no adventurers opened it yet. Probably all traipsing across the countryside looking for magic gems."

"So we need to find the gems?" Durham asked.

Thud snorted.

"Stones to that. Gryngo? Pop the cork!" This last he bellowed out to the dwarves behind them.

Gryngo was a dwarf who seemed to have perpetual wisps of smoke drifting off of him. He wore a thin cotton shirt that left his tattooed arms bare and squinted at things with his one good eye while his milky eye stared hauntingly. He gave a single silent nod to Thud, a gold tooth glittering in the slow grin that spread across his face.

Gryngo slung the pack off his shoulder and began pulling out several small wooden casks. Thud led Durham and Ruby back to the wagons then casually leaned against a wheel, eying the preparations. Several dwarves nearby were adding to The Diplomat. A modification that gave the ballista four separate firing bolts, two atop, two more beneath. The bolts had chains running between them. The vanguard had donned their full plate armor and carried tower shields. The six of them lined up behind the ballista, crossbows in hand, maces at their belts. Gong was obvious as he made up the middle and one dwarf to each side on his own but the others were anonymous with their helmets on. The bolts in their crossbows had metal balls on the end instead of arrowheads.

"Oi!" Gryngo yelled from the door after a few minutes.

"Knock first!" Thud called back. He grinned at Durham. "No reason not to be polite, eh?"

Gryngo produced a hammer from his pack and swung it at the doorjamb a few times, the clink of metal on stone echoing through the valley. He then strolled towards them, unspooling a roll of cord as he came.

"Why did we bang on the door?" Durham asked.

"You're a guard. S'pose you had a tomb full o' walkin' bloodthirsty killing machines that you didn't want no one comin' in. Where might you have them things positioned?" Thud answered.

"Guarding the door."

"Aye. And if you was guarding a door and there was a bangin' on it, what would ye do?"

"Take up position by the door to defend."

Thud grinned.

"'Xactly." He bent and touched his cigar to the end of the cord. "HOT SPOT!"

The cord caught fire and the spark raced hissing up its length, snaking across the ground, the same way that the cord on the signal flare had burned. It reached the casks that Gryngo had arranged. Durham noticed that all of the dwarves had plugged their fingers in their ears. He followed suit, remembering the noise that the flare had made.

Something punched hard, deep in his chest followed a mere moment later by a mind-splitting crack of sound. The ground beneath his feet jerked in surprise. A great cloud of dust and dirt burst from the cliff face, tiny pebbles showering down around them. The dust slowly began to thin, revealing a gaping black hole in the cliff where the door had been. Durham realized his mouth was hanging open and snapped it shut.

"What the..."

"Dwarven doorknocker," Thud proclaimed, yelling over the ringing in their ears. "And now anything close comes to see what in the hells that noise were..."

He turned to the dwarves manning the ballista.

"On my mark, lads. Hold..."

They watched the swirling dust around the entrance.

"Hold..."

In the darkness something moved. A glint of metal, a clatter.

"OPEN NEGOTIATIONS!"

There was a loud chonk noise as The Diplomat fired its four

bolts, the chains connecting them stretching to create a metal net spread between them. The shot disappeared into the darkness, followed by a great deal of clattering and clanking.

"SQUAD FORWARD!" Gong commanded.

The six dwarves in armor began a slow steady advance on the doorway, just enough gap between their shields for the readied crossbows. They reached the hole and stopped, hunkering down behind their shields, peering through the narrow view slots.

"No movement!" one called.

"BRACE!" Gong yelled.

The squad began fiddling with the shields. They unfolded clamps at the top and bottom, attaching the shields to each other and then unfolded metal braces that supported them all. Within seconds the six tower shields had been turned into a free-standing wall of metal.

"Light 'er up!"

One of the vanguard unslung a pack and pulled out one of the round pixie lanterns. It was about the size of a honeydew melon. He opened it up and poked at it with some fairy cake. After a moment light began streaming from it. The dwarf closed the ball back up, stepped back and flung it over the shield wall into the tomb. The ball bounced into the darkness, clanging as it went, a pool of light traveling with it as it rolled. Somehow the lantern inside remained upright and lit even as the ball rolled.

"Gyroscopic lantern," Thud said. "Keeps the pixie inside upright and happy while the outside rolls. Mungo's design," he added. "Little varmint comes in handy."

"Clear!" came the call from the squad.

"Reload and hold position!" Thud said. "Wanna let the rest of that dust settle. Should be plenty of time to see if we stirred anything else up in there."

Thud went to the weapon wagon and fished around a bit until finally producing a mace.

"Knew we had to have another one o' these in here," he said. "Swords ain't going to be of any use" he said, handing it to Durham. "Used one before, have ya?"

"Yes, a bit," Durham lied. The mace was like his guard cudgel but a lot heavier. He figured that the principles of using it were pretty similar. "Why no swords?"

"Most o' what we're gonna find in there that needs killin' is gonna be skellingtons. Blades ain't much use there. Slips between they ribs or just slide off the bones. Got to get a serious hit in to break a bone with a sword without just simply knockin' the damned skelly away from ya. A mace, on the other hand, will smash right through 'em. Like fightin' a pile o' sticks.

He gave Durham a long, contemplative look.

"So here's the deal," he said. "I needs to get you in and out o' here alive. Looks bad if'n the observer gets killed. S'pect that's in yer best interests as well, eh?"

Durham nodded.

"I want you to be my shadow. When I stop walking I want you so close you bump into me." He stopped, making a mental comparison between his height and Durham's anatomy. "Well, mebbe not quite as close as that. In any case, if things get hairy I wants you to hit the dirt as fast as ya can and stays there until I says, got it?"

Durham frowned and opened his mouth to protest.

"This ain't about yer pride, lad," Thud said. "This is about everyone comin' outta there safe and sound. Until ye've crawled through one o' these places a time or two it's hard to realize just what the word 'deathtrap' means. Are we clear?"

Durham frowned and nodded reluctantly. His visions of coming back a hero were growing wispy.

"I'll have Ruby write ya in somethin' noble," Thud said. "History's more wot gets writ rather than wot happened, eh?" He clapped Durham on the shoulder. "Buck up, lad. Ye'll have a story the envy of that lot back at your guard post and they'll be buying yer ales for weeks."

"Do you want the mace back?"

"Nope. Always the chance that this'll go arse-up and you'll be glad for it. If'n I'm still standing though just be sure you're swinging it higher than me head."

"Right."

"And take this pack." He tugged a bulky backpack from the wagon and handed it to Durham. It was the same sort of pack that most of the other dwarves were wearing and seemed to weigh about as much as a dwarf. "Full of exactly the sorts of things you might need in there, contents refined, improved, removed and consolidated by plenty o' experience. Lantern, chalk, rope, string, hammer, spikes and whatnot. Hopefully ya never has to even open it but ye'll wear it jest the same."

Durham managed to struggle it on with a fair bit of adjusting of strap lengths.

"Now," Thud grinned. "Let's go see wot wos'name has in store for us, eh?"

Durham followed Thud to the shield wall. Ruby was there already, waiting silently, along with a handful of dwarves.

"Report!" Thud barked.

"All quiet, sir," came the response.

"Fall in!"

The shields were unhooked, the vanguard reforming into a column two abreast with Gong at its head. Mungo scampered up and climbed onto Gong's shoulders. Thud stepped in just behind them, Ginny at his side.

They started for the tomb entrance, the armored dwarves accompanying, crossbows readied.

"I'm looking at my shadow and I ain't seein' no one in it!" Thud yelled from ahead. Durham jogged to catch up and they stepped into the darkness.

-9-

The smell arrived first. It was the smell of things that have spent many years alternating between periods of drying and rotting, the smell of things that grew in darkness and things that scraped on rocks. The air was thick and still, chilled. Water dripped somewhere, irregularly. Was the sun positioned perfectly to send ruddy rays of light through the swirling dust within, throwing their shadows long and stark across the floor? Of course it was.

They sent more pixie lamps in, their light spinning the shadows wildly as they rolled. Ginny followed after, crouching in the tomb entrance with what looked like a jeweler's loupe affixed to her eye. She moved forward slowly, one crouching step at a time. One of the pixie lamps was held high in her right hand, a bullseye lens throwing a cone of red light. She had a long pole in the other hand with which she poked and prodded at the floor before her. The vanguard moved in just behind her in a tight wedge, crossbows at shoulder, spreading out once they were through the breached door. Gong was the point of the wedge and Mungo rode Gong's shoulders. He had a leather cap on his head with goggles pulled over his eyes, cat-fur beard tucked into the collar of his gown-length coat. He had a long pole with a lamp on the end and was poking it into the shadowy recesses above, muttering, then poking it somewhere else and muttering again. Thud was tight on Gong's heels and an impatient shove from Ruby insured that Durham was right behind him.

The room was long and narrow, ceiling arched into darkness overhead, its beams curving down along the walls to give the room a tunnel of ringed shadow. The floor was abstract mosaic, each tile outlined with a fingernail of grime. It was littered with fragments of bone and stone and with pieces of rusted armor. There were dark recesses along the walls, between the arcs of stone and a dark archway at the far end, thirty yards away. Scattered pools of light from the pixie lamps broke up the gloom. Durham could see the chained ballista bolts tangled up on the floor against the back wall.

Ginny moved slowly into the room, tapping at the floor and walls with her stick, scrutinizing things through her eyepiece.

"Magazar Korra," she said. "Those corner joists are a dead giveaway."

"Is that a Dwarven name?" Durham asked.

"Most of these sorts of places are dwarven made," Ginny said. "Lot of money in dungeon construction. Same with fortresses. Dwarves is the architectural foundation of the entire adventuring industry."

"Magazar, eh?" Thud said. "Wasn't that bit over South of Song one o' his?"

Ginny nodded.

"Couple nasty traps, as I recall. That one with the molten lead coming out of the ankle level wall grate."

"Yes, but his trap seams tend to sink over time," she said,

pointing at a bit of floor utterly indistinguishable to Durham's eyes from the rest of the floor. "He cuts costs with the supports." She turned to the dwarves outside. "Barrel!"

There was a stirring and two dwarves jogged forward rolling a barrel between them, wood creaking with weight. Behind them two others spun an empty barrel into place and began shoveling dirt into it. Ginny pointed.

"Right down the middle."

They gave it a mighty shove and it rolled into the room, the fragmented bones cracking and crunching beneath it. It traveled all of ten yards before abruptly disappearing through the floor with a splintering crack and a cloud of dust, leaving a gaping hole in what had appeared to Durham to be completely solid footing. An enormous crash echoed up from below.

"They never get tired of pit traps, do they?" Thud asked.

"Least expensive traps up front," Mungo said. "Weed out the unobservant quickly and save the expensive traps for the clever ones."

"Bit of an effort would be nice though," Ginny said. "The next two pits are in a straight line with this one. Who does that?"

"Do humans weave when they walk?" Mungo asked.

"The ones that sing do."

"Rack it!" Thud snapped. "Is the room secure or ain't it?"

Mungo switched smoothly. "Three apertures left, three right. Symmetrical layout. Ceiling clear to at least the first pit"

"Middle one is an alcove," Ginny said. "Pretty sure. Floor seems clear apart from the three pits."

The vanguard dwarves swiveled to cover the sides, squinting suspiciously down the length of their crossbows.

Cardamon rolled the second barrel in, waiting as Ginny crept as far as the edge of the pit, Mungo scrutinizing the floors and walls in front of her through his lensed calipers. She waved them forward.

"Clear to here."

Gong pointed at the dark passages that flanked the pit. "Clink and Grott, take left. Rasp and Keezix take right."

Ginny pointed Mungo with Rasp then fell in with Clink.

The pit was about fifteen feet deep, upright spears planted in the bottom of it. The barrel had shattered at the bottom but seemed to have taken a good number of the spears with it. The broken hafts remaining looked just as dangerous as the spearheads.

Thud stepped back from the edge and gave a nod to Cardamon.

"Need a size B!" Cardamon yelled toward the entrance. Durham heard several voices outside repeating the call. A few seconds later two dwarves ran in, arms loaded. They unfolded hinged supports and placed them on either side of the pit then ran a beam across them. The middle of the beam had a block and tackle assembly. Nibbly favored Durham with a quick grin as he came in and then squinted contemplatively at the room. Two more dwarves followed in his wake, carrying empty sacks. They began kicking through the bones on the floor, collecting the skulls in the bags. Dadger Ben came in, wearing a harness, and clipped himself to the tackle rope. He dropped into the pit, swinging back and forth over the spears below. Nibbly took up position at one end of the frame and began cranking a wheel, lowering Dadger down into the pit.

"Spears is clean," he called up. "Looks like that's the first time this trap been triggered; ain't nothin' else down here."

Thud nodded. "That fits with the sealed tomb door. Ain't no adventurers been in here yet."

"Spearheads ain't nothing special but they's in good shape." Dadger said.

"Bag 'em up," Nibbly said. He locked the pulley into place. A sawing noise began emanating from the pit

"What do we got on them openings?" Thud asked, waving his finger in a circle at the recesses in the walls.

"Report!" Durham was fascinated by how Gong expanded and contracted in his entirety each time he yelled.

"Quit yer hollerin'." Ginny's head poked out from the hallway. "Small crypts back here. Some burial stuff in 'em. Guessin' they were conkybines, mebbe. Room is clear of traps."

"Same report," Mungo called from the other side. "Word for word save a correct pronunciation of concubine."

"What's your take, Nibbly?" Thud asked.

"Looks like there were about twenty of 'em," Nibbly said. He kicked at one of the pieces of armor, flipped another over with his toe. "Rusted crap. Rib-cages in them chest pieces, though, and skulls in them helmets. Reckon the ballista's what did for most of 'em." He studied the hall a minute longer, sucking on his teeth. "Reckon them armored ones was in them middle alcoves on the sides there. Skellies came from them halls in the corners."

"The wives and their defenders," Thud said. "Fits right in with the traditionalist theme." He glanced at Ginny. "Secure that other door and let's get this area sorted."

Nibbly whistled and more dwarves came with sacks. He directed them into the corner rooms. The dwarves with the bags of collected skulls had taken them to one side and were removing them from the bags, methodically smashing each one with a hammer before returning it to the bag. Gong's team set their shield wall up in a half circle around the arch and rolled the ballista into the room, reloaded it and positioned it pointing at the archway.

♬♬♬

The room behind them had been stripped bare by Nibbly's team, wooden covers sealing the pit traps in the floor and enough lanterns for a banquet. Durham waited with Thud and Ruby as Ginny and Mungo examined the archway. It contained a tall black door shaped to fit the arch. The door's surface was textured and glossy like leather. Ginny was examining the door latch with her loupe while Mungo went around the door edges with a wire. They finished by sinking an eye hook into the door and retreating behind the shield dwarves before tugging on a rope to pull the door open.

A breeze gusted thick with rot, as if the dungeon beyond the door was exhaling.

Mungo rolled a lantern through the doorway. It descended

rapidly, revealing a sloping passage with high walls with a stone door at the bottom.

"Seriously?" Thud asked after a moment of contemplation.

Ginny stepped to the edge of the arch, leaned in carefully and looked up. She aimed her lantern up at the ceiling behind the arch.

"Sure 'nuff," she called back. "Looks like it'll block the end of the hall if we drop it. We'll have to stabilize it."

"Find the trigger for me," Thud called back. "Mungo, Cardamon! In there with ropes, nets and spikes. Truss it up tight." He turned to Durham and Ruby. "Rolling boulder trap, if you can believe it. This guy believed in the classics. Not quite turning out to be the sort I 'spected."

"How do you mean?" Durham asked.

"Well, there's a type o' dungeon we call 'Mixers'. There was a bit of a Dungeon boom few centuries back. Fashionable among the nobility for a bit. Dungeon's a pricey kinda thing, though, well, at least the fashionable sort are. So if you was a lesser sorta nobility without them sorta resources, what to do? How ta keep up with the trend without emptyin' yer vault? Dwarves spotted a bizness opportunity. In comes 'Mixer' dungeons. Design a few score o' mix 'n' match rooms and hallways, the noble assembles what they want and kin afford, contract the work out, decorate and ya got a quick dungeon for a fraction the cost.

"This place seemin' like it might be one o' them types. Pit traps and a rolling boulder trap?" Thud rolled his eyes. "I jest 'spected more from a lich necromancer warlord, I s'pose."

Ginny reappeared in the archway.

"Trigger removed, boulder secured," she announced. "Rest o' the hall looks clear from up here but I'd recommend a barrel down it all t' same. Most interesting though is the trigger. Here, take a look."

She held it up and they all squinted at it in the lamplight. She was holding up a skull with a broken forehead. A skeletal arm descended from the neck in place of a spine, bony fingers dangling at the end.

"Animated?" Thud asked.

Ginny nodded. "The skull was sitting along the wall like it was just left lyin' on the floor, arm extendin' behind it through the wall. Walk into its view and the arm gives a yank on the pulley to start the boulder rollin'."

"An undead trap mechanism."

"Aye. Doesn't rust or jam. Easy maintenance." She frowned at the skull. "Prob'ly not what this bloke had in mind fer his afterlife but we sent him on his way."

Thud was silent for a minute, stroking his beard, puffing on his cigar.

"I'm 'spectin' that's relative in a way we ain't cognizant of yet."

He shrugged then nodded at Cardamon and another barrel of dirt was rolled forward then sent rumbling down the slope. It thumped loudly against the stone door at the bottom. Ginny followed after it, picking her steps with care. She had her trap pole in hand and poked and prodded the floor and walls as she went.

"Clear!" she called from the bottom of the hall.

They stepped through the arch, Durham glancing up nervously. The boulder was tucked away in a recess above the archway. The dwarves had netting up in front of it, spiked into the stone of the walls. He could see the hole in the wall near the floor where the skull trigger had been. The walls of the hall were carved with an elaborate stone relief of skeletons rampaging through a burning city and slaughtering the living. Blackened stubs remained in sconces above the carvings.

"The fall of Tanahael," Ruby said. "This had to have been carved before the city fell, wouldn't it? When the tomb was made? I wonder if anyone asked any questions about it."

"Not this wall," Durham said, examining the carving to the right. He pointed. "That building is in Karthor. I know because I look at it everyday from my post." It was the Rookery, a brewery in a tower that had once housed ravens. They'd co-opted the name and mounted a stone raven statue on the roof. The raven was unmistakable on the tower depicted on the tomb wall. "He never attacked Karthor though. And that statue has only been there for the last dozen years or so."

Ruby pursed her lips and frowned but was silent.

Nibbly examined it and clucked his tongue.

"Some fine work but pretty small market for something like this. No accounting for taste though."

"How would you even get it out?" Durham asked.

"Well, it's carved into the facing rather than the native stone so it's at least on the plausible side. We'd have to cut it into sections and restore it at its destination, all of which makes it pretty cost prohibitive. Here's hoping Alaham liked tapestries too. Much simpler all around."

Durham gestured at the sconces. "Do liches need light?"

The entire column stopped in a thoughtful pause.

"Don't rightly know," Thud said. "No eyeballs. Ruby?"

"It's theorized that undead see, but in a different way than we do," Ruby said. "They are usually capable of functioning in complete darkness."

"I don't know much about how wood ages but those torches aren't six hundred years old," Durham said. "And sconces bolted to the wall indicates intent. We're not the first ones to come through here and whomever came before was invited."

"Int'restin' proposition. You're startin' to prove yourself right useful," Thud said. "What makes you think they was invited?"

"Someone had to have let them in through the front doors."

"Brilliant! You could be our first non-dwarf member!" Mungo said. He stroked his cat beard.

The stone door at the bottom was wide with a split down the middle. Two great iron rings hung from it, one on each side. Ginny was scrutinizing them with her eyepiece.

"Somethin' peculiar here," she said. "These rings ain't fixed in tight. 'Spect they'd come right out if you gave 'em a tug."

"Trap?" Thud asked.

"Probably, give us a minute."

Mungo trotted down to her. He had a utility belt that he wore over his shoulder, loaded with an array of metal picks and files. He selected one and began poking around the door rings with it. Ginny and Mungo began muttering back and forth, an incomprehensible string of jargon. Thud sat on the barrel and puffed at his cigar.

Mungo had managed to insert no less than six picks around one of the ring settings before Ginny began to slowly ease one of the rings out of the door. Durham tensed, expecting something awful to happen any second. Ginny stepped back with the ring and Mungo peered into the hole left behind, holding one of the gyro lanterns up, focused in a tight beam.

"Non-lethal," he announced after a moment. "Apply sufficient door ambulation force to the rings, they dislocate and a metal bar drops inside. Undoubtedly secures the door to the floor via an internal slide-lock bar mechanism."

"Twist the rings a quarter turn and you can lock them into place," Ginny said. "They've got this little notch on them that..."

"That's it?" Thud asked. "Simple one, eh? Pull the rings like normal and yer blown. Twists 'em first and they works."

"Affirmative," Mungo said. "The egress is still secured from within, however." He took a long thin bar and carefully slid it between the doors near the floor then began to slowly raise it up, coming to a stop when it was just under halfway. "Cross bar at this location," he announced. He wiggled the end of his shim. "Twenty pounder, give or take."

The dwarves brought in a heavy gauge telescoping steel bar with a fork on the end. Cardamon placed it at the door and adjusted its length until the door shim rested in the fork.

"This is gonna make a helluva clatter, sir," Ginny said. Thud nodded.

"Door breach positions!" he called, then turned to Durham. "That means get yerself back up there next to Ruby. I'm right behind ye."

They stood at the top watching as the dwarves readied. The rings were twisted and tied with ropes. The shield wall was produced and secured, Mungo and Ginny retreating behind it. One of the armored dwarves clanked his way forward to the door with a large hammer in his hand. With a grunt he brought it down hard on the shim, levering it against the fork support. A split second later there was a loud crash from behind the door.

The dwarf dove behind the shield wall, the rest of them lined up with the crossbows at the ready. Ginny and Mungo pulled on the ropes and the doors swung open.

The dwarves at the bottom of the hall all whistled in unison as they got their first view through the door.

"Don't lose yer heads!" Ginny barked. "Last thing I needs is one o' you bargin' in there and gettin' impaled by somethin'."

"Whaddawegot Gin?" Thud called down.

"Looks like the museum."

Nibbly chortled and rubbed his hands together.

"Museum?" Durham asked.

"Just our term for it," Thud said, starting down the hall. "The sort of folks that build themselves tombs like this often has the notion that they gets to take all of their stuff into the afterlife as long as its buried with 'em. Granted, if'n you're a lichy sort and know that your afterlife is gonna take place inside the tomb I can see that bein' a fairly practical type consideration."

They reached the doorway and looked in. The room was crescent-shaped, the doorway opening through the middle of the greater curve. Couches were strewn about, topped with precarious piles of crates. Chairs were stacked in a corner, piles of paintings leaning against them. Clay pots were clustered here and there amid shelves crowded with small statues and pyramids of scroll casings. Half full cans of paint, stuffed animal heads, three crutches, a few ironing boards, a tourney dummy, a rowboat hanging from the ceiling…lacking only a vendor to be a flea market. Ginny, Cardamon and Mungo were creeping through it, poking at things with sticks. There was a clear path through the room to a large double door on the other side. The door looked to be covered in gold and carved with designs. It glittered in the pixie light.

"Form up!" Gong barked. The vanguard moved up with their shields facing the golden door. The Diplomat was rolled in, loaded and positioned.

"Don't want nothin' interruptin'," Thud said.

Dadger kicked a clay pot, shattering it.

"What are you doing?" Nibbly shrieked.

"Checking to see if there's anything in it."

"There is a hole in the top! Turn it upside down if you want to know what's in it!" Nibbly glowered. "Coulda gotten a silver for that pot, ya dafty. Now you're on pot-shaking duty. Check em all for the lich's shrively bits. I'll catalog the fun stuff."

"Gonna take a good while to sort through this lot," Thud said. He was beaming. "Looks like this'll put us in good financial shape for this venture though, eh?"

"I estimates it'll at least covers cost," Nibbly said. "Some nice stuff but I'm not seein' anything yet that anyone's gonna retire on. Apart from the couches." He laughed, a giggle that trailed off into a sad silence when no one else joined in. "We'll see what kind of shape it's in," he went on. "Pretty dry in here but them things is old. Don't hold out much hope for them couches and the paintings is going to be pretty questionable. Statues will all be fine and there's plenty of small ones. Sell good too. We'll start by loading those before we gets into any of the big stuff."

"Do you think the phylactery might be in here somewhere?" Durham asked. "There's a lot of vases and pots."

"Possible but I wouldna say likely," Thud said. "It might seem clever to hide something like that amongst all of the other vases in here but even a group of adventurers coulda gotten this far in. I'm still havin' a hard time believin' that this lich is as amateur as this dungeon is makin' him seem. Alright, Nibbly, you and your team keep working this room. Keep an eye out for a phylactery but don't dig down for sunlight. Ginny? Mungo? Let's have a look at that door."

"No dust," Durham said.

"Pardon, lad?"

Durham pointed at the piles of objects in the room. "Dusty." He pointed at the clear pathway between the doors. "No dust."

"Well spotted. What do ya make of it?"

"Someone or something has been through here. Can't say much more than that."

"Might be he has a skelly or two sweepin' the place up."

"Seems odd that they wouldn't dust all of the valuables also."

"It does, at that. Well, somethin' to keep in mind I guess. Might make sense of somethin' else later."

"Door is clear," Ginny called. "Doesn't even have a means of latchin'. Ornamental-like. Just pulls open."

"Brace one side. We'll open the other to give us a choke-point. If there's anything in there it already knows we's here."

The vanguard had their crossbows positioned and ready. Clink was in place on The Diplomat. Ginny and Mungo hammered wedges in under the left side of the door and tied a rope to the pull ring on the right. They moved back behind the shield wall and Ginny handed Durham the end of the rope.

"You wanna do the honors? On a three count so Gong's crew knows what's happenin'?"

Durham took a deep breath.

"One…two…THREE!" He yanked hard on the rope.

"Was expectin' more skellies, really," Thud said. They stood in the doorway, studying a room that, among its many qualities, was skeleton-free. "Think them bunch in the entry was his whole crew?"

"I suppose it's possible," Ruby said. "One expects a lich to have a bit more necromantic power than that, though. Particularly since he is in possession of the Mace of Guffin."

"Might be a lotta pyrite. Mebbe he's just a pretentious mummy."

The room was in the shape of a half-circle with a half-domed ceiling high overhead, the curved wall matching the crescent of the museum room. A tall statue stood in the middle, a robed figure in black stone with a freakishly long neck and a skull mask of gold, as if its face had been dipped in bullion. Its hands were clasped in front of it, holding a large crystal prism. A half-dozen other statues were scattered around the room, anonymous in hooded robes, each bearing a mirror.

"Light-beam puzzle," Ginny said. She pointed at a glimmering hole in the ceiling. "Beam from there, prob'ly. Has to be the right time of day. Or night, liches bein' what they is. Statues have to be turned to get the beam to reflect all the way to the center."

"Well, run the room for traps and get Cardamon in on

figgerin' out what 'xactly happens if the puzzle gets solved."

"Been a mighty slow day for the Vanguard," Gong said as they stepped away from the door. He was leaning against the shield wall combing his beard with his fingers.

"That's a good thing and you know it," Thud said. "Fightin' is the biggest wild-card. I like all me dwarves to come out with all their bits."

"Is there usually more fighting?" Durham asked.

"Depends on the type of dungeon," Gong said. "Some have open access and just about anything can move in and set up for itself. Beasts, monsters, whatnot. Place like this, though, sealed up for however many centuries and you're not going to see much alive in here unless there's been a breach over time, either from outside or from beneath. Then you might get big spiders, rodents, that sort of thing. A dwarf can make a fine living just clearing rats out of dungeons."

"I've heard stories about statues coming alive," Durham said, looking over his shoulder at the statue room.

"You get that sort of thing when there's a geomancer in the dungeon," Gong said. "Or a golemancer. A Necromancer type likely wouldn't know the first thing about getting a statue to move. Their closest trick is like we saw in the entry: sticking a skeleton in a suit of armor. Skeletons aren't too good at moving plate mail around though. Too big for them. They rattle around inside of it too much. Makes them slow and clumsy. They do better in chainmail. We'll be ready if those statues in there get lively but I'm not expecting that will be an issue. Gryngo will set charges up to blow them into gravel just in case and we'll have the pickaxes standing by for anything that survives."

Cardamon had strolled up during the conversation and stood, waiting, hands in pockets, his half-lidded eyes making him seem chronically apathetic.

"Center statue opens at the base," he said, once Thud arched an eyebrow in his direction.

"And?" Thud asked, after a few seconds of silence indicated that Cardamon had reached the end of his prepared briefing.

Cardamon shrugged. "Dunno. I expect monsters. Can't say until we open it. No exits from the room and no tomb yet so maybe the statue is a sarcophagus and Alaham will pop out. Maybe it's just hiding the door."

"Gonna think prob'ly the latter," Thud said.

"Oh, and it's been opened recently. Fresh scrapes on the floor."

"Hmmm," Thud said. His eyes narrowed and he stroked his

beard. Durham had noticed that when he did so he only used his fingertips, likely to avoid getting his beard hair caught in his rings. "You thinkin' what I'm thinkin'?"

"Probably not," Durham said after a suitable pause for reflective thought.

"No dust in the walkway out there, like you said. Them torches in the hall sconces. The other rooms and halls had clear floors too. Fresh scrapes in the next room where the statues opened. Thinking you were spot on about someone havin' been in here recently."

"That farmer chap didn't mention seeing anyone though," Cardamon said

"Because they paid him to be silent, maybe," Durham said. "He had new clothes. Expensive ones."

"Which raises the question of who would visit a lich?"

"More importantly," Cardamon said, "Is they still here?"

⚑⚑⚑

Everyone was in position. Shield wall arrayed, ballista aimed, precautionary explosive charges laid. Leery had been called in. Leery seemed eccentric, even among the dwarves.

Instead of the kilts the rest of them wore she had a pair of trousers that were missing the legs, revealing knees and shins crisscrossed with scabs and long scars parting the hair. She had a green leather jerkin that was too small for her and wore her beard in a long braid that seemed to whip about with a life of its own.

Her first act had been to just shine a lantern on the crystal.

"Sometimes that works," she said, after it didn't. "But usually it doesn't. Light sensitive trigger mechanisms are expensive. The light beams are likely just gilding. It's the position of the statues that matter, like tumblers in a combination lock."

"The configuration to achieve proper light reflection is relatively simplistic," Mungo said. "Shall I position the statuary?"

Leery nodded.

Mungo's idea of positioning the statues turned out to be directing other dwarves on positioning the statues. In all fairness, Durham wasn't sure whether the gnome had either the height or the muscle to move them. The statues were all moved into place with no results.

"Is that right?" Leery asked.

"I assure you that were a beam of light to come through the ceiling aperture that it would be reflected into the central prism," Mungo said.

"Maybe it's positional AND light sensitive?" Leery held up her lantern to the prism again. A grating sound rumbled through the floor. Leery somersaulted backwards through the air as a seam appeared in the base of the central statue, the halves of the base moving apart to reveal stairs leading further down. Leery rolled her way to the top of the stairs.

"Looks like the main burial chamber," she yelled back.

Thud snorted skeptically.

"Too easy," he muttered. "Too small, too simple, too basic."

Mungo extended his lantern-pole into the room at the bottom of the stairs.

"Negative adversaries. Type C Room."

"Send in the chickens!" Ginny called.

The order was relayed back toward the entrance. Goin jogged in a minute later, a pole on each shoulder, a coop dangling from each end. He set the cages down behind the shield wall, removed one of the chickens and began attaching some sort of complicated harness to its head, the chicken providing a running commentary on his efforts.

"What's he doing to them?" Durham asked.

"Chickens is pretty useful for finding traps in cramped or cluttered areas where barrels ain't so good," Thud replied. "They sees somethin' outta place an' they pecks it to see if its food. The difficulty is in getting' them to go in the right direction in the first place. So Goin puts a little harness on their heads with a worm hangin' on it. Donkey an' a carrot kinda thing. Catch is that chicken's got eyes on the sides o' their nogs and don't do so hot at seein' somethin' dangling right in front of 'em. So Mungo fixed that by adding lenses o'er their eyes that reflects the carrot with li'l mirrors. Problem then was that the chicken was seein' the worm on both sides and would stand still outta pure stupid while it tried to decide which way to go. So he added a little springy mechanism thingy on top that swings the worm back and forth so the chicken only sees it one side at a time. Tha's workin' well enough to get it to run forward in a zig-zag which is random enough that it seems to get us pretty good coverage."

"Wouldn't it be easier to just, I don't know, yell and wave your arms a bit?"

Thud nodded and then gave a 'whaddaya goin' ta do' shrug.

"I figgers if Mungo keeps at it long enough, eventually he'll just remove the chicken entirely and we'll have some new li'l thingwhirly that might be good for somethin'."

Goin had distributed the harnessed chickens amongst the shield dwarves.

"Release the chickens!" he yelled.

The dwarves flung them down the stairwell and a great deal of squawking and flapping commenced.

"One chicken down," Ginny said. "Flaming dart trap at W915, trigger on FC2."

Mungo began scribbling in his notebook.

A loud thump came from within the room.

"Chicken two down," Ginny said. "Block trap FD5."

A surprised squawk came from within. Ginny winced. "Ouch. Three down. Pivoting spear wall at W1220, trigger probably at FD8."

She waved her arm in the air.

"All right, team, form up. One survivor. Looks like Miss Cluck at 4-1 odds."

Several of the shield dwarves muttered curses and began exchanging coins.

Ginny and her team advanced slowly into the room. She poked her head out a few minutes later.

"Clear!"

Thud strolled down the steps, Durham and Ruby close behind.

The first thing Durham saw was the glint of gold. It seemingly came from everywhere—the walls, the objects piled around the room, the massive sarcophagus in the center. The walls were hung with ornate tapestries, gold thread woven amongst bands of color and panels of sigils, shining from woven demonic faces. Vases, armor and chests were draped with strings of pearls and jewels, baubles and beads. Rolls of rotted silk were stacked in a far corner beside a massive weapon rack arrayed with glittering swords. A large stone block sat on the floor near the coffin with chicken oozing out from under it. A second chicken was impaled on a spear that extended from the room's far wall and the third was slumped smoking in the corner with a quizzical expression.

The golden sarcophagus in the middle was shaped like a temple, arches, pillars and windows carved in detail along its sides. The lid was sloped and fashioned like a tiled roof, peaking in a jewel encrusted snake depicted in a sinuous weave along the coffin's length. Miss Cluck was standing awkwardly atop the sarcophagus. She'd managed to eat her worm, the string still leading from the rod to her beak and now just appeared to be confused by the array of lenses strapped to her head.

Thud stood in the doorway, contemplating the room.

"Ginny? Mungo?"

"Traps disabled and clear. Take a look at this, though." Ginny held out a lit candle. She stepped near the coffin with it and lowered it to the floor. The flame suddenly flickered and leaned in towards the base of the sarcophagus.

"Somethin' under that thing, I figger. Hole of some kind."

Thud's grin split his face.

"I knew there had to be more to this place."

Ginny shrugged.

"Might just be some kinda oubliette. Maybe for his necessaries."

"Necessaries?" Durham asked. "What sort of necessaries would a lich have?"

"Dunno. Moisturizer, mebbe?"

"Well, we'll see in a bit," Thud said. "Ready for you Nibbly!" he yelled. Ginny's team scurried out, leaving only Ginny and Mungo. Nibbly, Dadger and Leery appeared and began shuffling around the room, bags in hand, squinting at things and poking them. Ginny and Mungo were crawling around the base of the sarcophagus, prodding at it with rods.

"Leaf and paste," Nibbly said sadly after a minute or two.

Thud arched his bushy eyebrows.

"Most o' the gold here is leaf," Nibbly said. "Scrape that coffin clean and ya might have enough to make a ring. Same with them chairs and such. Lotta them jools is glass and paste. Some real, mebbe. Tapestries is good, though."

Thud nodded but didn't look overly disappointed. In fact, if anything, his grin got bigger.

"Show tomb for the locals. 'Nuff to make an amateur happy and send 'im on 'is way," he said.

They stepped out of the way as Nibbly's crew began carting out furnishings and loading their sacks. Nibbly himself was busy removing tapestries and rolling them up.

"So is there a lever or something that lifts the coffin?" Durham asked.

"Yup," Thud said. "Three of 'em." He held up a crowbar and winked. "Nibbly, keep on with what yer doing but I also want that sarcophagus secured and prepped to be hauled out of here. No telling what sorta surprise might 'ave been left inside of that thing and I wanna open it outdoors in the clear. Ginny, I want traps team to help. Lend dwarfpower where needed and supervise the sealing just in case there's sumthin dodgy waiting."

He nodded at Durham. "Back into the fresh air, shall we?"

Durham and Ruby followed Thud back through the dungeon and outside into the field tent that had been erected behind the wagons. A large table filled most of it, a dozen or so chairs around it. The walls of the tent had been lowered against the evening breeze and the pixies and mosquitoes it brought with it. A large metal pot was on the ground next to the table, filled with water.

"We aren't going further in tonight?" Durham asked.

"Patience, lad," Thud said. He lit a fresh cigar and blew a large smoke ring with a contented sigh. Gammi appeared with mugs of ale and began distributing them.

"Got to take these sorta things slow and careful," Thud said. "No such thing as 'too cautious' with these sortsa places. And it ain't all about delving in—we gots the clerical side o' things to handle also."

Nibbly arrived from the tomb with a bulging sack and hoisted it onto the table. He had donned thick leather smithing gloves, goggles and a half-mask that covered his mouth and nose. Thud stood and waved everyone back from the table.

"Keep yer distance a bit here, 'til we knows it's clean."

"Clean?" Durham asked.

"Aye, some o' these ol' timey bastards liked to dip their jools in various poisons before entombing them. This is the jewelry from the wives. Some rulers like using it when they've got a bunch o' still breathin' wives that's s'posed to be laid to rest with them. Give 'em some poison rings and out they go."

Nibbly upended the sack and jewelry spilled out across the table. Necklaces and rings, pearls and gold and gemstones. Durham's breath caught in his throat. Thud sucked on his cigar a moment, regarding the pile.

"Seems Alaham liked glittery wives, eh?" Thud said. "Nice little haul for first day's work."

"Little haul?" asked Durham incredulously. "I could buy a house with what's on that table."

"Not once it's been split twenty-two ways," Nibbly said. "And that's only what's left after we subtract expedition costs. Might be enough for you to get a small shed. I reckon there's more where this came from. Never know how deep these things are gonna go but ol' Alaham had plenty o' opportunity to hoard up some nice bits."

Ruby had begun sorting through the jewelry with a pair of tongs, examining each piece and making notes in her journal before dropping it into the pot of water next to the table.

"Now we gotta boil these clean, record 'em for posterity and appraise 'em for prosperity," Thud grinned. "That'll keep us busy until supper."

♝♝♝

The boiled jewelry had been placed in one of the chicken cages, along with Miss Cluck, who proceeded to plop herself down on it like the world's most pathetic dragon. Her purpose was to determine if any danger remained from the jewelry. It provided an odd sort of suspenseful entertainment over dinner, everyone periodically glancing over at the cage to see if she'd toppled over dead yet. When Mungo stepped up and threw a blanket over the cage he immediately had everyone's attention.

"A philosophical conundrum for your edification and perturbation; your discussion betwixt mastications," he squeakily proclaimed.

Thud's eyes narrowed. "Er...jest go behind a tree er sumthin' 'n' wash yer hands after, eh?"

"A riddle to discuss while we eat," Ruby translated.

"Ah, go on then." He winked at Durham.

The gnome gestured grandly at the blanket covered cage.

"Is the chicken alive or is it dead?"

"Got five eagles says it's alive!" Nibbly called. "Less'n it keeled over in the last few seconds."

"Ah, but theoretically it could be either, yes?" the gnome said. "No one can know for sure."

"Reckon the chicken's got a solid notion on the matter," Gryngo said.

Goin put his ear next to the blanket. "I kin hear it movin'"

"Ain't much as far's riddles go," Thud muttered.

Mungo sighed. "Don't you see? It could be either! And therefore, until we observe it, both answers are correct! It leads to speculation of parallel realms with every possible outcome, each echoes of the others!"

"Like mirrors, kinda?" Goin asked.

"Precisely! Except each reflection has a minuscule difference. Imagine an infinity of other worlds, each just slightly different but sharing most of the same things. Events, people, even such small things as words. Even our words which seem obscure and strange could be commonly used in the world next door and they'd know immediately what you were talking about!"

"Like slintwhiff or banglypang?" Thud asked. "Never did think them words was proper."

"Exactly!"

"Mooshwort!"

"Precisely!"

"Chinfig!"

"Undoubtedly!"

"Kangaroo and boomerang!"

"Well," Mungo said. "Not sure I'd quite push it that far."

Durham tuned the discussion out and turned to Ruby. "What exactly is the point of building a dungeon?" Some big underground maze full of traps and monsters. Seems like a lot of unnecessary expense and effort. And why are they called 'dungeons'? I thought dungeons were places where prisoners were kept."

Ruby looked up with the spark in her eyes that Durham had come to realize appeared whenever a question was asked that fell anywhere near the history category.

"Well, once you place prisoners somewhere, you place

guards and locks there as well," she said. "Eventually someone realized that they could save a bit of coin on guards by replacing them here and there with a few deathtraps in choice spots. Now you've got an underground place with locks, guards and traps — only natural for it to start looking like an ideal place to keep your valuables as well. Once you start keeping valuables down there, it makes a certain sort of sense to move the criminals elsewhere. Or to maybe just lop their heads off. The idea caught on well in Keine. They think whatever is buried with you goes with you beyond. They fill their tombs with treasure and virgins..."

"Virgins?" Durham asked. "People virgins? Alive ones?"

"Well, they don't stay alive for too long once the tomb is sealed, but yes, people virgins. Well, maybe some other varieties of virgins too but that isn't something they tend to advertise. Afterlives, regardless of their religion, tend to have a common theme in that they last a very long time. One needs to pass the time somehow and un-virgining virgins might seem a more appealing prospect than rereading all of your books again. You give them poison jewelry, light them on fire or wait a few weeks for them to starve to death. The notion is that if someone robs your tomb that you lose your treasure in the afterlife as well. But even if someone takes all of your gold it's pretty good odds that they'll leave you your virgins. Far lower resale value.

"No one wants to lose the gold, however, Keine or elsewhere. Paying guards to watch your tomb for the length of an afterlife is cost prohibitive, not to mention that it greatly increases the likelihood of prematurely losing your virgins. Owners of dungeons took pretty readily to the idea of filling the places with traps, tricks and puzzles as a means to guard their treasure. What's more secure than a locked vault full of gold? A locked vault full of gold at the end of a maze filled with spiky bits that slam down on anyone trying the maze.

"After a time someone figured out a way to add guards of a sort. There are plenty of dangerous things out and about in the world and many of them are perfectly happy living underground. If you included habitats for them in your dungeon then you get free guards. Likewise, some of the fae races that prefer living underground figured out that if they could move in to part of a dungeon that it gave their homes quite a bit of free security. The idea spread to underground lairs that weren't tombs. Since the fae races tend to have belongings, outsiders came to view their homes as dungeons as well. Break in, dodge the traps, kill the monsters and you could maybe haul off enough treasure to retire on. Particularly after the daemonwars when the remnants of the hordes scattered and hid, often in the same places their fae allies were living. Going in and slaughtering anything that moved was encouraged as an act of public service."

"That's us," Thud said. "Public servants." He'd wandered over from Mungo's chicken audience and stood just behind and to the left of Ruby, sipping at a mug.

"There are going to be demons in there?" Durham asked, looking toward the crypt. A bit of his stomach seemed to have relocated itself into his throat, leaving him queasy and swallowing.

"Probably not here," Thud said. "See, dungeons tend to develop based on what started 'em. Here we got a crypt with a lich in it. Place is as much its home as it is a dungeon and they can be right particular about anyone else livin' there. Demons ain't known for their suitability as tombmates. Demons ain't big fans of the undead, either, considering how the daemonwars ended."

Durham frowned. "The whole Bonebin thing? Isn't that just a bard tale?"

Ruby shook her head. "Not according to the histories we

have in the Athenaeum.

"Five centuries ago, when the daemons came, the kingdoms fell quickly. No army could stand against their numbers. The Hermits gathered in council and determined that their best course was an even larger army. An army that grew for every loss it took and for every enemy it defeated. What they had in that number were the dead. They tasked the grey Hermits with it. Not only was death under their domain but their neutrality insured that balance would remain after the war. They crafted a set of bone weapons and armor and bestowed them on one of the Archons of Grimm, raising him to be the first of the Avatars. Though the grey Hermits directed the crafting, all of the Hermits lent their aid. Each of the items they made was an artifact greater than any before or since and, as a set, they made the wearer almost a god. But the greatest of all of them was the crown. It allowed the wearer to control the dead as an army. If one fell, it rose again. Anything the army killed rose and joined its ranks. They were unstoppable and they destroyed the daemon army in less than a month. Afterward the dead were laid to rest in a secret place that came to be called the Bonebin and the bone artifacts hidden away in guarded places known only to the gray Hermits. Should the daemons ever return, the dead are still there, in numbers far, far greater than what we saw here, waiting to be called again."

"And there's where the avatar's name came from? The bonebin?"

Ruby nodded. "Only the grey Hermits know who he was before he was raised."

"Odd earned-name, Bonebin," Thud mused, "but guess it's better than 'Larry' or whatever it was beforehand."

"Liches aren't concerned with keeping their treasure for the afterlife as they've chosen to remain in this world for their afterlife," Ruby said. "All liches were necromancers when they had a heartbeat as it's the only line of magic that allows someone to figure out how to become a lich. What drives necromancers, initially, at least, is the lure of forbidden knowledge. You tell them that they're not to know something and they immediately want to know it, partly so they can figure out why they're not meant to know it. There's power in knowledge and a little power feeds the desire for more of it. If the knowledge is something that few others have then it makes the power rare and especially seductive. The thing about knowledge and power is that there's always more of both to be had and each increases the other. Suddenly a human lifespan begins to look ridiculously short compared to the amount of knowledge and power left to acquire. And so the necromancer first conspires to extend his life. A common aspiration among wizards as sorcery offers many ways to artificially stretch your life thin to cover more years. Necromancy goes a step further in that it offers the possibility to keep going, even after death. It's not an easy thing, however, and most necromancers fail. Liches are fortunately quite rare. Unfortunately, it is only the most powerful of necromancers that achieve it. Add in the knowledge and power that they acquire after death and they become increasingly dangerous as their years add up. Alaham has been a lich for centuries. He will not be an easy foe. Every lich has a critical weakness, however."

"The phylactery?" Durham asked.

Thud nodded. "If I have me way we won't even see the lich. Grab the mace, smash the phylactery and get out. Probably won't work that way, however. A lich guards his phylactery like an elf guards his salad."

"And there lies his motivation for creating a dungeon," Ruby said. "It's a place hidden away, to continue the pursuit of forbidden knowledge and power and, more importantly, a way to guard the phylactery that allows him to do so."

"Lich dungeons grow o'er the years," Thud said. "The

necromancers got all them skellies wandering around, doin' whatever they tells 'em to do. They never tire, they never need feeding or paying. You just set 'em to work, digging, building. East, beyond the Hammerfells, there's a land where necromancy ain't forbidden and the dwarves have always found less work there as they're competin' with skeleton crews which come a lot cheaper and build faster. Alaham's had a lot o' years secreted away underground. We ain't see it yet but I'm guessing he's put a load o' work into the place."

"The small favor is that there's a limit to what a necromancer can animate," Ruby said. "Each corpse they have up and walking requires a little of their power to maintain. They have to balance their number of servants with the amount of power they can manage."

"So every skeleton you kill increases the lich's power?" Durham asked.

"Well, sorta," Thud said. "Likely he just uses the fresh power to make more of 'em. Never ending stream of reinforcements, least 'til he runs out of intact skulls. Based on the number of dead that Ruby says was in that graveyard don't make that seem too likely of an occurrence. Walking dead things is the primary means for a necromancer to defend themselves. They got some other tricks too, granted, but most of their magery requires their target to already be dead. I may not know much about the specifics of necromancy but I do know that the best way to defend against it is with big, heavy things that crush bones. They needs an intact skull to animate the rest o' the bones that go with it. Break the skulls and the skeletons go down for good."

He finished the last swallow from his mug. "Figure that's enough time we killed by jawin."

Thud gestured toward Mungo.

"Reveal the chicken!"

Mungo whipped the blanket away with dramatic flare.

The hen blinked unhappily at the lantern light.

"Go ahead and move that jewelry to the strongbox. Miss Cluck there will live to see another adventure."

-12-

Morning in a tomb was much the same as evening in a tomb. At least nobody had objected to Durham bringing his mug of coffee in with him. Breakfast had been boiled pupae with mossbeard leaving Durham to settle with an extra cup of coffee as his pancake supply had dwindled to irrelevance. Thud and Ginny were next to the sarcophagus, crowbars in hand. Mungo was between them with an awkward looking metal contraption. Steel bands had been bolted to the sides of the sarcophagus, holding the lid securely in place. The two dwarves hoisted at the corners enough to raise the coffin an inch or so and Mungo slid one end of his contraption underneath the edge. He began working a lever on it and, with a great deal of clanking, it began to slowly raise the edge of the sarcophagus revealing a dark oblong hole in the floor.

A smell rose from the darkness. A smell so strong it was a flavor. The sort of smell that coats one's sinuses like a glaze. A smell like the forgotten container of cabbage, the potato at the bottom of the bin, a week old battlefield in summer, a rotting skunk drowned in a communal outhouse, a mummy's breath and boiling giblets, all rolled into one, tied with a bow and then left to ferment for a century.

"Wasn't me," Nibbly said.

"Masks," Thud ordered. The dwarves began rummaging through their packs, one by one producing a small cloth covered dome-shaped frame with affixed leather straps. A large pan was produced from somewhere and filled with water. Ginny added a few splashes of scented oils to it, gave it a stir then stood back as each dwarf dipped their mask into it. Durham found the mask in his own pack and followed suit. Once it was on his face it managed to at least take the edge off of the reek, dulling it with what seemed a combination of vinegar, clove and rose. The room now smelled like a funeral home rather than a home funeral. Thud's mask had a hole in it just large enough to allow his cigar to extrude.

"All right," Thud said, his voice slightly muffled. "Anyone starts feelin' woozy down there you pulls out. Trust me when I say you don't wants ta puke into one o' these masks. Like havin' a bowl o' Keldorian soup strapped to your face."

"Are we going to open the coffin?" Durham asked.

"Aye, we'll get to it," Nibbly said. "This bein' a fake tomb removes a bit o' incentive. At best it's going to be empty. At worst there's a trap or some nasty dead bloke just waitin' for the lid to open so he can jump out an' yell 'boogy boogy'. We'll cart it outside in the sun and open it from a distance with the ballista pointin' at it."

Mungo was wielding his lantern pole again, lowering the light into the hole in the floor. The faelight revealed a flight of narrow stone steps descending into the darkness.

"Different," Ginny said.

"Eh?" Thud asked.

"The stonework. This ain't part of the original tomb. Amateur work. Not Magrazar's."

They rolled one of the dirt barrels in and sent it down the stairs, counting about thirty thumps before the final thud at the bottom.

"Al'ight," Thud said. "Marchin' order. Gong, you're up front. Mungo on Gong's shoulders, Ginny jest behind. Two crossbows af'er that and then I'll bring up rear with the humans." He glanced around at the looting team. "Dadger, you follow us down to act as order runner if we need to bring a specialty team in. Nibbly, make sure everyone outside is ready to move. I 'spect this is where things are gonna start to get lively."

Gong waddled and clanked forward, his plate mail causing him to resemble a temple bell. Mungo was able to easily perch on one of his ham sized shoulders, dangling the light in front. He'd donned a new pair of goggles along with his breath mask, an array of different lenses fanned out around his head, each on a swivel arm allowing them to be moved in and out of place.

Durham stepped in behind Ginny and the two crossbow wielding dwarves. One was Goin, the chicken keeper, Clink the other one. Clink was squat with a massive beard which he'd braided, drawn up at the sides and then wrapped around the top of his head like a turban. Durham tried to assume that this was possibly very stylish among dwarves. He had one glass eye that never quite seemed to line up with the real one which gave him a half-crazed look. Ruby stood next to him and Thud brought up the rear with Dadger.

The stairs were steep and narrow. They opened out into a tall dome-shaped cavern, the carved stone of the stairway giving way to natural rock that had been worked and smoothed, the walls filled in places with stonework. Shadowy openings around the circumference suggested multiple passages and caverns beyond. Dozens of crates were stacked precariously in the center of the room. Ginny advanced cautiously, poking at the floor in front of her with her stick as she went.

"These crates are new," she said once she'd reached them. "Got merchant stamps on 'em"

"Recognize any?" Thud asked.

Ginny shrugged. "Nibbly might. Looks like most of 'em is empty. Ones I can see at least. Some of 'em got letters on 'em. 'L'. 'S'. This one got some papers in it." She produced a pair of tongs and extracted a scroll from one of the smaller crates, carrying it back as if it were a snake. Ruby spent a moment examining it.

"The seal on it is from a scribe in Keine." She took the scroll from the tongs, cracked the wax and unrolled a few inches of scroll. "The letters are Karthorian but I don't recognize the words. Poetic form. Possibly a chant of some kind."

Thud spat. "Ain't a fan of mysteries in my dungeons," he said. "We seen all them signs o' someone bein' here recently. Seems unlikely it was all just for deliverin' crates though."

"This one got an 'XL' on it," Ginny called. "Maybe they's Bronjian numerals? That's 40, ain't it? There's one with an 'M'. That's one of the big numbers. A hunnert or a thousand methinks. Don't know what an 'S' would be though."

"Clothing sizes," Durham said. There was a brief silence as everyone considered this.

"For playing dress-up with the skellingtons?" Dadger asked.

Durham shrugged. "Haven't figured that bit out yet."

"We'll have Nibbly go through 'em all, see if anything else is in 'em," Thud said. "Gong, what's yer take on the exits?"

"Seven of 'em, all natural stone that's been worked. Best course is pick one and barricade the others."

Thud nodded. "All right, maintain ready status. Alaham knows he's got company and there's bound to be some blastback at some point. Dadger, bring Giblets in and tell Nibbly we need some constructin' done down here." He held his fae lamp high and approached one of the dark openings in the cavern wall. "Let's at least 'ave a peek, eh?" Gong frowned but rearranged the vanguard with a few quick gestures.

"Catacombs," Thud said, peering into the gloom. "Shelves cut in the walls. No bones though."

"It connects through," Durham said, pointing. Light from the fae lamp was dimly visible at the next opening to Thud's right. A few minutes of experimenting with the lantern once Giblets arrived revealed that six of the openings were three looped passageways, all with empty internment shelves. The seventh had internment shelves like the others, choked with cobwebs, some containing a few scattered brown bones. It led straight, deeper. Nibbly set the construction crew to explore and secure the loops while he began going through the crates. The advance team reassembled at the seventh hall.

They waited a minute while Ginny did an initial barrel check and then sent a chicken after it for good measure.

The height of the dwarves in front of Durham allowed him a clear view of the dark passageway ahead as they moved forward. He felt like he was walking into a throat. Mungo's light bobbed in front as the gnome examined the ground and walls for potential dangers. Ginny followed just behind him, holding her lantern pole up high and watching the ceiling.

The passage twisted back and forth, rising and falling but mostly falling. Though the stone had been worked it was still uneven in spots, knobs of cave-stone or dips to catch the unwary foot, seeping cracks in the walls. Small stalactites crowded the ceiling, providing a perpetual drizzle. Their shadows bobbed long and dark in the swaying yellow light. The floor was wet beneath their feet, the air thick and still. They moved forward slowly, Ginny and Mungo constantly pausing the line to double-check various bits of debris and tangles of bone. The dwarves in the second row stared fiercely at the bones they passed, as if daring them to move. Occasionally they jabbed at the air with their crossbows. Miss Cluck wandered on ahead of them, zig-zagging and giving the occasional annoyed squawk as she pecked at the fresh worm dangling in front of her.

"A moment," Ruby said after a few minutes. She stepped to one of the shelves and used her lantern pole to clear the drifts of web aside. After a moment of looking she stepped to a different shelf and did the same.

"None of these are complete," she said. "Most of the skulls

are missing, many of the major bones..." She moved to a third shelf. "No spine on this one, There's a skull but it's broken."

"Spare parts and leftovers, mebbe," Thud said. "Only reason I can think of wot 'splains these just lyin' about rather than crawlin' after us."

"You need a whole skeleton for it to animate?" Durham asked.

"Well, at least enough of it that it's of actual use," Thud said. "No good just animatin' a ribcage and some teeth. Gotta have an intact skull, though. Without that you might as well be trying to animate a bunch o' sticks."

"Many of them empty, like the ones back in the cave," Ruby said. "No dust either."

"It's like the world's creepiest bunkhouse," Thud muttered.

"Archway ahead," Ginny announced. They all turned their attention forward. Mungo rolled a gyrolantern ahead. The cave passage terminated into a hallway, bare and plain, constructed rather than natural cave. Miss Cluck stood about ten feet in, unharmed but no longer advancing as she'd finally managed to secure her worm. She peered about myopically, occasionally pecking at the floor.

"Well, now, I'm s'picious as all hell o' that," Thud said.

"Dadger, go tell Nibbly to bring the team in and start working this hall and tell the support team to move up. I want help close."

Dadger scurried off, soon becoming just a light bobbing in the darkness behind them and then was gone. Ginny had rolled the barrel up and she and Mungo moved into the hall slowly, pushing the barrel ahead and scrutinizing the walls. Gong followed them closely, Goin and Clink just behind with their crossbows raised. Thud let them get about fifteen feet ahead before stepping forward, waving Ruby and Durham to follow. The silence lay thickly across them, the shuffling of their feet seeming shockingly loud. Halfway down the hall Durham felt his stomach lurch madly. Everyone froze.

"Y'all felt that?" Thud asked.

"Aye," Ginny said. She squinted at the walls suspiciously. "Sumthin' jest happened. Felt like I fell offa wall, kinda."

They waited a long silent minute.

"Hmph," Thud said. "Well, nothing seems to 'ave come of it. Maybe that was just Alaham wakin' up."

"Shouldn't Dadger have returned by now?" Ruby asked.

"Yeh," Thud said. "Reckon he should've." He peered back down the hall behind them. "All right. Ginny, mark yer spot there. Time to backtrack and make sure we've got ever'thing secure from the entrance to here. I'm suddenly gettin' a bad feelin' an' I want ter make it go away."

They retreated down the hall, Miss Cluck bobbing behind them apparently having decided that the light was a good thing to stay next to. They arrived back at the arch.

"Well, shit," Thud said.

-13-

The catacombs that should have lain beyond the arch at the start of the hall were gone. A crumbled stone alcove was all that was visible through the arch.

"Ambulatory chambers!" Mungo squeaked excitedly.

"That was so smooth, too," Ginny said. Her voice was hushed and breathless with awe.

Thud arched an eyebrow at her and emitted an impatient puff of smoke.

"Uh, sir, sorry, it's just…" Ginny paused, her gaze never leaving the walls. "We used to discuss the possibility back in my buildin' days but I've never actually seen…"

"Pull it together," Thud snapped.

"Yes, sir. Moving dungeon parts is what we're talking. That lurch we felt back there was the actually the entire hallway moving. Did it so clean we scarce even noticed. Dunno if we went up, down or sideways but we's in a diff'rent place than wot we was. We'd kicked the idea around, like I was sayin', but couldn't think of a way of doin' it that wouldn't end with all the involved mechernisms corroding into junk within a century or two."

"Tellin' me this Alaham figgered somethin' out that was stumpin' all o' you architect types? Dwarven architects? Finest in all the lands 'n' all that?"

"Ermm, yes sir, it would seem so," Ginny's voice was slightly abashed.

"Was it sumthin' we triggered?"

"Not unless there's some sort of counterbalance involved that we caused to shift by walking in the hall. Possible, but a system like that would..." her voice trailed off. "Actually, with the engineering required to have a moving hall I 'spect a counterbalance trigger might not be too much of a stretch. Ordinarily that's some pretty tricky building, especially one that will maintain over time. Other than that, someone or something would have had to have known where we were and have manually triggered it. Unless…that animated mechanism that triggered the boulder trap?"

Mungo shook his head. "An animated trigger, perhaps, but you'd still need well maintained machinery. Oiling and repairing seems an impractical use of limited animated resources."

Thud pulled the mask off of his face and gave the air an experimental sniff.

"Well, the stink ain't so bad at least." He puffed furiously at his cigar as if attempting to rectify that. "Gong and Mungo, you go down and see what's at the other end of the hall. Gong should be enough to trigger a counterbalance if there is one and from here we can sees what happens. I'm also good and curious to know what's at the other end o' this hall now that it's moved. Safe enough here so Goin and Clink, go with 'em jest in case there's anything clatterin' around down there." The dwarves moved off slowly, their pool of light and Miss Cluck following them into the darkness. Thud turned his attention to Ginny.

"Now, I ain't callin' you out or nuthin' but seems to me that if this hallway moves around there's a seam somewhere that didn't get spotted. Might be good to get eyes on that so we know what to look for."

Ginny nodded silently and began studying the corner of the

hallway by the arch. Thud knelt at the threshold with a piece of chalk and drew a chalk line across the threshold with a number 1 at each end.

"This is a new one so I'm inventin' this system as we go," he said. "Figure if things start movin' around again then this might be a way to tell where and how much."

"The seam is here," Ginny said. She was standing in the archway, looking at the frame. "It's bisected right down the middle of the lintel work."

"Wot's that tell us?"

"Tells us that the hall likely moved horizontally or vertically rather than spinning. Corners would grind if it tried to spin...less'n they're sheared or rounded...hmmm. Concentric circles, maybe..."

There was a whistle from far down the hall.

"OI!" Thud yelled.

"Room down here." Goin's yell was distant but clear. "Forty yards of hall, room with...WAIT! STOP!"

Thud's head snapped around at the yell and he was off down the hall at a sprint, the rest of them following on his heels, not having anything more pressing to do. The far end of the hall was in darkness. They reached it quickly. Beyond was a pentagonal room, archways evenly spaced around it. Gong, Mungo, Goin and Clink, however, were nowhere to be seen. Miss Cluck stood at the hall end, alone, blinking at the empty room, apparently mid-catharsis.

Thud grinned.

"Well, looks like we found us an adventure after all," he said happily.

"I thought you hated adventure," Durham said.

"Aye, that I do." He dabbed at his eyes. "That don't mean I don't miss it sumthin' fierce though.

"Seems we got a new objective," he continued, switching to his leader voice. "Split up ain't no way to proceed so's we need to figure ourselves outta this and find whatever is controlling this so we can get everyone lined back up."

"They must have gone into one of those arches and found another moving hallway," Ginny said. "Might be all of the arches are like that. Most likely thing is that we're in a big cave or some such with the movin' bits built inside so they got space to move about in. If we can find a way to break through a wall somwhere's..."

"Gryngo's back there, unfortunately," Thud said, waving his hand vaguely in a manner indicating he had no idea whatsoever which direction Gryngo might be in. "No 'splosives in these packs we got; too dangerous to tote around. Some small picks though."

He knelt down and drew another chalk line across the threshold, adding a 2 at each end.

"Dunno if this'll end up helpin' in any way," he muttered. He stood and brushed chalk dust from his hands. "All right, leave one lantern here as a marker. Everyone grab hands and let's step through all at once."

Ruby's hand felt dry and papery, Thud's like lunchmeat. Durham braced himself and then, with a nod from Ginny, they all stepped forward.

The dungeon moved.

Miss Cluck stood in the now empty hallway, alone in the pool of lantern light. She blinked once or twice at the dark, empty room and came to the conclusion that she had no compelling interests located within. She pecked aimlessly at the number 2 on the floor, the small pool of light around her an island in darkness.

Nibbly and Dadger Ben stood silently gazing at the archway, the narrow ledge and the dark emptiness beyond.

"Right as I came out," Dadger said. "Whole damned thing dropped right behind me. Voop! Gone."

Nibbly rubbed at his beard about where he believed his chin would be.

"Well…" he began.

"Hmmm…" he continued a few moments later.

"Methinks you're in charge," Dadger said. "All the team leaders is in there cept'n you."

Nibbly nodded slowly. "Go fetch Cardamon and Gryngo. Maybe Giblets too, if he seems coherent enough." He wasn't entirely sure if they'd be able to help but it would serve to remove his audience for a minute while he stood there not knowing what to do. Leading the looting team hadn't really prepared him for anything that involved anything other than looting. Hopefully the three dwarves he'd asked for would be enough to form a good argument amongst themselves about what should be done so that he'd have a few ideas other than the nonexistent ones he already had.

The trio arrived a minute later, Dadger bobbing about

behind them, trying to peer over their shoulders.

"Whole hall dropped, eh?" Cardamon asked. "Kind of a pit trap, mebbe. Instead of a hole in the floor, drop the whole hall. What's in there?"

"Ain't looked yet," Nibbly answered. "Didn't want to stick my head in until you'd had a chance to look at it lest something lop it off."

"Pfffrt," Giblets said, stepping forward onto the ledge. He extended his lantern into the dark.

"'S' a bell cave," Giblets said in his rapid-fire mumble. "See't'wall behin' us, curvin' in up, out down, round'e'sides. Big bell we're in, wot? Reckon dere's a stactite runnin' right o'wn'e'middle, there, eh?"

He cupped his hands around his mouth. "OI!" His voice echoed back.

"Hunnert yards 'cross' giv'er'tek, mebbe half that up and a long ways down." He dropped his lantern into the hole and watched it fall. There was a distant clang a long moment later.

"Hallway down there, fi'ty feets. Rope down, easy." He turned and strolled back up the hall, punching Dadger in the shoulder as he passed. "Look there, wot? Hey!"

"Ow," Dadger said.

"Well, there's that," Nibbly said. "Gryngo?"

Gryngo shrugged. "I could blow it up if'n yer want but might not be a good idea if they're still in there."

"Noted," Nibbly said, hoping he sounded authoritative. The discussion he'd been hoping for was failing to materialize though the rope idea seemed pretty good. "Dadger, go get Leery." Dadger nodded and scurried away.

Leery arrived a few minutes later. Her hair and beard were braided back and her cheeks trimmed to little more than a five o'calendar shadow. Her pale knobbly legs stuck out from the brown shorts she wore, shockingly exposed. At least she'd combed her leg hair.

"Whaddaya reckon?" Nibbly asked.

She stood on the ledge, studying the cave for a minute then began pointing

"I can leap over there, grab on and shimmy round that ledge there, drop down and grab that lichen and then backflip over to that rock knob below. Then hand over hand around the side, jump across that bit there, slide right down to that dip then grapple across and drop right down on the top safe and sound."

"Yeh, well we'll tie a rope around you just the same," Nibbly said. He'd watched Thud perform the routine with Leery at least a dozen times.

They attached the rope to the clip on her belt and tied the other around around a clamp, hammered securely into the wall. Leery edged herself out on the ledge and then leapt for her first handhold. She missed it completely, bounced face first off of the wall and dropped like a rock. There was a loud "Glurnk!" from below as the rope went taut. Nibbly looked down. She dangled at the end of the rope, swinging slowly back and forth.

"You almost had it that time!" he called.

"My fingers slipped!"

"All right, we're lowerin' ya down."

A moment later and she stood atop the hallway below. She stomped up and down on it. "Hello in there!" she shouted, and then, "Anyone hear me?" and then, "AHHHH!" as the hallway began ascending back up through the cave.

The sudden acceleration knocked her flat. Nibbly braced himself, waited, and then yanked as hard as he could on the rope. Leery came bouncing back into the room, tumbling end over end as the hallway arrived just behind her, slotting back into place as if it had never been gone.

There was no sign of anyone within.

"Braces, quick!" Nibbly yelled.

Cardamon ran forward with iron bands and began bolting them across the joining seam. Nibbly helped Leery untangle her arms and limbs then helped her to her feet. She wobbled a bit but seemed intact. Nibbly had figured out long ago that Leery's value to the team was her pathological lack of self-preservation accompanied by seeming indestructibility rather than her questionable acrobatic skill. Dwarves excelled at somersaults but that was both the beginning and the end of the dwarven acrobatic legacy.

"There was another room down there," Leery said. "I saw it when the hall started coming back up. Looks like that hall dropped them down and they moved on."

"That gives us a target at least," Nibbly said.

Cardamon stepped back from the hall entry. "Secured," he said. He'd affixed the iron bands across the trap's seam on all four sides of the hall. "This end ain't goin' nowheres less'n something hits it really, really hard. Also, there's a number 1 chalked on the floor here."

Nibbly went and looked but Cardamon had pretty much summed up the extent of the information that the '1' offered.

"Guessin' one o' us did that," Cardamon said. "Can't figger skellingtons going around chalkin' things."

"All right then," Nibbly said. "Time for us to launch a rescue mission."

ℓℓℓ

Mungo stood in the middle of a hallway, stroking his cat fur beard. Gong was technically in charge but the situation they were in was going to require thinking to get out of. Gong was no slouch in the thinking department but he was no Mungo. He stood clustered with Goin and Clink a few yards away, all three of them watching Mungo expectantly in the silent acknowledgment that he was their way out. They'd moved through several halls and several rooms, all identical, sometimes they'd felt the lurch of movement, sometimes they didn't.

Mungo looked up at the corners where the walls met the ceiling. He idly calculated the quadrilateral binomial hypotenuse vectors, even while knowing that it wouldn't lead to anything. He stuck his hands in his pockets and rocked back and forth on his heels. There was a piece of lint in one of his pockets. He could think of forty seven potential uses for the lint, forty eight if it were cotton, but none of them seemed overly applicable at the moment. He stuck the lint in his beard, use number seventeen. The beard was key to his dwarf disguise and he made sure to maintain it well. He wasn't quite sure the beard was enough on its own, however. Maybe he needed to get a hat as well.

He studied the floor, silently calculating the total volume of empty space constituted by the seams between the stones then estimated the weight of each stone followed by the amount of quarry hours and number of wagons required to transport it. He licked his lips to determine air speed and direction then spent a few seconds spitting out cat hair.

"Clink," he finally said. "Might I briefly appropriate your eyeball? The glass one, not the biological one."

Clink arched his eyebrows then shrugged and pulled his glass eye out. It made a little schloop noise. "Yeah, if ye'd asked for my good one I'd probably have to turn you down." He held the eyeball out.

Mungo took it and placed it gently on the floor in the precise horizontal and lateral center of the hallway. He studied it for a moment then reached out and gave it a poke with his finger. It rolled a few inches then stopped. He picked it back up, went further down the hall and repeated the poke and roll. And then a third time, still further down. He retrieved the eye and trotted back to the trio of dwarves, handing Clink his eye back. Clink scrutinized it carefully with his remaining eye, wiped it on his sleeve and then popped it in his mouth and rolled it around. Mungo could hear it click against his teeth and mentally charted the route that it was taking through Clink's mouth. Clink retrieved it and poked it back into its socket then winced.

"Ah! Always burns somethin' fierce when I do that."

"Then don't do that," Mungo murmered, more to himself than to Clink. He was staring down the hall, preoccupied with calculations. "Salts in your mouth," he added. "Membranous tissue. Bad mix." He scurried down the hall a few yards, stopped and thought for a moment, then retreated back a step.

"Goin, could you come stand right here?"

Goin nodded and plodded over. Mungo adjusted his position a few times before he was happy.

"And Clink, stand right here," he said, demonstrating. Clink did so. Mungo fished his chalk out of his pack and carefully drew an X on the floor. He then went and stood further down the hall.

"All right, Gong, whenever you're ready I want you to go to that X and jump up and down on it four times."

"Four times, eh?" Gong said. He walked over to the X.

"Well, three and a half would suffice but it would require

you to jump to the X from elsewhere then up and down on it three times and, as four times in the same spot will achieve the same result with less complication to the instructions I choose to go with the simpler option."

"Naturally," Gong said. "You know, I'm not exactly known for me jumpin' skills."

"That's quite all right," Mungo said. "We're more interested in your landing skills which I suspect that you will achieve admirably."

"Fair 'nuff," Gong said. He jumped.

An immensity of dwarf such as Gong, launching himself into the air, is a sight few have the opportunity to witness. Parts of him still seemed to be going up as the rest of him came down, and then those same bits went down as he propelled himself back up. His plate mail creaked and the floor trembled slightly with each impact.

As he hit the floor for the fourth time, the hallway moved.

"Eureka!" Mungo yelled. It was a word that wasn't actually a word but which he'd mathematically proved to exist in a parallel realm and he quite liked the sound of it when it came to needing something to yell in moments of cerebral triumph.

Goin squinted at the walls suspiciously. "Wot just

happened?"

"We counterbalanced the hallway and forced the mechanism to trip."

"Ah," Goin said. "Well that's good then, right?"

"It means that we can manipulate the parts of the labyrinth we occupy. Most labyrinths follow a larger design. If we explore a bit more I can ascertain the underlying pattern and deduce much of the rest of the labyrinth."

"Meaning we'll know how to solve it?"

"Precisely." Mungo grinned and cracked his knuckles. "And as the corridors can be manipulated we can maneuver them to provide a direct route through for the rest of the team. Logically, such a route exists as it is implausible that the designer of an adaptable labyrinth wouldn't provide themselves with a path through it for their own convenience."

"Makes sense," Gong said. "Wouldn't want to have to do a maze in the middle of the night when you're just trying to get to the jakes."

Mungo's eyebrows knotted together. "I don't believe that liches micturate."

"I don't reckon I want to think about that enough to form an opinion," Clink said. "If exploring is what we need to do let's get to it."

"All right," Mungo yelled. "Dungeon protocol!" He attempted to bark the order and succeeded, albeit with more of a chihuahua result than intended.

Clink and Gong took up position side by side. Mungo clambered onto Gong's shoulders.

"You expecting many traps in here?" Gong asked.

"No," Mungo said. "But like Thud says, there's no such thing in a dungeon as being overly cautious. Forward, ho!"

"I ain't a horse," Gong said. "Yell that again and I'll forward-ho you into the wall."

"Yes, sorry," Mungo said. "Quite right. Proceed in your own good time, sir."

♋♋♋

"Vertical," Ginny said. "I watched it that time. Up 'n' down like ellyvaters."

Ruby had her journal out and was silently scribbling away at it, her brow furrowed. Durham frowned at the six archways spaced around the room. Beyond each lay seemingly identical hallways.

"There's no guarantee any of these are the right way, is there?" he asked. "These could just keep moving us around in circles, never leading out."

"Likely functions like a sort of combination lock," Ginny said. "Know the exact order of doors to take and it'll get you through. Bugger one up, however, and yeah, all bets is off. Probably a way to reset it from within but that's just gonna be another code, as it were. Stumblin' onto it by happenstance is some slim odds."

"Well, I never been much for rules," Thud said. "Durham, come on over here and get me up on yer shoulders."

Durham crossed to the middle of the room and knelt, letting Thud climb aboard. The dwarf was far heavier than he had expected but, fortunately, less moist. Thud stood and maneuvered himself so that he was standing with one foot on each of Durham's shoulders. It occurred to Durham that he could look up and answer a number of questions that he'd had about Dwarven kilts but made the snap decision that there were things man was not meant to know. Or, at least, things that this particular man didn't want to know.

Thud had procured a small pick from his pack and began tapping at the ceiling with it.

"Mortar's old an' crumbly," he said. "We'll be through here in no time!"

"No time" turned out to be rather longer than it sounded. Durham's shoulders quickly went numb and then began radiating alarm messages down his spine. He tried to shift a little.

"Quit yer wrigglin', lad," Thud said. "An' watch yer head. First stone coming down!" Durham glanced up in alarm and instantly regretted it, though he no longer had any unanswered kilt questions. Their chins weren't the only place that dwarves grew luxuriant beards. Thud dropped the ceiling stone he'd loosened and it crashed to the floor.

"Reckon two more o' them and it'll be big enough," he said.

Durham was close to whimpering out loud by the time the third stone dropped. Thud pulled himself up through the hole and the sudden relief gave Durham the happiest moment he'd had in weeks.

"Dark as a nostril up here," Thud's voice floated down from above. "Big space, lotsa echo. I kin hear some sort of clicking noise but nothin' seems ter be jumpin on me. Climb on up."

They could hear the clicking noise from below as well. It wasn't loud but it gave the impression of coming from many sources.

Ginny helped Ruby climb onto Durham's shoulders and then Thud pulled her up through the ceiling. She seemed to have the weight of a bird in comparison to Thud. Ginny was next, her kilt giving Durham a lesson in comparative Dwarven anatomy that he suspected would be the source of more than one unpleasant dream in the future. She scrambled clear of the hole and then reappeared, along with Thud, extending their hands down to try and pull Durham up.

He reached up to grab hold and, as he did so, the floor beneath him opened and he found himself falling, Ginny and Thud's surprised faces rapidly receding until they were lost in the darkness.

"Well, don't that bugger all," Thud said. His voice hissed through clenched teeth. "That lich bastard always got another trick up his sleeve." He leaned over the hole and cupped his hands around his mouth. "OI!" His voice echoed in the pit below. The echoes died out and only silence answered. He slumped to the ground looking defeated.

"If anythin' happens to that lad, then...then..."

"Surely you've had losses before," Ruby said. She rested a wrinkled hand on his shoulder.

"Aye, but not many and never an observer. I put me dwarves in jeopardy 'cuz that's our jobs, ain't it? Him, though, he weren't even s'posed to be here. He's s'posed to be back safe at home, searchin' sheeps 'n' sech." Thud wiped at his eyes and Ginny handed him a grubby hanky.

"We don't know yet what happened to him, boss. Might be he's ok down there somewhere."

"Well, we ain't leavin' him behind one way or the other," Thud said. "We may have lost team members before but I ain't never, ever, left one behind."

"I know, boss. We even swept up Bili that one time so we could take him to 'is mum. We'll find him."

"What happened down there? With the floor?" Thud asked.

"If there was a seam, I...well, I missed it," Ginny said. "Some sort of retractable retaining pins around the circumference, maybe..."

"Aye," Thud said, waving his hand to cut her off. "Another trick we ain't seen before."

"It's my fault, sir," Ginny shuffled her feet nervously. "First them hallways movin' an' now the floor droppin'. I missed 'em both an' now we're scattered an' lost ever' which way."

Thud was silent, neither contradicting nor forgiving. Ginny stepped quietly away from him, out of his line of sight. He began rolling past events through his head, altering, discarding, revisiting. Ginny and Ruby were quiet, waiting. The only sound was the faint clicking noise that seemed to be coming from some distance all around them. It was like an entire army continuously cracking their knuckles

After a long minute he sighed deeply and stood.

"If you'se to blame, I'm even more so. Had me whole team an hour ago and now I'm down to jest you, me and a scribe along for the ride. Can't think o' too much we coulda done different. We jest got outplayed by Alaham and now we gotta try to live long enough to learn from it. Fault or not, pointin' fingers ain't gonna fix it."

He stroked his beard glancing around at the darkness. "Need to figure out our own situation 'afore we can do anything 'bout the others, though. Echoes make it sound like we're in a damned big hole in the ground. Figger it'd be good ter know wot's makin' that clicky noise, too. Got any them costonflagrationater thingys in yer pack?"

"Probably," Ginny said. She slid her pack off and began rummaging through it. "Mungo likes to hide 'em in my pack when he makes 'em cause he doesn't want to carry 'em around in case they explode." She produced a metal tin from her pack, opened it and pulled out a footlong paper tube. "Right about now's when a crossbow'd come in mighty handy. This one ain't mortar style."

"I can help with that," Ruby said.

Thud arched an eyebrow at her. "Got a crossbow under yer robe somewhere's?"

"No, just a trick I learned when we were in Akama," she said. "Do you have a small knife?"

Thud nodded and produced one from his belt.

Ruby took it and sat down. She began carving out bits of wood from one end of her walking stick. "That was my first outing with you, traveling up the Marea river from Kalaim."

"Aye, we did that old temple ruin," Ginny said. "Nasty snakey buggers in there."

"Our third night on the river we stayed in that Fae village," Ruby said. "They did that initiation dance, remember?" The pile of wood shavings next to her was growing. She seemed to be carving a hollow into the head of the walking stick. "I learned this trick from one of the hunters there. They use it to throw spears. This will take a few minutes. Sit tight."

Thud and Ginny sat, nervously staring into the darkness, the clicking noise surrounding them.

-15-

Durham woke up cold, wet and in pain. A brief bit of splashing about informed him that we was laying in a large puddle of water, which explained the first two issues. The memory of the fall arrived a moment later explaining the third. All of his limbs seemed mobile, at least, though none of them seemed too happy about it. He was laying on his back, his backpack squashed underneath and leaving him in a reclining posture like a sideways parenthesis. It was also extremely dark. Ridiculously dark. The sort of dark that had a bit of enthusiasm about it regarding just how dark it was. Save over there, perhaps fifty yards away, a single dim torch flickered. It was set in a cave wall beside a dark opening.

Durham flopped about a little bit atop the backpack, turtle-like, until managing to roll off of the side of it with enough momentum to maneuver himself onto all fours with the pack on top of him. He still wasn't sure exactly what the pack had in it but, based on what it now weighed he had to assume that it was full of lead sponges. Another minute of wiggling and he managed to extricate his arms from the straps. He began fumbling with the buckles on it, searching by touch until he found one that released the top. He reached in, gingerly feeling around. Everything was moist and much of it sharp. He finally found a hard ball shape that he hoped was one of Mungo's gryo-lanterns. One side of it was dented badly enough that he doubted it would be particularly good at rolling anymore. He tapped firmly on the side.

"Hello? You alive in there?"

After a moment there was a bit of sputtering followed by a few tiny coughs. A dim light flickered to life. The pixie inside looked bedraggled and miserable, her wings limp and soggy. She glared at him and shook herself, a tiny spatter of water misting against Durham's face. A final contemptuous snort and then her light grew until it became strong enough to provide some meager illumination. Durham glanced around first, figuring that having at least a slight notion of where he was could help determine if he should be fleeing in terror or not. He was on a natural stone surface, smoothed by erosion. He could make out the wall of the cave a dozen feet away, surface runneled with limestone ridges.

Nothing seemed to be about to leap out at him so he turned his attention back to the pack and began fishing through it.

Broken chalk, rope, some iron spikes. A waterproof package of hard bread that had been reduced to powder and crumbs. Flint and a cube of shaved wood pressed with wax. Quite a few other small bits and pieces the nature of which he wasn't quite sure of. There was a sodden blanket toward the bottom which seemed to be the primary source of weight. He tugged it free and tried to twist some of the water out of it with limited success. He settled for draping it over the top of the pack in hopes it would dry a bit but was felt he was being overly optimistic in that regard. He tugged the pack back on and held the lantern up over his head, looking about.

The space he was in seemed far larger than what his lantern had any hope of illuminating. He could still hear the clicking noises coming from somewhere far above him. Quite a lot of clicking noises. Whatever was making them was well beyond his light but he was certain that whatever it was was unpleasant and that finding somewhere else to be was a good priority to have. He made his way to the wall of the cave, figuring that, as it and the torch were his only landmarks, it was his best bet. He began following it toward the lone torch, picking his way carefully over the uneven floor. It had seen much less work than the passages above and large piles of stone debris made the footing treacherous. The torch was ensconced beside an opening cut into the wall. He cautiously extended the lantern through. Beyond was the worked stone of the dungeon. The opening seemed to have been cut through as a 'back door' of sorts. He wasn't sure how far his fall had been, but figured it was enough that he was at least a level deeper down in the dungeon, perhaps two. More than that and he figured that he'd be a bit more broken. The dungeon, however, hazardous as it certainly was, likely offered a better chance of finding the surface again, if not a better chance of living to see it. Something, after all, had to have lit the torch.

Through the arch was a small antechamber with an iron-bound wooden door. He started to step in then froze, memories of the traps above springing to mind. He wasn't really certain what exactly Ginny and Mungo had spent all of their effort looking for. He recalled them mentioning seams and triggers. He felt he could possibly spot a seam but the only trigger he was familiar with was on a crossbow and he felt it unlikely that there would necessarily be a resemblance. He poked his head through the arch, holding the lantern up. The room was bare, the corners showing a build up of muddy silt that told him that the cave, on occasion at least, had enough water in it to encroach on the dungeon. There were certainly seams between the worked stones but none of them seemed continuous. The stones were all interlocked in the usual manner. He took his pack off and dropped it down on the floor in front of him. Many different deadly things failed to happen to it. He nudged it forward with his foot and stepped in to replace it. It was a slow way to cross the room but eventually he nudged the pack up against the door without anything unexpected having happened during the process. He carefully examined the door. No visible wires. Nothing that looked like something anyone would call a trigger. He fished around in the backpack and found a long thin metal rod. He inserted it between the door and the jam, sliding it carefully around the edge of the door. It hit obstructions about where he expected the hinges would be and another where the latch was. Feeling slightly silly, having taken ten minutes to walk five feet across an empty room he took a deep breath, grabbed the door latch and pulled.

It was locked.

He leaned his forehead against it in frustration. What was that Thud had said about there being no locks in dungeons? Alaham must have missed that discussion. How would the dwarves have done it? One of them would come trotting up with picks or an axe, maybe explosives. He assumed that there was some sort of lockpick in the pack but the door had no keyhole, at least that he could see, which ruled out managing to lockpick it through sheer dumb luck. You're a guard, idiot, his brain informed him. How would a guard open it? He gave a snort of laughter, took a step back and kicked the door in.

It flew open in a crash of splinters followed by a resounding thud as it rebounded against the wall. He caught it on the backswing, pushed it open and peered in.

He blinked.

He considered the results for a moment then he blinked again, in hopes of greater success.

The room beyond was a well appointed parlor. A thick red rug covered the floor. Tables and chairs with curly wooden legs were scattered about amongst cushion adorned couches. Gilded lamps hung from the walls, casting a warm golden light through the room. The air smelled of mothballs and seemed thick and still. A thick layer of dust lay over everything. He stepped in, immediately reprimanding himself for not looking for seams and triggers but nothing instantly killed him so it seemed that, for the moment, luck was on his side.

There was a plate of cookies on one of the tables alongside a teapot and a teacup. A book lay open on the chair beside it. The book was dusty but the cookies looked fresh and the teapot was not only dust-free but still emitting a wisp of steam. Durham crouched, drawing the mace from his belt. He could see no one in the room but it gave every sign that someone had been there recently and was about to come back. Factoring in the room's locale told him that it was probably someone whom he wouldn't get along with. He moved cautiously over to the chair. He tried to imagine if the sort of mind existed that would leave poison cookies and tea in a dungeon parlor on the off chance an adventurer would wander by. It seemed, to him, unlikely. He picked up one of the cookies and sniffed at it then took a very small bite. It was still warm and tasted of honey. He wiped the inside of the empty teacup and poured himself a cup of tea. A bowl beside it turned out to contain sugar and another held cream. He added a bit of the sugar but decided to forego the cream as he couldn't think of a reasonable way for there to be fresh cream in a dungeon. It seemed unlikely that they kept a cow down here anywhere and he didn't want to dwell on what sort of creature might be serving as a substitute. He couldn't imagine where the fresh cookies and tea had come from either but they seemed a safer prospect than the mystery cream.

He sipped at the tea then examined the book. It was about a thousand pages long and was written in a language he didn't recognize. There was an illustration that Durham decided not to dwell on after the briefest of glances. The spine made little crackly noises when he tried to close it. The binding was a deep red leather.

There was a door on the far side of the room, which Durham felt no particular hurry to get to. A trail led through the dust from the doorway to the table where the tea and cookies were. What would the dwarves do here? He contemplated the notion for a moment, picturing the dwarves stripping the room down to the bare stone and carting it off to their wagons. Yes, that's exactly what they would be doing. It didn't help him much in his current situation, however. Any answers he was going to find to the mysterious tea and biscuits were going to be beyond the door. Any exit out of the dungeon was going to be beyond that door as well. If he answered the tea and biscuit question along the way then all the better. He set the cup back next to the pot, readied his mace and went to the door. Just as he reached it the handle turned and the door began to open.

Durham quickly dodged behind the door as it swung open into the room. He crouched, trying not to breath, wondering if his leap for safety had made enough noise to be heard. He heard a faint noise from the other side of the door as someone entered the room. He gripped the mace tightly but whomever it was didn't seem to have an interest in looking behind the door. After a moment he peeked around the edge.

It was a skeleton. It moved slowly across the room with a curiously stilted gait as if someone or something had to pull each limb through every motion. It clattered its way to the table Durham had just left and began gathering up the tea and cookies.

A skeletal butler? Durham supposed it made a certain kind of sense. If you had an army of mindless slaves, why not command one to bring you snacks? No one had used the room in a long time and it occurred to Durham that the skeleton had probably been faithfully serving tea to no one, day after day, year after year. Were there other skeletons somewhere, making the tea and baking the cookies? His stomach gave a twist, reminding him that he'd eaten one of those cookies. Had it been mixed and shaped by long bony brown fingers? He blanched at the thought and felt the cookie leap its way back up his throat. Through sheer force of will he scrunched his face up, clenched his teeth and forced it back down, feeling that vomiting on the rug would likely draw the skeletal servant's attention. He needn't have bothered. Mouth full of honey flavored bile and face twisted into a grimace he looked back up to find the skeleton standing and staring at him with its dark and hollow eye pits. It had the teapot in one hand and the plate of cookies in the other. Its jaw hinged open as if to scream, producing a chilling hissing sound that was more of a memory of a sound than something he could actually hear. Durham had just long enough to wonder how it was making the noise before it flung the teapot at him.

Teapots are not generally known for their aerodynamic qualities, hence the proclivity for their use during breaks between fighting rather than as an actual weapon of war. Durham easily dodged it and it shattered on the wall behind him, dousing him in hot tea. The plate came spinning after, shedding cookies along the way. Contrary to teapots, plates bear a striking resemblance to certain weapons of war and the plate demonstrated this by carving through the air straight into Durham's forehead. It clanked loudly against the front of his helmet, the inside of his head giving a flash of light with the impact and sent him staggering back against the wall where he slipped in the tea and sat down firmly on shards of broken teapot as cookies pelted down around him.

The skeleton came sprinting across the room at him with terrifying speed, running in a strange half-crouch motion, its hissing scream grating down his spine like fingernails on slate. He grabbed at the open door next to him and pulled it towards himself just in time for the skeleton to crash into it with a sound like a bag of antlers. Durham braced against the wall and kicked the door as hard as he could. It slammed shut with a hollow boom, knocking the skeleton in a backward stagger to hit the back of a couch and go tumbling over it. Durham scrambled to his feet and charged. He could see it struggling up on the other side of the couch. He dove headlong over the couch, bringing the mace down on its brown skull with his full flying weight behind it. The impact pulverized the back of the skull, slamming it down to the floor with a crunch. The skeleton's bones instantly came apart, collapsing into an unruly loose pile which Durham promptly landed on, the air whooshing out of him, the bones breaking beneath him and poking into him.

He rolled to the side, gasping for breath but still alive. Blood was trickling into his eyes from his forehead but the helmet seemed to have taken most of the hit and the cut was shallow. His head throbbed, however, and he didn't expect that to go away any time soon. He dislodged a few pieces of broken rib from the front of his armor. They hadn't pierced through but he anticipated a few bruises. Burning pain from his rear, however, told him that he hadn't gotten quite so lucky with the broken teapot. He stood gingerly and felt around behind himself. He'd taken at least one fairly deep jab back there and his hand came away wet with blood.

He stood for a minute, contemplating his medical options and came up mostly blank. He limped his way back to where he'd left his backpack, feeling the blood trickling down his leg. There were long linen strips in it, sopping wet but serviceable as bandages. He couldn't think of a way to secure one in place however without wrapping it completely around himself which seemed like it would be both awkward and immobilizing. He retrieved a pair of iron spikes and a wooden mallet instead. He pulled his backpack into the room and closed the remnants of the door to the cave then used the mallet to pound the spike into a crack between the flagstones to secure the door shut. The mallet thumped loudly with each hit but not quite as piercingly as a metal hammer would have. He went back to the door that the skeleton had come through and repeated the process. He hadn't got a look at what lay beyond the door yet but was pretty certain that he didn't want to find out at the moment.

With both doors spiked shut he went back to the couch and eyed the skeleton suspiciously. It gave no sign of movement. He remembered Thud telling him that the skull was all that had to be broken and he had certainly achieved that. Having made himself as safe as he could manage, he dropped his trousers, peeling and cutting them away from where they were sticking to the wound. It was time to do some creative bandaging.

♫♫♫

Chickens are true creatures of zen-they live only and absolutely for the moment. Their actions one particular second will not necessarily have any influence or bearing on their actions in the next second, nor are they necessarily influenced by their actions of the prior second. Chicken thoughts arrive in their tiny mad little minds like flashes of a strobe light, each light being an action, each flashing with the brilliance of a not very brilliant thing. Each action utterly random. The complete randomness of chaos. Chickens are notorious escape artists, not due to their ability to devise cunning plans as they huddle together in their coop beneath a bare light bulb, scratching out complex diagrams in the dirt, but simply out of sheer unpredictability. They are the pachinko balls of the animal kingdom, effecting their escapes through the simple device of, say, turning left for no particular reason.

Miss Cluck waddled out of the maze and into the cavern.

♪♪♪

Ruby held up the stick and eyed it critically. "Yes, I think that just might do."

"Yer made a four foot long spoon?" Thud asked. Ruby smiled, which Thud didn't recall having seen her do before. He wondered if the smile came from the fact that this was the first thing she'd gotten to do that actually affected the mission. The scribes were known for going to great lengths to avoid having any significant effects on how events played out, present simply to record what happened. "We don't make the history, we write the history," she'd told him once. Later, on reflection, Thud had decided that the two were one and the same. History wasn't what had happened. History was what someone had written down about what happened.

Ruby raised her walking spoon up over her shoulder, holding it by the narrow end, the spoon end extended out behind her.

"Try and balance that on the end there. Be ready to light it"

Ginny carefully placed the costonflagrationator on the end of the stick, balancing it on end. Thud took a big drag on his cigar then touched the tip to the fuse.

Ruby swung.

It flared into brilliant white light, high above their heads, arcing through the emptiness. The light lasted but a second or two which was both just long enough and, having seen what it revealed, not nearly long enough at all. The light faded and went out, leaving them in their suddenly very small pool of lantern light, surrounded by the immense darkness and the clicking sounds.

"Holy shit," Thud said.

ℓℓℓ

They advanced into the hall in as best of a formation as

Nibbly was able to manage with their reduced numbers. He'd appointed Rasp as the temporary leader of the vanguard team and he and the other three remaining vanguard were in front, shields up and crossbows poised. Cardamon was just behind them as the only available member of the traps team, his pack sagging and Cardamon listing backward with the weight of the extra gear he'd loaded up on. His trap poking pole was the only thing that seemed to be holding him up. Nibbly followed behind with Leery to one side and Gryngo to the other. Dadger took up the rear as message runner. Nibbly didn't have much of a plan formed. He knew that the lost dwarves were down below him somewhere and his hope was that somewhere up ahead there would be a more conventional means down. If that failed then the time it took for it to do so would at least give him a chance to come up with a plan B. He hoped. Provided that plans of action arrived fully formed from the ether without requiring much pondering on his part.

They advanced, taking it slow. Cardamon was the newest member of the trap team, having replaced Kengi a year ago following the incident with the pit full of whipped cream in the haunted harem. Nibbly wanted to make sure Cardamon had every opportunity to spot anything before Rasp stepped on it.

The dwarf's perpetual half-lidded eyes didn't do much to inspire confidence in either his being particularly alert or his ability to spot things. Still, he had Ginny's confidence so Nibbly extended the benefit of the doubt.

That was when they met the daemon.

♪♪♪

"This gonna take much longer?" Clink asked. He and Gong had been watching Mungo scribbling on a piece of parchment for several minutes.

"Well," the gnome said, "if you think you might be of any assistance you are more than welcome to help. All we have to do is postulate the layout of the maze based entirely on knowledge of the route through it. As this is, typically, the opposite of how mazes are usually solved it is taking slightly longer." He stared at the paper for a moment, sucking on the quill tip. It had stained his lips black causing them to blend in with his faux beard. He scribbled a few more lines then studied it again. "Gentledwarves, I think I have it!"

They crowded around him.

"If we activate this hall here it should move to connect to

that one. We move through it without activating it then activate the next one twice and that should give us our passage through."

"And if it don't?"

"Then I'll have learned something useful about the maze and can correct my error. One way or another, we're bound to succeed."

"Yer makin' a lot of assumptions there," Gong said, gesturing at Mungo's piece of paper. "Symmetricality, no accountin' for possible rooms in the maze, levels we don't know about, pattern breaks, consistency of the rules-set…"

"Yes, yes, as I said, if it doesn't work then I'll have learned something useful and make necessary corrections. Now, this way!"

"That's the way we come from," Clink said.

"Sorry, got turned around. This way!"

ΩΩΩ

If you'd asked the dwarves, they would have said it was a demon. Only the humans were pretentious enough to add the superfluous 'a'. The spellings had identical pronunciation but the humans felt the extra letter added a more occult feel to the word to better reflect the danger of the things. They felt justified, having borne the brunt of the daemonwars with dozens of cities and hundreds of villages being sacked. The dwarves placed less importance on the war, having followed their usual strategy of holing up in Kheldurn, their city beneath the Hammerfells. The dwarves had long advertised Kheldurn as being impregnable but were very taciturn as to what they'd done to make it so. People took them at their word, as they'd also built everyone else's fortresses and knew a thing or two about how fortresses worked. That the daemons had attacked Kheldurn was widely known. It was also widely known that Kheldurn had not fallen and that the dwarves had spent the next month burning piles of deceased demons. Kheldurn still held its secrets.

This particular daemon looked like a toddler-sized monkey with yard length tentacles in place of its arms and legs. The tentacles had monkey paws at their ends and were covered with monkey hair. The thing hung from the ceiling by one arm, swaying gently back and forth, looking at them. There was a door behind it and Nibbly wondered if the demon had been put here to guard it. It didn't seem particularly interested in attacking them. Not yet, at least.

"Hello?" Nibbly said, figuring it was at least worth a try.

The demon monkey picked at one of its nostrils and then spent a moment examining its finger, tentacle undulating. It sighed.

"Hello," it finally responded. Its voice was saturated with boredom and ennui.

"We'd like to go past."

"No."

"What are you doing talking to the damned thing?" Rasp hissed. "We should stick it to the wall with a dozen bolts and then burn the carcass for good measure. Only way to be sure with that lot. Standard Plan A for demon encounters. I can show ya where Thud put it in the manual."

The monkey demon tilted its head. "Are you desiring to commence with the hostilities now? I'd been hoping for at least a minute or two of conversation first. More to prolong the amusement of the distraction you're providing, really, than any hope that the conversation itself will be interesting. But, if you insist, just say the word."

"There's a lot more of us than there is of you," Rasp yelled. He stepped forward to yell it then stepped back again just as quickly afterward.

"How adorable; the dwarf can count. I'm sure your superior

numbers just fill you with inspiration and courage." It yawned.

"What's your name?" Nibbly asked.

"In order to pronounce my name you'd have to cleave your tongue in half, tie one half in a knot and choke on the other. I'd be more than happy to provide that service, should you wish. If not, call me whatever you like. Your choice will be utterly irrelevant within a few minutes."

"Why are you here? Everything else we've seen has been a bit more…skeletony. You seem a bit out of place."

"Alaham's teenage experimental phase, I suppose you could say. Hormonal angst sort of thing. Necromancy or demonology, however to decide? One can appreciate the difficulty, perhaps, in making the choice. He summoned and bound me then decided on necromancy. Here I still am, centuries later, still following his command." It cast a sidelong glance their way. "I would take this opportunity to point out than none of you are particularly skeletal either. As you are also not demons, you would seem to be even more out of place."

"You're his wyrd?" Dadger asked.

Cardamon gave him a sidelong look. "His wot?"

"His wyrd. 'S a demon necromancers keep around so folks think they're actually demonologists."

"That's somehow better?"

Dadger shrugged. "Messing around with dark and sinister entities in the pursuit of power, well, folks can understand the allure. Playing with dead things, however, not so much. So they have a demon to parade around and keep their skeletons in the closet."

"Both types of magic smells about the same," Rasp said. He gave a disapproving sniff in the demon's direction.

"Do go on," the demon said. "I'll just be over here."

"We can free you," Nibbly said. "You won't have to be bound to Alaham no more," Rasp made a hissing noise and glared at him.

The demon shook his head. "Not interested. I'm from the Plateau of Leng. Freezing cold wasteland of ruins, cultists, and spiders the size of moon beasts. Being here is like a vacation. And Alaham nailed the luxury resort ambiance. I can't think of a single good reason to leave."

"What's behind the door?"

The demon gave him a look of surprise. "Asking? Well, I don't think anyone ever mentioned any rules in that regard and the heritage of my species pretty much demands that I take the opportunity to undermine my master's intentions while still following his commands to the letter."

"Exactly," Nibbly said, mentally filing that information away so that he could use it on purpose next time rather than by happy accident.

"Beyond this door is where the necromancers are."

"...Oh?"

"Quite a lot of them, as a matter of fact."

"But they need you to protect them?"

"Oh, no," the monkey demon laughed, displaying a mouth full of teeth that looked like coffee icicles. "That's not why I'm here. I'm here to make sure they aren't interrupted."

"Erm...interrupted?" Nibbly scratched at a drop of sweat that had suddenly trickled into his beard. "What sort o' thing might they be up too?"

"Oh, no, now that would spoil the fun," the demon grinned. "Suffice to say that you will most certainly notice when they've finished."

"Well that don't sound like something I wants to wait around fer," Rasp said, just loud enough for Nibbly to hear. "Still thinking Plan A is looking pretty good."

He'd switched to speaking Dwarvish, insuring that even if the demon heard what he'd said that it wouldn't understand. The extremely strict Dwarven laws over who could learn Dwarvish (dwarves only) guaranteed that dwarves could openly discuss strategy in front of their enemies, as long as they weren't fellow dwarves. Some countries had come to consider a dwarf speaking Dwarvish to be an act of war and had, thus far, been spot on. It was the linguistic equivalent of a crossbow being cocked.

The demon dropped to the floor and rolled its neck around, loosening up. Its neck made a sound like a batch of popcorn. Rasp gave a snort and cracked his knuckles with a sound like a troupe of tap dancers falling into a pit full of castanets. The demon arched its eyebrows, impressed. A split second later and it was flying through their air at their heads.

It grabbed onto Cardamon's pole with one hand, arcing sideways mid-flight to angle between Rasp and Nibbly. It caught onto each of their heads with one arm and one leg each, its hairy tentacle limbs wrapping around their heads as it flew between them. It reached the end of its tentacles, hanging for a moment in mid-air just in front of Dadger's face. It had just long enough to hiss and snap at him before its tentacles rubber-banded it backwards, giving it the momentum and strength to bring Rasp and Nibbly's heads together with a sound like a frying pan on a metal coconut.

Against humans this would have been a reasonably brilliant tactic. Dwarven skulls, however, are more akin to granite than to bone. The two dwarves, unfazed by the impact, jerked their heads apart, pulling the monkey tight between them and yanking it back right into Dadger's fist. The impact spun the monkey horizontally, braiding its tentacles on each side. Rasp and Nibbly grabbed hold and began swinging it in loops between them like a jump rope.

The monkey demon wailed, its voice oscillating as it swung. The noise was cut off with a bass drum thump as Cardamon swung his staff down hard, the blow meeting the monkey on its upswing. Rasp quickly tied the demon's limp tentacles together in a complicated knot he'd learned from a yo-yo he'd kept in his pocket as a boy. He tossed it into the air, flip-kicked his crossbow into his hand and fired, pinning it to the wall mid-flight.

"That was Plan B," he said. "It works good too."

It was a good line, to be fair. The sort of line that bards like to latch onto and deliver in gravelly drawls to trigger a round of audience cheering and applause. It would have been all the better had Rasp not still had the bone-breaker ball-tipped bolts loaded. As it was, rather than the expected pinning to the wall the monkey demon just made a 'wuff' noise then slid to the floor, a tangle of tentacles and hair reminiscent of a Mondilinian appetizer. The demon's head snapped up, face twisted into a snarl, tentacles writhing as they unknotted.

"Is there a Plan C?" Nibbly asked.

"Yeh," Rasp said. "Reload afore it gets that knot undone." He had his foot in the crossbow stirrup and was tugging the string into place.

The demon had one tentacle arm free. It grabbed up the blunt bolt, arm snapping forward with a whipcrack followed directly by a loud clank noise. Rasp keeled over backward, a fresh round dent in the front of his helmet.

Nibbly grabbed Rasp's crossbow from where it had fallen, having to give it an extra tug to free it from Rasp's foot. He aimed and fired. The pointy bolt definitely worked better in the 'pin the demon to the wall' department. It screeched, displaying far more teeth than Nibbly felt any creature needed to have.

The thing was not out of tricks, however, demons being what they are. Its tentacle arms and legs detached and came slithering across the floor with terrifying speed. Hairy, sucker-covered snakes with grasping monkey paws for heads, fingers flexing, nails long and ragged. Nibbly suddenly had a compelling desire to do everything in his power to prevent one of those from getting under his kilt. The demon's tail was still attached and it was using it to tug at the bolt pinning it to the floor. Black goo bubbled from where the bolt had impaled it.

Unloaded crossbows are notorious for not being much good in the ranged offensive category. They can, however, make for a fair club in a pinch. Nibbly grasped it by the lathes and brought the stock down hard on the paw of the tentacle that was coming for him. There was a satisfying crunch and the monkey demon yelped from across the hall.

"What're you doin' to me crossbow?" Rasp yelled, having sat back up, followed by, "Ack!" as he saw the tentacle wriggling up his leg. He grabbed the paw as if he was shaking its hand and began flailing it about. Cardamon was having less success. He had a tentacle wrapped around his neck, squeezing, the paw clamped over his mouth. He was trying to leverage his staff in between to pry it off. Dadger Ben was scurrying around in circles, the fourth tentacle chasing after him, paw grasping.

"Ceiling!" Rasp yelled. The tentacle was wrapped around his arm and he was swinging it frantically as if attempting to fly. Nibbly looked up and saw the glyph.

In order to be bound demons had to be imprisoned. Surrounded by a glyph that created a magical barrier that the demon was unable to cross, either physically or dimensionally. The occult equivalent of a pinning crossbow bolt. The glyph covered the ceiling of the hall, a bewildering array of angled lines, curlicued with sigils. It was carved into the stone of the ceiling to prevent it from being easily disrupted. It had not been carved to contend with dwarves, however. Just as some elves could meld wood, so could some dwarves with stone. And Cardamon was such a dwarf.

Not that Cardamon was in a position to do so at the moment. He'd managed to get his staff in between the tentacle and his face but hadn't had the leverage to actually pry it loose. He'd gotten the other end of the staff between his legs and was trying to sit on it, bouncing up and down in an attempt to use his weight to apply enough force to break free. Physics was making the process rather awkward.

Nibbly ran to him, dodging around Dadger as he ran past yelping, tentacle still in pursuit. The demon had unpinned itself but was short on ambulatory limbs at the moment. It snapped its tail, throwing the bolt toward Nibbly but had less luck this time as Dadger ran in between, the bolt pinging unnoticed off of his helmet.

Nibbly stuck his head between Cardamon's knees and stood,

hoisting the diminutive dwarf to the ceiling, grabbing the end of the staff to lend stability. Being wedged between Cardamon's face and the tentacle let it act as the third leg of a tripod. Cardamon, fortunately, had the presence of mind to have grasped the plan. He let go of the staff, reached up and drew his finger through the edge of the glyph. The stone was like clay beneath his touch. The glyph flared with red light, bathing the hallway in eerie crimson. The monkey demon screamed, the sound rapidly dwindling as if it was moving away at an astonishing speed, pulled across vast dimensions. It faded from existence.

Cardamon gave an undignified squeak as the tentacle around his head vanished, robbing him of the staff's support and sending him tumbling backwards off of Nibbly's shoulders. He crashed to the ground just in time for Dadger to trip over him and grab at Nibbly in an attempt to stay up, pulling all three of them into a tangled pile.

Rasp snickered.

"I'm lookin' forward to tellin' Thud about whatever the hells you lot is doin' so he can write that up as 'Plan D'."

Everything hurt.

Durham opened his eyes to complete darkness. His brain reminded him that he was laying bare-assed on a couch next to a shattered skeleton in a parlor deep beneath a necromancer's crypt. His adventuring legacy, so far, seemed to frequently involve him being without pants. Taking all of that into account he tried to convince himself that things could only get better but he wasn't very convincing. He sat up slowly, every muscle protesting. How long did I sleep? Long enough that all of the lanterns in the room had burned down but beyond that? He eased himself to his feet and realized that there was a pillow stuck to his butt. He peeled it off gently and poked carefully at the wound. It was crusted and sticky but no longer bleeding. Where did I leave the lantern? He remembered setting it down when he was trying to open the door from the cavern. Had he moved it inside with his pack? He carefully made his way across the room, navigating by banging his shins into various unseen pieces of furniture that all seemed to be comprised entirely of sharp corners. Eventually he encountered a wall which was stubbornly not the door that he'd been trying to find. Right? Left? He chose left and felt his way along until he came to a corner. He sighed and began feeling his way back the way he'd came.

There was a noise.

A scratching sound that sounded exactly like claws against wood. Insistent, loud, deep and grating. Something from the cave, trying to get in. The door latch had been bent to uselessness when he'd kicked it open, hanging loosely from the shattered frame. The only thing holding the door shut was the spike he'd wedged into the floor. It occurred to him that his mace was back by the couch somewhere. Lantern or mace? How had he managed to scatter every useful thing that he had to every part of the room other than where he was?

Scritch, scritch, scritch.

He had a pretty good idea of where the mace was but if he went after it he'd still be in the dark. He had only the vaguest notion of where the lantern was but if he managed to find it then getting to the mace would be much easier. Unfortunately his idea of where the lantern had ended up was in the same direction where the something with claws was. He made for the door. Whatever it was hadn't gotten in yet. If the spike could hold just long enough…

Scritch, scritch, scritch.

It grew louder as he inched closer. His mouth was dry and tasted like revisited cookie.

He found the lantern through the expedient method of kicking it with his foot. It flared to light as the pixie woke up but promptly went rolling across the room. He scrambled after it, scooping it up with one hand and then dashing to the couch and grabbing his mace. He spun around to face the door.

The scratching had stopped.

On the inside of the door he could see long fresh grooves.

Not outside trying to get in. Inside with him and trying to get out.

The pixie was low on cake and the lantern wasn't enough to light the whole room. The corners lay deep in darkness. The furniture cast long wavering shadows across the rug.

Something moved in the far corner, the same corner he'd found in the process of trying to find the lantern. Stalking him from the darkness while he stood like a fool in a pool of light. A situation easy enough to reverse. He rolled the lantern across the room.

Whatever sort of creature it had once been it was now a twisted thing of bone and hair and and dried meat, crouched in the corner, poised to spring. Its shadow was huge and distorted against the wall. It was precisely at this moment that Durham realized that he still didn't have any pants on.

The thing leapt.

Durham dove backwards over the couch which did absolutely nothing to improve his physical condition. He scrambled into a crouch, mace in hand and risked a look over the back of the couch. The skeletal thing had leapt at the lantern rather than at him. It now held it in its massive jaws, the light shining out from inside of its skull giving it the appearance of a pumpkin-jack. Its bony tail flickered at the sight of its prey and it dashed across the room at him. He readied the mace and braced himself to swing.

The monstrosity skidded to a halt a few feet away and dropped the lantern. It bounced once and rolled to a stop at his feet. The thing waited in a half-crouch, chest to the floor, hindquarters high, tail vibrating back and forth like a snake rattle.

Durham hesitated. He gave the lantern a light kick, rolling it away. The skeletal thing scampered after it, tail wagging. Durham let out a long breath and lowered the mace. He'd found someone's undead pet dog. It looked to be, or have been, some sort of terrier. It had patches of curly hair in places, bushy eyebrows that hung over its eye-sockets and a beard that looked like the mop in the guard's loo back home. It bounded back over to him and dropped the lantern at his feet again. He knelt down and tentatively scratched it on the side of its skull. The dog leaned into his hand, tail still wagging, then gave his hand a lick. The experience was exactly like being licked by a mummy. The dog spun around in a circle and then began bouncing up and down with little grunts. Durham imagined that the skeletal butler hadn't been much for playing fetch. There was a chain around its neck. More of a bracelet, really, considering its neck was a spine.

"Sit!" Durham said.

It sat. Its mouth hung open as if it were panting. Durham examined the tag on the collar. "Squitters" it read. The name had been inked on in the handwriting of a child.

An image came to Durham's mind of a boy, weeping over the death of his best friend. Anger at death. Beginning the search for a way to reverse it. A long and strange path from there to Alaham the Lich Lord.

♨♨♨

Nibbly carefully eased the door open. They'd shuttered the lamps and Cardamon had gone over the door for traps and then oiled its hinges. The door led onto a wooden balcony overlooking and encircling a cavern chamber with the size and look of a church. The floor of the cavern was crowded with robed figures, lined up on benches, their attention on a tall figure on a podium at the end of the room. The candelabras along the walls did little to penetrate the shadows of the balcony. The dwarves crept in, peering down on the proceedings.

"Now you all received the scroll with the chant on it yesterday," the tall figure was saying. "Has everyone had a chance to memorize it?" His voice was dry and his face was withered and pinched as if someone had stuck a straw in him and sucked out most of his juices.

A hand was raised in the congregation. "I thought it was written down so we didn't need to memorize it?"

The withered man sighed. "You're going to have a fine time reading a scroll and doing the gestures at the same time, hmmm? It's not a long chant. Just muddle along with the repetitions until you pick it up. Now, did everyone get their packet of dried fleshwasps from the bin in the back? Those are your components,"

"I thought those were a snack," came a voice.

"You ate them?" The witherman looked amused. "Well, that should prove a very brief educational experience for you. With any luck someone will take pity and reanimate you. I hope they were delicious. Now, I've been informed that there have been some complaints about your skeletal minions being commandeered. Please understand that for the purposes of the ritual, all animated entities must remain under Alaham's control. Don't worry though. At the conclusion of the ritual there will be plenty of skeletons to go around, eh?" He winked. "Please remember that the human involved in the ritual is not to be harmed under any circumstances that are outside of the ritual. Alaham has vowed that if anyone damages him prematurely that they will spend the rest of their eternal life chained to a wall with a skeleton guard whose sole purpose is to repeatedly remove and reattach random body parts."

"I make about five hunnert, give or take," Rasp whispered in Nibbly's ear.

"Recommendations?"

Rasp gave a glum shake of his head. "Barrels of oil and a torch but don't think we gots the time to bring 'em in. Think they's preparin' to leave for this ritual thingy."

"We'll have to figure a way to hit 'em there then, once we know where they're going."

"Remember," the witherman continued. "There's going to be a lot of energy generated over the course of the ritual. If you have anything metal I strongly advise leaving it in your tray on the way out. I'm not sure what being a conduit to that much necromantic energy would do to you but we'll have an interesting discussion about it while we scrape you off of the walls. I've also just received word that there is a group of dwarves within the dungeon." He held up his scrawny hands to settle the murmuring. "Alaham assures me that the dungeon will keep them occupied and out of the way. However, on the off-chance that they stumble down into the caves you have complete license to kill them."

"How are we supposed to manage that without our skeletons?" an angry voice called.

"I expect that necromancers worthy of inclusion in the ritual would have means of defending themselves that didn't rely on minions, no? Try feeding them your fleshwasps, maybe. Likely a dwarven delicacy. Now, are there any other questions?"

"Point of order…" someone in the audience began.

"No questions? Excellent," the witherman interrupted

smoothly. "Remember there will be coffee and bagels in the organ pit after the ritual. Now, everyone line up by height and we will proceed into the cavern."

The room devolved into milling and muttering.

"Is that a necromancer thing?" Leery whispered. "Being all shrively like that?"

Nibbly had noticed it too. It wasn't just the speaker that looked like he'd been drained dry; all of the necromancers were withered looking, their skin pale and papery. He'd noticed something else interesting as well. He motioned with his hand and the dwarves silently followed him back out into the hallway. They eased the door shut again and opened one of the faelamps a sliver.

"They's all wearin' the same robes like what we found," Nibbly said. A search of the crates back in the catacombs had confirmed Durham's idea that the labels were clothing sizes. Several of the crates had had a few robes left in them, black and embroidered with occult symbols.

"You ain't seriously suggestin'…" Rasp said. "That's the oldest and dumbest trick there is. Don't know that any dwarves has done that in eight centuries lest they been clownin' in a circus ring."

"That means they'll never see it comin," Nibbly said.

⚘⚘⚘

The door on the left side of the hall turned out to be a bathroom. Durham stood for a moment, blinking stupidly at it, trying to rationalize why undead would need a bathroom. Undead physiology was something he hadn't gotten around to speculating on much but now his head was full of questions he wasn't certain he wanted answered. Had there been someone alive down here at some point? Had Alaham lived here as a necromancer before achieving lichdom? There was a lidded chamberpot in the corner, above it hung a semi-fossilized sponge that appeared to have been used followed by having not been used for several centuries. The other corner held a washbucket, long dry and adorned with cobwebs. A row of decorative clay pots lined a shelf on the wall, some with remnants of what may have once been flowers. Durham lifted the lid of the chamberpot. It smelled precisely how Durham imagined lich poop might smell. Durham closed the door on Squitters—he'd never been a fan of pets watching him in the bathroom. He made use of the chamberpot and then, feeling a bit better about things in general, went back out to check the door on the other side of the hall, Squitters clicking along beside him.

It opened to reveal a study. A large wooden desk, sagging with age, piled with books and scrolls, quills and inkpots. A skull sat on the corner with a flickering candle melted on its head. Durham wondered if the skull's prior owner would be happy knowing his head would spend its days as a candleholder and then wondered who had lit the candle. Another skeletal servant? The far wall was filled with dusty jars filled with murky liquid and floating things. The ceiling was hung with strange animals, stuffed and glassy eyed. Some sort of preposterously sized lizard with rows of carrot sized teeth, a squirrel that appeared to be wearing a tiny suit and top hat, an owl posed as if about to pounce on the squirrel, a peculiar mummified half fish, half humanoid that Durham would have identified as a mermaid if the human half hadn't looked like a shaved monkey.

Shelves were laden with carved boxes and vials, small statues of metal and stone, amulets, pestles, incense burners and several old coffee mugs. It reminded Durham of a shop he'd once visited where he'd somehow been persuaded to pay a handful of silver talons for some polished pebbles in a felt bag.

He examined some of the books, handling them gingerly lest they disintegrate from age. The Infantinomicon was on top, which was full of baby names. A book of recipes called Unaussprechlichen Kuchen. De Feminae Mysteriis was just below that and seemed to contain dating advice. None of them struck him as being much help at the moment.

"Could you tell me the time?" came a voice from behind him.

Durham spun around. The room was still empty or, at least, empty of things that he would expect to talk.

"It's only that I want to be polite," the voice continued, "but I'm not quite sure whether to say 'good morning' or 'good evening'. Perhaps 'good afternoon'?"

The voice seemed to be coming from the skull on the desk. Durham narrowed his eyes at it.

"I could, perhaps, just go with 'good day' but that always sounds to me like a farewell and I do hope that you're not intending to leave just yet."

"Who...?"

"Ah, quite. Don't quite recall my name, sadly, but I'm the one with the candle on my head. Pleasure to meet you."

Durham looked around the room suspiciously.

"Right here, on the desk. Pale, big smile," the voice added helpfully.

"Whoever that is, come out!" Durham said.

"Just me, just me. I'd tell you something that only the two of us know to prove it but I can't think of anything that actually qualifies. Perhaps this will help?"

Two glowing pinpoints of green light appeared in the skull's eye sockets. They flickered a couple of times as if blinking and then steadied.

"Ah, there we go. Been a while since I've had call to do that. Bit out of practice, as it were."

"How are you talking?"

"Well, I'm not. Not really. I'm...what would you say...thinking out loud? Yes. Thinking out loud. I'm just able to do it much more loudly than most people are."

"Skulls don't think, either."

"Well, no, but their contents do, eh? The skull is more of a house, I suppose you could say. Much like yours. A little house for you to ride around in."

"That's not the sort of thing that's usually possible."

The skull's pupil lights moved in such a way that would constitute rolling them had it any eyeballs to speak of.

"You're in a necromancer's study and you're taking issue with a skull that talks?"

"Fine," Durham said. "So you're a talking skull. Now what?"

"I'm still hoping that you'll tell me what time it is. Or the year, at least. I lost count some time ago."

"Ermmm, late afternoon? 875 is the year."

The skull made a sighing noise.

"Nearly six hundred years, then," it said.

"Six hundred years as a talking skull?"

"No, six hundred years since anyone's come into the study. Nothing else in here talks so it's been a bit dull.""

"Why would Alaham animate his candle-holder?"

"Think he was having a bit of a laugh, really. After that I was someone to talk to when he was in here working. Most risen dead aren't much in the way of being conversationalists."

"So, you know quite a bit about him then?"

"Alaham? I suppose. It's been a very long time. I'd actually assumed he was dead."

"He is, but apparently that doesn't seem to have inconvenienced him much."

"Ah, so that lich thing ended up working out for him, did it?" There was a long pause. "I guess...I guess he must be very busy now."

There was a noise like someone performing a drum roll on a set of teeth and Durham turned to see Squitters in the doorway, scratching his head with a bony foot.

"Ah, is that Squitters?" the skull asked.

At the sound of the skull's voice Squitters jumped up with one of his ghostly barks and began bouncing up and down with a sound like a drunken tap-dancer.

"Guess you two have met," Durham said.

"Well, naturally. It has been rather a long while but memories don't really degrade when your head is a skull."

"I seem to be collecting Alaham's cast-off friends," Durham said. "Are there any more of you down here?"

"There's a butler somewhere. He comes in to dust once a decade or so but isn't much for conversation. He makes biscuits and tea but it's been a while since I've had any tasting apparatus, as it were, so can't say if I'd recommend them or not."

"Right, tall chap. Skinny. We met."

"So…" the skull said. There was an awkward silence. "What brings you here?"

Durham thought about that for a bit.

"A string of accidents, I suppose you could say." He sighed.

"This is not where I'd ever had any intent of ending up at the moment."

"Ah," the skull said agreeably.

"A few days ago, bored in a guard hutch. Now I'm in a necromancer lich's study in a crypt beneath a ruined city with a bleeding butt and no pants. I'm not sure how I got here and I'm not sure how to get out of here. The place is full of death traps and roaming dead things that seem intent on having me join their ranks."

"Well, I can help you there!" the skull said, a shining note of brightness in its voice. "I know this place inside and out. Was right here while Alaham worked out the designs for it."

Durham scratched at his beard. "That's quite the tempting offer."

"Well, of course it is! Your situation is bound to improve with a guide."

"Look, let's drop the pretense shall we Alaham?"

The skull fell silent. Squitters sat down with a click.

"Clever, clever," it finally said. "What gave me away?"

"Several things. First being that you have complete intelligence in a dungeon where all of the other skeletons have nothing of the sort. Second, you claimed that you couldn't remember your name then a minute later claimed that memories don't degrade for undead indicating to me that you were being deliberately obtuse. Third, Squitters was happy to see you in spite of the fact that I can't think of much a talking skull could do to endear itself to a dog other than letting him gnaw on you, which you don't show any signs of. Plus you referred to cookies as 'biscuits'. Everyone around these parts calls them cookies. According to a history I read on Alaham he's from Abilane, where they call them biscuits."

"That's a remarkably thin stream of conjectures, impressive though they may be."

"Yes, which is why I confronted you with it and let you confirm it for me."

"Squitters, I believe I've been outplayed," Alaham said. "Subterfuge was never my strong point." Squitters wagged his tail.

The skull rose from the desk, the candle flame on its head dancing with the motion, sending shadows skittering around the room. It floated into the air, hanging in a position approximate to where it would be had it a body beneath it.

"Most impressive," Alaham said. "Most impressive indeed. Quite delightful, really."

Durham pursed his lips and arched his eyebrows. "That's a good trick, floating about without a body."

"Ah, thank you. Rather simple really, comparatively."

"Where IS your body, if you don't mind my asking?"

"Oh, it's around here somewhere. Think I might have left it in the hall closet last time I used it. With the umbrellas. That's why I had it out, if I remember correctly. Went topside and needed something to hold an umbrella with."

There was a rattle from the hall. A headless skeleton, the bones smooth and polished, stumbled into the room. It reached out and took the floating skull with both hands and placed it on the stump of its neck, twisting it back and forth a bit as if screwing it into place.

"There we are," Alaham said. He reached out and plucked a dusty black robe from a hook on the wall and shrugged his way into it. Durham found it disquieting watching the bare bones twist and move. The robe was a bit of a relief.

"You're not what I expected." He said.

"Met a few necromancers before, have you?"

"Well, no."

"Liches, then?"

Durham shook his head.

"Quite all right. You're not what I would have expected from a city guardsman either."

"How do you know that?"

The skull's grin glinted. "Oh, you'd be surprised what I know. For instance, you came here with a group of dwarves that call themselves 'The Dungeoneers' in search of the legendary Mace of Guffin." He said the last in a deep dramatic tone, mocking. "An artifact so horrible, so powerful that nary a word is spoken of it and its dangers are completely unknown." His voice went back to normal. "Bit suspect, that, don't you think? To be fair, I do have a green mace around but it's green because it's made of bronze and I left it lying on a shelf for a few years."

"You're very well informed…"

"I should be. After all, I'm the one who hired them to come and arranged for you to be with them."

"ME? My being here…"

"…was an accident? So you said. A mis-delivered message from a thin pageboy with curly blond hair and a missing tooth, eh? Not all of my minions are skeletons." Alaham laughed. "You're a clever one, yes, but you seem to have completely missed the big lie in favor of finding the little ones."

"You actually think I'll believe that the dwarves are in on

this?"

"Why would they object to escorting you to visit?"

Durham felt a lump of pure unease in his chest. It seemed to be gnawing on things indiscriminately.

"You did all of that to bring ME here?"

"Well, yes. I couldn't just send you an invitation. 'Dear Durham, please come visit crypt beneath ruined city, love, Alaham the necromancer lich.' Can't imagine that you'd have exactly leapt at the opportunity."

"But why me?"

"Because, dear boy, you are my last living descendant. You are my heir."

Durham opened his mouth then realized that he had nothing to say and closed it again. He opened it again, certain that there really was something he should be saying but, once again, came up blank and closed it once more. Perhaps the third time would be the charm?

"Er…"

Nope.

"Yes, yes," Alaham said. "Quite a lot to take in, no mistake. Follow me and perhaps I can clear things up a bit for you. This way." He swept out of the room, robes trailing behind him,

Squitters bouncing relentlessly at his feet.

"I've been at this for a long time," Alaham went on. "And I'm ready for a change of scenery. To travel. To see the world. But I can't very well leave my tomb with no ruler, now, can I?"

They reached the end of the hall, passing through an opening into a small room with a strange contraption in the middle. It was made of bones and looked almost like a very large basket. A spine with a skull atop it extended up from one end of it. Alaham stepped through an opening in the side and sat on a row of femurs that extended horizontally across the middle. Durham realized the the thing was a cart of sorts, though it seemed lacking in wheels. Alaham patted the bone bench next to him. Durham swallowed, climbed in and sat. Squitters leapt in after them, putting his paws on the front of the cart and wagging his spindly tail. The cart rose in the air with a lurch, skeletal legs unfolding beneath it. It began to walk, carrying the three of them down another hallway.

"There's no creature that looks like this, is there?" Durham asked, having tried and failed to mentally resolve the cart into something with muscle and skin.

"No," Alaham said. "And that is why I'm widely regarded as the greatest of all Necromancers, if you'll pardon my saying so.

I'm the only one with the skill to recombine bones into new and wondrous things. My imagination is the only limit and I have an excellent imagination, again, if you'll pardon my saying so. I can combine the bones in any way I like, add a skull and animate away!" He reached up and rapped a knuckle against the skull that adorned the cart. It hung just above and behind their heads, looking out between them. "This chap here is our cart. We rest within him and his legs carry us forward."

"How did your body move with no skull?"

"Ah, that was a different bit of magic entirely." He pressed a finger to where his lips would have been. Durham understood the gesture but could have done without it.

"I thought that you…uh…animated things by tying their souls back to their skeletons."

"That is what many think. In fact, if you were to ask other necromancers, that is likely what they would say as well. But what is a soul other than a swirl of magical energy in the shape of what it inhabits? I learned that one can make the shape and then form the magic to it. And magic, why, magic can take any shape at all. I'd warrant, for example, that you've not seen one of those before." He pointed as they emerged into the most horrifying place Durham had ever seen in his life.

The room appeared to be a workshop. Long tables were arrayed in even rows, their surfaces stained dark and covered in piles of bones. Half formed creations were scattered about, mid-assembly, from tiny and delicate looking to larger ones made from bones that must have come from great beasts. Beasts with tusks and claws, horns and spikes. Shelves lined with dozens of skulls ran the length of one wall, some human, many not. Charnel stench hung above the tables with the solidity of a mist. The room was lit with guttering light from chandeliers above. The chandeliers themselves were made of bones, artfully placed together in intricate patterns of macabre beauty. The candles rested on skulls at the center of whorls of scapula atop arching arms adorned with dangling humerus. The ribs of the arched ceiling had more bone ornamentation, arranged into elaborate designs. The room buzzed with clouds of flies, making the room's surfaces seem to writhe in the flickering light. The thing Alaham was pointing at lurked in the shadows across the room from the skull wall. It had a long body, low to the ground, six freakishly long legs along the sides, extending above its back and folding at the knee like a spider. Its torso curved up like a scorpion tail, a bull skull instead of a stinger adorning the top. Four arms extended from the front of the thing, two with claws, two with massive pincers. The thing advanced out of the shadows, talons clicking on the stone floor. The spiked tip of its tail weaved back and forth like a dancing snake.

"No," Durham said. "Can't say that I've seen one of those before."

"One of dozens of my masterpieces!" Alaham was rubbing his hands together with the delight of showing off his creations. His fingers made little raspy sounds. "If you'll forgive my having dispensed with modesty long ago, I am the greatest artist in bone in all of history!"

Durham would have hoped that a single bone creation would be enough to elevate one to the greatest artist in bone. It wasn't a list that he felt it proper to be lengthy. He tore his gaze away from the thing's dark sockets and fixed it gaze straight ahead as they moved through the room, trying to see as little of it as possible. That first look was going to haunt him until the end of his days, whether that moment came years from now or tomorrow. Durham was starting to reconcile himself to the fact that the lich really didn't have any intent of killing him.

Heir.

That was a word Durham's brain poked at as if it were a rotten tooth, shying away each time he tried to mentally latch onto it.

Their walking bone chariot left the workshop and they entered a vast space of darkness. The return of the clicking noise and the natural stone floor told Durham that they'd emerged back into the central cave chamber. The cart carried them within the wavering pool of light coming from the candle that still flickered atop Alaham's head. They came to a wall, rippled and melted looking. A long row of skeletal spines were attached to it, extending end to end up into the darkness. Each had a pair of shoulders with arms and hands affixed to it. The hands on the lowest spine grasped the edge of the cart and lifted it, raising it up so that the next pair of arms could grab them and lift them still higher. It wasn't exactly a smooth process but definitely an effective one as the cart rose slowly up the wall. Up and up it went, the darkness around them still filled with the clicking and clattering noise.

"What am I hearing?" he asked.

Alaham made a bemused 'hmmm' noise. "Just wait," he said. "You will see."

The cart finally arrived at its destination, stopping next to a narrow span of stone, a bridge through the darkness. Alaham stepped out of the cart and beckoned Durham to follow.

Squitters came after, stepping gingerly on the narrow path.

It led them out to a platform, rising from the cave floor far below. The dais was round, a great stalagmite that had been cut across, large enough to have held a small farmer's market. At its center was a second dais, rising up to hold a great throne and an altar before it. The altar was carved from the cave rock and hoary with hanging lichen, the throne a conglomeration of bones. A stalactite, thick as a tree hung over them from the shadows above, a snarled knot of metal suspended below it with a dozen flickering torches at its ends. Around the edge of the dais stood a terrifyingly eerie ring of figures, robed and hooded in black, the hoods tall narrow cones with with shrouds covering their heads and faces. A wide flight of stone steps began at the edge, descending into the darkness toward the cavern floor.

"Are you ready?" Alaham asked. He didn't wait for an answer.

"Behold!" he cried, gesturing grandly. The cavern bloomed dimly with points of light at Alaham's gesture, giving Durham his first view of the boneworks, a merciless sense of its extent. And to think that he'd thought the workshop was the worst thing he'd ever seen.

They were in a massive cave. So massive that the light was

almost lost within it. And all around them were the boneworks.

Hundreds, perhaps thousands of skeletons, clasped together into spinning gears, their skeletal bodies rigid, grasped hand to foot, arcing to form sweeping curves. Gigantic gears with tangled masses of bones as teeth, small gears with the skeleton's spines interlocked. Gears both horizontal and vertical, some alone, some in intricate layers, clicking their way through their rotations along hubs, rails and spindles of skeletons with arms clasped around each other. Still more skeletons stood amidst the gears working the cranks, acting in place of springs and ratchets. Others clumped together as weights, raising and lowering as the wheels turned. Long ropes woven of sinew ran between the great wheels, pulling them, rotating them. The corridors of the maze hung in the midst, each section in its own twisted mockery of an orrery, ready to be spun, to be dropped, lifted, moved.

"What is it?" Durham asked. It seemed a phrase that didn't quite cover the scope of the question.

Alaham was almost dancing with delight. "I call it the Boneworks," he said. "I must confess, I started out just trying to make a clock. Back when I was alive, ruling Tanahael. I had the idea for machines made of bone, animated bone to provide their power and motion. I figured that a clock for the city might be nice. Experimentation and civic improvement rolled into one. Once I realized my breakthrough, however, it became so much more.

"I made it of bones from the crypts. It was much larger than the clockworks but still only a third the size it is now. I conceived it and built it, animating skeletons to assist me. It still took years. And then that glorious day when I turned it on. The day that has gone down in history as the death of Tanahael. I gave the command and it awoke, hungry for power, thirsty for life. And it took it, just as I'd planned, pulling on the souls of all of the life in Tanahael, drawing them all in, feeding itself until it had the strength for all of its mechanisms to go into motion. I'm a bit embarrassed to admit it but I may have even cackled maniacally when it began to work."

"You killed thousands," Durham said.

"No," Alaham said. "I gave them immortality as part of my greatest creation. And I've been adding to it and refining it ever since, adding all of the bones from the city above until now, when it has become this thing of sheer magnificence. And now its construction is finished. Which is why I finally invited you here."

"But what is it for? What does it even do other than murder

cities?"

"Ah," Alaham said. "I could tell you but that would spoil the surprise! Suffice it to say that it shall be an even greater work of magic than its creation. Perhaps, dare I say it, the greatest work of magic the world has ever seen. Even the Hermits will cower before what I am to achieve."

Durham wasn't quite sure yet how he was supposed to fit into Alaham's plan but was very sure that he didn't want to know. He looked nervously at the ring of hooded figures surrounding the dais.

"Who are they?"

"My assistants!" Alaham said. "Not everything here is dead. Necromancers from across the entire face of the world have come to be a part of this moment. There are many more than what you see here. They are all about, preparing for the ceremony."

"What ceremony is that?" He didn't recall a ceremony having been mentioned. Alaham seemed to have an entire parade of horrors to shuffle him through and now a ceremony to add to the end of it? A ceremony involving who knew how many necromancers and, presumably, the boneworks?

"The magic, of course," Alaham said. "The boneworks are

finished, the necromancers assembled and now you have arrived. There is no reason to wait any longer. Tonight shall be the night that I have spent centuries working to bring about. Tonight you and I shall change the world."

"Ah," Durham said. "THAT ceremony." He wondered where the dwarves were, what they were doing, if they were even still alive. Surrounded by necromancers, skeletons and a lich, Durham felt excruciatingly alone.

"I do have a few other matters to consider so I must beg your patience," Alaham said. "There are no traps on the dais here and I've given the order that you're not to be interfered with so you should be perfectly safe. Tea and biscuits are available- just ask one of the necromancers and they'll see to it. Plenty of books to read as well and Squitters here to keep you company. Oh, and the green mace is lying about here somewhere if you care to dig it up so that you feel you've accomplished something."

The skull lifted from its body, letting it collapse, and floated down to rest on the arm of the throne. The lights in its sockets dimmed then went out.

"This shouldn't be possible," Ruby said from Ginny's left. They were sitting on the edge of the hallway ceiling, legs dangling over the side. Thud was to Ginny's right, wreathed in a haze of cigar smoke, having been utterly silent through a cigar and a half, frowning at the darkness. They sat atop their room with its six hallways extending out, only one of the dozens like it that the costonflagrationater had revealed, criss-crossing above and below each other in a spiderweb of stone corridors, all hanging high up in the emptiness of the cavern. All around them the boneworks clicked and rattled.

Ruby had made some tea and they sipped it from their wineskins. It was as red as wine and tasted of raspberries.

"Do you mean the bone machine?" Ginny asked. "It seems to work well enough for moving hallways around but I have to think there's more to it. Far too much effort for just a maze trap."

"No," Ruby said. "The level of necromancy involved. We don't know a lot about Alaham's background. He was an obscure hedge wizard for most of his life until he suddenly rose up and took over Tanahael and then destroyed it. That right there was enough of a mystery to bring me on this expedition in hopes of solving it. No mortal should ever have managed such a feat of necromancy. But this…" she gestured around her. "Thousands of undead simultaneously animated. Only the Hermits have ever managed such a thing and even then it took three of them to work the sorcery and at least a dozen more to feed them power. Maintaining even a few dozen should be enough to have fragmented Alaham's mind."

"Right, but the Hermits didn't do the animating, did they?" Ginny asked. "They made that Bonebin fellow to raise and lead the army against the Daemon. You don't suppose…"

"That Alaham is actually Bonebin returned?"

Ginny nodded.

"The thought had occurred to me but, no, the Hermits laid him to rest and locked him away somewhere in case they ever needed to pull him back out. It requires three keys to release him and each Hermit faction only has one of the keys. It would require some threat grave enough to unite the Orders against it before there'd even be a chance."

"Maybe he figured out the spell they used. Or maybe he's made some major breakthrough in necromancy."

Ruby was silent, frowning into the darkness much as Thud was, a quill in her mouth substituting for a cigar. Ginny sighed. They seemed out of her area of expertise at the moment.

That was when the lights came on.

Were the yellow orbs merely dim? Or was their light bright but simply lost in the immensity of the cavern? It was hard to say either way. They were affixed to the walls and ceiling of the cave, their sickly yellow light just enough to create a twilight luminance. It backlit the machine, turning the gears into huge silhouettes, their shadows methodically rotating across each other and stretched long on the cavern walls.

Thud was instantly on his feet, crossbow in hand, provided 'instantly' can include a second or two of panicked scrambling and flailing.

"What…" he began.

"Hush," Ginny said. She was in her element now, the workings of the machine above her laid bare. She began reassembling it in her mind, finding each gear's purpose, the meaning of each belt of sinew. Her mouth moved, offering its own stream of speculation alongside the stream in her head. Her hands opened and closed, twisted, poked at the air, fingers circling to describe invisible axis and pulleys.

"I didn't 'hush' you while I were thinkin'," Thud grumbled but then fell silent.

"So sorry to interrupt," a new voice said. They spun around.

One of the nearby gears had detached itself, the circle unspooling into a long twisting tentacle of skeletons. It had extended down to them, a skull prominently affixed to the end, weaving back and forth with the bone tentacle's snake-like undulations.

"I have to admit," the skull continued, "I'm rather impressed at your means of escaping the maze. If I'd known I was to have had visitors out here I might have dusted a bit."

"Alaham," Ruby said.

"Why yes," the skull said. "Though I'm at a bit of a loss as to whom you might be. I don't recall inviting any scribes. No matter, you are welcome all the same. Delighted to have a scribe here, really. Not inviting you was an egregious oversight on my part. Most welcome indeed. Though we can hardly have you perched up here in the rafters, as it were, where nothing of any interest seems to be happening or likely to happen, now can we?"

Ruby yelped as another bone tentacle unfurled from behind them and grasped her around the waist, snatching her into the air. It passed her to another and then another, skeletal tendrils unfolding from the different gears to grasp her and carry her along. Within moments she was gone. Thud spun back around and fired his crossbow bolt into the skull's face, shattering it.

Alaham's laugh came from behind them. A new tentacle, a new skull.

"Now that was a bit on the rude side, but, circumstances being what they are I suppose I can understand the decision, futile as it may have been."

"What have you done with her, lich?" Thud spat out the last word as if it were a curse. He cranked a fresh bolt into place.

"Not to worry, she is quite unharmed," Alaham said. "I am just relocating her to where she'll have something worth recording. Something other than watching you attempt to stretch your brain around your current predicament. You are but a tiny bit of grit amongst the gears. A leader reduced to one follower, your party scattered and lost."

"What do you mean, 'invited'?" Ginny said, figuring it couldn't hurt to interrupt. She knew that Thud's ego tended toward the unassailable side but Alaham rubbing it in was unlikely to improve the dwarf's mood.

"Sorry?"

"You told Ruby that you didn't recall inviting her, implying that there was someone here that you did invite."

"Ah, yes, thank you so much for reminding me. Why, I

invited all of you, of course. Except for the scribe, as I believe we've established."

"You didn't invite us," Thud said through clenched teeth. "We was hired by…"

"'WERE hired', I believe you mean. Really, dwarven accents are so tiresome. But yes. You were hired by a man in a black cloak with chalk dust on his elbows, claiming to be from the Royal Vault Keeper and presenting you with a sack of coins and a contract, yes? The chalk dust was my idea. Little details like that add so much to believability."

"Why would you bring us here?" Ginny asked. "We've sacked half of your tomb."

"Are you referring to that little play area I put in at the entrance? Oh yes, wonderful job with that. I brought you here as a means to bring Durham here, of course. He's the one that I'm specifically interested in. Now that I have him the rest of you are largely irrelevant."

"What do ye know about Durham?" Thud asked. "Where is he?"

"Oh, he's perfectly safe, right where I want him to be. By the way, I may have left him with the impression that you were aware that it was I that hired you and that you've been in on the plan all along. I do sincerely apologize for any future awkwardness that may cause if you attempt some sort of rescue. Not that I expect that a rescue attempt would go well enough for it to even become a concern. Now, I've other things to attend too so I'll leave you two to explore the many possible excruciating deaths the dungeon has to offer. Ta!"

The long spine of bone twisted away into the murk of the machine, its laugh fading into the grinding of the gears.

Thud's fists were clenched and his face was a level of red that Ginny mentally placed as a tentative nine on the Thud rage scale.

"Why, that…" he began and then launched into an amazing stream-of-consciousness mass of expletives.

"Ermmm…" Ginny said.

"…bilious crotchboil of a weevil ridden hag taint…"

"Boss?"

"…maggoty canker egg…"

"Boss!"

"…worm riddled ogre nipple…"

"BOSS!"

"What?" he roared.

"Behind you."

Thud turned.

It was made of bone, which came as no huge surprise. It was, however, the skeleton of no creature that Ginny had ever heard of. Eight legs ending in long, curved claws; three pronged scorpion-like tail; four heads that seemed to be largely comprised of teeth. It was the size of a catapult and half as user friendly. It lurked just at the edge of their lantern light, scuttling back and forth, taunting them to attack. Thud obliged. The thunk of the crossbow was followed quickly by the clatter of the bolt bouncing its way uselessly through the monster's excessive number of ribs. It charged, scuttling forward with startling speed. Ginny dove to the side, realizing in midair that the edge of the platform preceded her estimated landing point. She flailed into open space, her stomach lurching with a wrenching twist. She drew in air to scream then landed hard, far sooner than she'd expected. Her breath poofed out of her in a cloud of garlic pupae scent. She bounced and was falling again, through one of the gaps in the horizontal gear she'd landed on, landing on a second gear below. It spun her swiftly around, feet first, below the hallway hanging above. She pressed herself as flat as the gear just above her spun the opposite way, the bone struts a blur inches from her face.

Her throat unseized and she was able to take in a deep gasp of air.

"Jump!" she yelled.

Above her she glimpsed an airborne Thud through the blur of the gears and had a moment of gratification that he trusted her enough to leap into the darkness. She twisted to see where he'd landed and her beard got caught by the gear above with a huge yank of pain. It instantly pulled her beard up over her face, clogging her mouth and nose, covering her eyes. She was dragged across the bone gear below, bouncing across its knobbles and knuckles. Her beard smelled and tasted like her shampoo, Eau de Mouse. She grabbed at it, tugging it with her own hands like it was a rope, pulling herself up to relieve the drag on her chin. She had a panicked flash of an image of her head getting caught against a strut of the gear below, folding her in half backwards and promptly focused her efforts at trying to keep her head up. Both wheels jolted to a stop with a great crunching noise, bringing an abrupt end to her predicament. Momentum kept her moving only until she reached the end of her beard length where it jerked her to a halt, yanking her mouth open with a crack of her jaw hinge and a rip of pain from her chin.

"Oo," she said.

She took a shaky breath and scooted down just enough to allow her to close her mouth and tried again.

"Ow," she said.

Her back felt like she'd shoved it into a bad pair of boots and marched twenty miles on it. Her face felt like it was what had been marched on.

She arched her head back to try and see in the direction from which she'd heard the crunch. Thud was wedged upside down between the gears, a twisted cluster of broken bones around him from where the gears had cracked around him. He grinned at her. Since he was upside down and she was looking at him upside down the grin was right side up.

"Ow," he said. "Guess I was a tougher piece o' gristle than what they kin handle."

Ruby nodded in agreement, which turned out to be an awkward thing to do while laying on her back and looking above her head.

There was a crash from immediately above her as the skelescorpiarachnohydra thing landed on the gear above. It reached down with three of its claws, They scratched and scraped, trying to reach her.

Ruby saw Thud reach down and grab hold of the gear she was laying on. She quickly rolled over so she was face down, knowing what he was about to do. Thud tugged hard, pulling himself free from the gear above, barely clearing the break before the top gear spun back into motion. The monster was carried with briefly until it met up with the side of the hanging hallway with a clatter like a bundle of canes spilling on marble. It was knocked down between the gears and promptly ripped into shards between them, pieces of bone clattering across the gears.

"Hold tight," she heard from Thud's direction. She heard him pulling himself along the gear, crawling until their heads were together.

"Conference time," she said.

"Not quite yet," he said, and pointed. Ginny looked to more bone creatures moving toward them, climbing spindles, hopping across gears. None were as large as the first but all were strange, malformed accretions of parts that had no place in nature. There were at least a dozen.

"Starting to think he don't like us," Ginny said.

"No accounting for taste," Thud said. "Got your mace?" he asked, gesturing with his as if she might not know what one was.

She felt at her belt. "Yeah, never even got a chance to draw it on that last thing." She pulled it out, the weight and solidity of it a comforting feel in her hand.

Thud had crawled to the side and was peering over the edge. "Walkway below us. Less claustrophobic." He heaved himself over the side and was gone.

Ginny decided to look before she leapt. Her mind was still chewing on the machine. It was something she'd always been good at—looking at things and being able to discern how and why they did what they did. The scope of the boneworks was too vast and shadowed to grasp the whole of it and she had not even the faintest idea of the overall purpose of the thing but she'd seen enough to have a good grasp of how the parts she could see fit together and worked with each other. She could see that Thud was not so much on a walkway as on a gear track which made it a likely sort of place for a gear to come rolling along before too long. The first of the bone things had arrived in front of him, hunched low, claws clutching the narrow rail, spikey knees jutting out to the sides.

"Hot spot!" she yelled. It was a dwarven term, used to announce a location that was safe for the moment but very soon wouldn't be. Demolitionists used it when they lit the fuse. Smelters used it when the molten iron was about to be poured.

Soldiers used it when the shadow of an incoming catapult stone fell across them. Ginny used it now to tell Thud to move, fast, because now she could see the gear spinning its way toward him. It was about all she could do for him as two more of the monsters were closing in on her fast.

She saw a counter-weight the size of a barrel drop past and realized that it was descending on a chain. She holstered her mace and leapt for it, grabbing the chain in a full body hug. The chain swung out from her impact causing the counter-weight below her to swing out of place and miss its slot. The chain went slack for a moment as the weight stopped, giving Ginny an abrupt jolt when she hit the end of the slack. She lost her grip with her hands but managed a death grip with her feet to keep from falling. This promptly swung her upside down on the chain. She was briefly annoyed with herself that her first reaction was not toward self-preservation but to grab the hem of her kilt between her knees to protect her modesty and then annoyed with herself for much longer when she saw her mace go falling past her head. She grabbed on her with her hands again and let go with her feet, swinging down to grab hold again just as the weight began its ascent. Some part of the machinery above was pulling it, bringing it up faster than it had fallen. The original drop had carried her far enough below the two skeletal creatures that had been coming for her that they had turned their attention to Thud. Now she was rising fast and she could see one of them above her, crouched on a cog as if to leap. She swung out with her feet as she soared past it, catching it in the chin with a high speed kick. Its skull sailed off into darkness, the rest of its body collapsing below her as it dropped out of her view.

She'd caught a glimpse of Thud, jumping from the rail and hoped that there was somewhere for him to land. One of the creatures had latched on to the counterweight below her and was starting to climb up. Another came skittering down the chain toward her from above. Ginny saw a spindle go past and grabbed for it, swinging all the way around it just in time to catch the creature on the weight with another swinging kick, scattering it.

The impact was enough to knock her from the spindle, however. She landed on a row of vertical cogs, each the size of a wagon wheel, with teeth made from what looked to be scapula. They were all spinning the same direction, meshing with another row of cogs just to the left and beneath. Ginny scrambled to her feet, trying to run in place and maintain her balance against the rotation. The skeletal thing above dropped onto her back. It seemed to be made mostly of arms and legs, sharp fingers clutching at her.

She fell backwards, keeping it between her and the grinding point between the cogs below, bridging the gap between the cog rows, half turned over with her head and shoulders on the lower spindle and her feet on the one above, the conflicting rotations trying to fold her in half and feed her through. Her shred of hope was that the thing on her back would choke the gears for at least the briefest of moments. There was a sharp clattering as the skeletal horror got pulled between the cogs. As she'd hoped, they seized for one brief, merciful moment. She shoved hard with her feet, sending herself sliding over the lower cog spindle, into the unknown darkness beyond it.

ℓℓℓ

Thud had landed on a narrow wooden catwalk in his leap from the rail. It had seemed a thin place of relative safety, an illusion broken quickly as the bone monstrosities began arriving on the walkway as well. He wondered how Ginny was doing, how many she'd taken down. His advantage so far had been that the things weren't sapient enough to know their own weak point and went to no extra effort to protect their heads. He'd bashed in three of them but the fourth and fifth were coming at him simultaneously, one from in front and one from above, achieving a semblance of strategy through the sheer accident of their timing. He lowered his head and charged at the one in front of him, his mace arm cocked behind him. Horrific looking as the things might be they didn't have much in the way of mass. He knocked it back, all six of its legs splaying out, then swung forward and caved its skull in as the one from above landed on him, sinking its claws into the meat of his back. He roared and jumped into the air, flipping himself over to bring his full weight down on top of it. It broke apart but its stabbing pincers went even deeper with the impact. He lay there a moment, gasping for breath, a white spear of pain stabbing at his thoughts. He didn't seem to be able to move his arms. Another skeleton monster came into his view, looming over him. Its shape reminded him of a mantis, legs straddling the catwalk rails. Its arms began unfolding, pincers poised for the strike.

And then it was gone. He'd had just a brief glimpse of Ginny, sailing past in its wake. He rolled over to see Ginny and the creature roll off the end of the walkway, landing back on the rail. She'd had just enough time to get to one knee when the great gear came rolling past. There was a spray of red and when the gear rolled out of view both Ginny and the skeleton were gone.

It had been the last of them. The things didn't seem to have much in the way of autonomy and without Alaham around to send in reinforcements the attack was over.

And Ginny was gone.

Durham was captured.

The rest of the team was lost, scattered through the dungeon, maybe some of them dead as well. Thud let his head sink to the catwalk, the wood rough against his forehead. Around him the boneworks whirled on, clicking its secrets.

-18-

Durham stood next to Alaham's throne, watching the boneworks spin before him. He'd considered sitting on the throne, as it was the only seating option available that wasn't the floor or the altar but a quick examination of the throne's seat suggested that Alaham had spent many years sitting there while his mortal form was still in the process of decaying away, leaving a residue of goo that made sitting an unappealing prospect. The robed figures circling the dais didn't seem to be paying him much attention. The altar was stained with a color that Durham tried to convince himself was spilled coffee. A cloud of flies did their strange whirling dance over the altar and throne but Durham felt better standing next to them than to the silent necromancers.

The details of the machine were difficult to make out, the lighting leaving most of it shrouded in spinning shadow. Consequently he was rather startled when the gear in front of him rotated Ruby into view. She was in a rib cage that hung below the gear, looking even more annoyed than usual. The cage opened as she rotated over the dais, dropping her onto the edge next to the figures. Her fingers scraped on the stone as she tried to crawl away from them. Durham ran forward and grabbed her under her arms, pulling her away and to her feet at the same time. They ran to the altar where Ruby spent a moment brushing and straightening her scapular, catching her breath before looking his direction. At his feet.

"What is that?"

Durham was left with his mouth hanging open. He'd been expecting a different greeting and had been preparing to say something along the lines of, "Yes, I'm glad I'm still alive too",

"You're welcome" or "Yes, I'm alright" or even, perhaps, "Nice to see you!"

He looked down.

"That's Squitters. He's Alaham's dog."

Squitters pranced a few steps and wagged his tail.

Ruby pursed her lips disapprovingly, squinted suspiciously at the candle wax coated skull on the arm of the throne and then around at the hooded figures encircling them.

"And that's Alaham," Durham said, pointing at the skull, feeling that it was rather more important than the dog. "He said he had things to think about and has just been sitting there ever since."

Ruby pressed her finger briefly to her lips, indicating silence. She picked Alaham up from the arm of the throne and thumped the skull hard against the arm's edge, knocking off the candle and most of the wax. She held it out to Squitters.

"Here, boy! Fetch!" She sent the skull rolling briskly across the dais, Squitters scampering after it. Durham's face was frozen into the sort of expression one might have while watching someone wave their genitals about at a wedding.

"Listen," she whispered. "That's not Alaham. None of these are."

Squitters scampered back with the skull. Ruby wrestled it away from him and threw it again, further this time. Squitters was after it instantly.

"But I talked to…" Durham began.

"No," Ruby said, still whispering. "You talked to Alaham's voice in your head, yes? It was Alaham but he wasn't in the skull. He can control any of them, animate them…" She paused to throw the skull again. "…see through their eyes, but they're not actually him. It's a puppet show. He's still hidden away somewhere, toying with us. He can observe us through any of the skulls, including these two," she said, as Squitters returned with the skull in his jaws, tail wagging furiously. She threw it hard this time, off the edge of the dais. Squitters charged after it, leaping into the darkness to follow. A barely audible clatter reached them a moment later as Squitters met the ground somewhere below.

"Always wondered if dogs were actually that stupid," Ruby said.

"You just killed Alaham's dog," Durham said.

"It was already dead, idiot."

Durham swallowed the lump in his throat. He'd rather liked Squitters. "Alaham probably won't be happy about that."

"Good," Ruby said. "But unlikely. He can just put the thing back together again. Meanwhile, he's not going to be able to spy on us with it and those others are too far away to hear as long as we keep our voices down. Over here—" she gestured for him to follow and stepped between the throne and the altar where the two fly clouds blurred together into perfect storm conditions. "The noise will help cover our voices." She spat out a fly then pulled her scapular up to cover her mouth. "Now, I've figured out part of this charade but I still don't know why. You say he talked to you. Tell me everything he said. Sorry. Hold off on that. First tell me why you aren't wearing any pants."

"I had to cut them off and they were soaked with blood."

"Fair enough. Now, what did Alaham say?"

"He said that he hired the dwarves to bring me here because he's retiring. Wants to travel. And that he's giving this dungeon to me. Because I'm his heir."

Ruby let out a cackle of laughter. She pressed her fist to her mouth to cut it off.

"I think it's safest to start with the base assumption that everything he told you was a lie," she said. "We may find a jot of truth between the lines, though. You being his heir, as a start. You said that you never knew your parents?"

"Yes."

"And the dwarves felt that a potentially serious liability?"

"Yes."

"Not exactly poking any holes in that theory, are we?"

Durham was silent, awash in unjust guilt.

"What else did he say?"

"Something about a ceremony and a big magic thing that he's going to do now that I'm here."

"Hmmm. Now that sounds like it might have a grain of the truth."

᯽᯽᯽

Thud did not allow himself to mourn for long.

He took stock of his situation. His pack was somewhere far above, lost somewhere in the machine. His arms were too weak to even think of climbing to retrieve it, however. He still had his mace but could barely lift it. His duoculars were laying nearby, one of the scopes crushed, its lens shattered. Bones, some broken and splintered, lay scattered across the walkway. He could feel his blood, in a tickling trickle down his back and soaking into the waist of his kilt. He pulled his jerkin off and then his under-tunic, his pale skin almost seeming to glow in the dim light. The under-tunic was already sodden with blood but he tied it tightly around himself anyway, binding the wounds on his back as best as he could. The pain had turned into a teeth grinding sting, waves of heat searing through him with each heartbeat. He tugged his jerkin back on and laced it tight to help keep the bandage in place. It was tight enough to make it a nuisance to breath but at least he was still breathing.

He struggled to his feet and made his way to the rail where he'd last seen Ginny. It was made of two rows of femurs, end to end, scapula spacing the rails apart, gaps between for the teeth of the gear. The bones were wet with blood, a spatter of red out onto the catwalk where he stood. His brow furrowed. The blood didn't look right. He crouched and touched his fingers to it. It was thin, watery. He sniffed his fingers.

Tea.

Not blood.

Ruby's red tea that she'd shared with Ginny. And there, caught between two of the scapula, Ginny's wineskin.

"Ginny!"

"Down here, boss." Her voice was thin.

He poked his head over the edge of the catwalk. Ginny was

twenty feet below on top of a vertical spindle, cradling her arm and rotating slowly as the spindle turned.

"Wotcha doin' down there, lass?"

"Thinking you was dead. Glad you ain't. Wouldn't happen to have a rope handy, would ya?"

"Naw, lost me pack. I can climb down to ya though, maybe."

"Can't say the spot has much to recommend it."

"How bad are ya hurt?"

"Don't rightly know. All my bits are still movin' but everything hurts like a hangover. Arm got a bit squished but I don't think it's broken. You?"

"I'm leaking a bit and'll have a nice new set of scars to show off come Honor Day but there's enough o' me left to keep breathin'."

"So what's the plan?"

Thud's shoulders slumped. "Dunno. Think we're on the losin' end of this one."

Ginny snorted. "Not 'til we're all cold and dead. Relentless assault? Instant death? All odds against us? Just another day at the office, boss." A grin split her beard. "This dungeon played it's hand but we's still kicking. We're the godsdamned Dungeoneers, boss. Time to show this place what for."

"Don't happen to have a plan to go with that speech, do ya?"

"Well, sittin' here spinnin' for a few gave me some more time to look at this machine we're in. Pretty sure I've got it sussed."

Thud looked up at the incomprehensible contraption of whirling bones. "How do ya figger?"

"Them hallways we was in ain't hallways. Well, not as such. The whole point of this machine is to move 'em around, mostly into places where they ain't much use as hallways. Don't know why that is but that's what it's for." She frowned. "Think it also may be a clock."

"Not sure what good knowin' that does us."

She grinned up at him again, her face rotating slowly in the dim light.

"Pretty sure I can break it."

🙢🙢🙢

Durham sat on the edge of the stone altar, Ruby next to him. She was frowning and sucking on the end of her quill, her journal laying unopened next to her. The robed figures still circled the dais, backs to them, apparently completely unconcerned with anything that they might get up to. Not that they'd come up with anything to do other than sit on the altar and try to avoid the stained spots.

There was a scraping noise behind them. Durham turned and saw that the throne was moving. Or, rather, the bones were. They were unknitting, folding out from each other like a flower blooming or hands unclasping, turning the throne from a chair into an array of jabs and spikes, moving apart to reveal a dark hole in the heart of the stalagmite floor. A figure rose from the darkness, smoothly and slowly as if raised by unseen hands.

The robe it wore had, perhaps, once been a brilliant red. It may have once had intricate gold filigree traced across it in whorling patterns. The sash that bound it may have once hung with silver ornaments. The thing within the robe may have once been human, once had pale skin and flowing black hair, may have once been sane.

But now it was a thing of rot and tatters. Skull the color of a fish's underbelly with shriveled raisin eyes gleaming madly in the sockets and a crown of finger bones adorning its pate, raising its rag-adorned skeletal arms imperiously, throwing its head back with a spine curling laugh that echoed through the cavern.

Ruby bustled over and gave it a swift quick in the shin, cutting the laugh short.

"Ow!" There was a note of hurt in its voice.

"The real Alaham, I presume?" Ruby asked. She spat on the floor at its feet.

"Yes," it said. "And the occasion warrants a bit more decorum if you don't mind. Behave yourself or I'll add you to my collection."

Ruby humphed but backed away from him, arms crossed, face glowering. Then she seemed to realize something. Her eyes widened briefly then narrowed into a suspicious squint. "Well, that puts the cob right in the cornhole," she said.

Alaham had begun raising his arms grandly again. At her interruption he stopped and put his bony hands on his hips and sighed.

"There is an order and tone I desire for this ceremony, madame, and you prattling on about cornholes is not in my order of operations," His voice hissed through clenched teeth. "I've been planning this for centuries and if you can't contain yourself I will have you peeled. I mean that quite literally. You are here for one reason and that is to record what you see in your capacity as a scribe. Get out your book and start writing. I'll hear no more out of you."

Ruby's mouth twisted back and forth a bit before settling

into a rather alarming grin. She retrieved her journal from the altar, extracted a fresh quill from her hair and produced an inkpot from within her robe. She uncorked the top, licked the tip of the quill, dipped it in the ink, opened the journal, poised the quill above the page and raised her eyebrows expectantly.

"Better," Alaham said after a moment, seemingly mollified. He raised his arms again, quickly this time as if determined to be back on his mysterious schedule.

"Attend!" he cried. His voice rang out, filling the cave. "The ritual of ages is upon us. All of our work, all of our plans have led us to this moment. Be witness to the dawn of a new era!"

The figures surrounding the dais turned in unison to face inward. They lowered their hoods. Ancient men or shriveled and withered mummies—Durham wasn't quite sure and had little intention of feeling one for body heat. He wasn't sure which would be more horrifying—to find their wrinkled sags warm and moist or to find them cold and rubbery. The withermen knelt and bowed the heads forward, stretching their arms toward the lich king. Far below them on the cavern floor Durham could make out skeletal and robed figures gathering. Dozens, then hundreds, streaming out of the darkness, coming up from hidden holes and secret pits. The audience was assembling. A slow drumbeat began somewhere below, deep and hollow. The thin call of a flute joined it, long notes, discordant and haunting. A procession began up the long fight of stairs to the dais. Row upon row of black robed, hooded figures, five abreast. At their fore was a horrible amalgamation of bone, one of Alaham's twisted creations. A giant lumpen skull atop a ring of a dozen long thin vertical ribs that walked it forward like a stiff-legged spider. They had to have been the ribs of some great beast-a titan whale perhaps-for the thing stood a full three meters in height as it clacked its way up the stairs. It moved with rapid jerky motions as if its limbs simply appeared in each new position with no visible movement in between.

It arrived at the top and stood before the altar. The figures behind it came to a halt, the stairs choked with their numbers. Alaham turned toward Durham, apparently not having been fooled by his attempt to hide behind the throne.

"Durham, our guest of honor, come forth," his voice boomed. The glittering eyes of the nearest withermen told Durham that his choice was to walk or be dragged. He stepped out, legs shaking hard enough that his kneecaps clicked. Alaham gestured towards the ribskull monstrosity. "Please, take your place." Two of the massive ribs splayed apart, creating a doorway of sorts and Durham came to the horrifying realization that the thing was a walking cage.

Durham shot a nervous glance at Ruby. She gave a slight jerk of her head, eyes widening meaningfully as if extolling him to do something. She flipped her journal around quickly, then back again, giving Durham just enough of a look to see that she had written a single giant word across the pages.

"CROWN"

He took hesitant steps toward the cage but glanced back over his shoulder at Alaham. He was, indeed, wearing a crown. It looked to be made of twenty or so skeletal fingers, arrayed around his head, pointing upward. They were brown and old. Older, perhaps, than any of the other millions of bones within Alaham's kingdom. He looked to Ruby again but her head was lowered over her journal again, quill feather seeming to dance as she wrote.

As slow as his steps had been, they had inevitably moved him forward and he found himself standing before the ribskull cage. He stopped, looking back over his shoulder at Alaham.

"Step in," the lich said. His voice was as sharp and cold as an icicle.

"I never believed you," Durham said. He turned back and

stepped into the cage. The ribs closed behind him.

ЯЯЯ

High above the dais, perched on the edge of a bonegear,
Thud watched the ceremony through the battered remnants of
his duoculars, squinting to look through the one scope that still
had lenses. Ginny crouched beside him, sucking thoughtfully on
her teeth. He'd climbed down to her and followed her, hopping
from spindle to gear to rail until they'd gotten to where they
could see Alaham's throne. He'd seen what Ruby had written and
was now intently studying the crown on Alaham's head.

"That's it," he said. "The crown."

"What about the crown?" Ginny asked.

"Bugger the mace, the crown is the real artifact here. Ruby
spotted it."

He lowered the duoculars and gazed off into space,
thinking.

"There's only one thing leaps to me mind and I hopes to all
the hells that it aint what I'm thinking."

"What's that?"

"Bone crown, thousand of animated skellies. What's that put

you in mind of?"

Ginny swore under her breath. "You don't think…"

"Aye, I do. And methinks Ruby does as well. That Alaham bastard has the Crown of the Bonebin. Damn well explains everything, don't it?"

Ginny let out a long whistle of breath. "Might be above our pay grade, boss."

Thud chuckled. Thousands of skeletons, a lich king, a giant bone machine and only now did Ginny think they might have taken on too much.

"No, lass," he said. "That lich got a skull full of rotted brain and he's made a critical error that's going to throw his whole damned scheme, whatever the hell it is, right under the minecart wheels."

"Oh? What mistake?"

"He brought us here. And we're the godsdamned Dungeoneers."

Ginny grinned at having her speech thrown back to her.

"Damned straight," she said. "So what's the play?"

"We gots three main objectives, seems to me. Rescue the lad from that cage, interrupt the ritual and gets that crown offa the lich's head."

Ginny nodded. "Straight forward enough. Have a plan?"

"Nope," Thud said, "but seems to me there's a dozen and a half more dwarves around this place somewhere and that's a whole lot of gremlins in the works for Alaham that he seems to have discounted. So, I thinks step one is to start coordinating the problems." He reached into his pack and pulled out a rock and a small hammer.

The Dwarven race is largely known, by the non-Dwarves of the outside world, for their proficiency at mining. It is a well deserved reputation, as mining to Dwarves is akin to eating or talking for other races. Dwarven children receive their first rock hammer in the crib, along with stones to bang on with it. They receive interesting rocks to break apart on their birthdays and their own mineshaft when they come of age. Dwarven music is comprised almost entirely of the sound of things hitting stone in complex rhythms and many a happy adolescence is spent burrowing deep into the bones of the mountains, accompanied by the sounds of all of one's peers doing the same. Over the centuries, the Dwarves built up a complex code comprised entirely of hammering, allowing them to chat and gossip through the bowels of the deep as they each dug ever deeper in their shafts. It was a language even more secret than the the

Dwarven language, a language so secret that most people didn't even realize that it was anything other than the rhythm of metal on stone.

Thud began to tap the hammer against the rock, the clink of each impact ringing out, carrying through the halls of Alaham's crypt, hoping there were others to hear.

After a minute, the tapping sounded back.

-19-

Something else had arrived at the bottom of the dais stairs. Durham squinted to try and make it out in the gloom. Four figures carrying an ornate chest on a litter. There was barely enough room for them to ascend the stairs amidst the throng waiting there and they moved slowly, those they passed reaching out with reverent hands to touch the chest as it went by. Alaham walked forward to stand next to the Durham's cage.

"Most of what I told you was entirely true," he said, a note of defensiveness in his voice.

Durham snorted.

"Really," Alaham said. "If you hadn't noticed, I have you in a cage, completely under my control. What cause would I have to lie to you now?"

Durham was silent. It wasn't difficult to come to the conclusion that whatever was in store for him was going to be unpleasant. The cage made that pretty clear. The skull at the top looked down at him, grinning.

"You are indeed my only living descendant, and you are to be my sole benefactor. The nature of the, ah, inheritance, however, is perhaps where I gave the wrong impression. Rest assured, however, that this will be a moment of glory for you. You should feel greatly honored."

"Which is why I'm in a cage?"

"Well, some reticence is anticipated, I suppose. Better safe than sorry, eh?"

The chest had reached the halfway point on the ascent. The drumming seemed to grow louder with each step that it rose and the tempo of the notes from the flutes had quickened. There was a new sound too—a high pitched rhythm of clinking that was almost lost amidst the other noise.

"An amazing feat of necromancy will occur here tonight," Alaham said. "Something never accomplished before. A rite that previously only the Hermits could have achieved, had they even the will to do so." He did not look at Durham as he spoke, his attention focused on the chest. "This body is old. It can no longer sustain me. I require a new one."

Durham's mind very rapidly filled in a lot of blanks with answers he wasn't happy about.

"Switching bodies…well, nothing like this has been attempted before," Alaham said. "So much of our identity is tied up in the form that carries us. The more similar the bodies, the better that chance of success."

"And you think I'm similar to you?"

"More so than any other," Alaham said. "You are my only living descendant. All that I was is carried within you and, during my life, we were not so dissimilar looking, you and I. You will be the new form of the continuance of my reign."

"Your reign over a hole in the ground full of puppets made of bone?"

"Oh, no," Alaham said. "This is but the beginning. The boneworks is the greatest thaumaturgic engine ever created. It's influence will sweep across the land, sucking life as it goes. We will stream forth and create a new world. A world of the dead and of their masters. A world of necromancers, each living like kings, waited on by their animated minions. All of the menial tasks, all of the farming, the building, all performed by the dead. Uncomplaining, never tiring. A world of endless luxury and ease and we shall rule over all of it, your body, my mind."

"And what of my mind?"

"Not particularly relevant," Alaham said. "A situation, I believe, which won't exactly be a novelty for you, no?"

Durham clenched his teeth and fists. There was knot of fury deep inside of him that was twisting all of his thought into it. The chest arrived at the top of the stairs.

Alaham turned towards Ruby. "Getting all of this, I presume?"

"Yep." She barely glanced up from her journal. "Do you prefer being described as crazed or mad?"

"Whichever you feel more likely to persuade me to keep you alive as my court scribe rather than as a dessicated hag corpse that licks the chamber pots clean."

"Ah," Ruby said, pausing to consider a moment. "That would be 'batshit lunatic' then."

"I'd hoped that at least one of you would appreciate the majesty of this moment, but it shouldn't surprise me. You will appreciate it in time, I'm sure." The chest had been set to rest atop the altar. Alaham strolled slowly around it, looking at it.

"It's a very delicate procedure we're attempting here. My phylactery resides within that chest, and within it, my heart. Within the heart, of course, lies my essence. My mind. My soul. We shall prepare a new phylactery and place a heart within it, still beating." He cast a meaningful glance toward Durham, making it clear whose beating heart he was referring to. "Then I shall let this body drop to the dust it longs for, and my essence will rise free from my old heart, and take up residence in the new. And a new form shall be mine."

Durham prodded at the ribs on the cage, testing their strength. It had occurred to him that the noble thing to do, were he to manage to escape the cage, might be to fling himself off of the dais, letting his body be crushed in the fall. Unfortunately, the noble route didn't offer much personal incentive over Alaham's alternative. Maybe he could bash his head against the side of the cage really hard? Unconsciousness probably wouldn't be much of a hindrance for Alaham but might make the experience more personally endurable. Maybe he could try to pluck his own eyes out, out of sheer spite in order to stick Alaham with a blind form. None of the options were sounding particularly good.

Alaham gestured and two of the withermen raised the lid

from the chest, then pulled at pins on the corners, allowing the sides to fall way, revealing an ornate vase, slender and filigreed with silver. Two of them reached out and lifted the vase while the others pulled the chest out from beneath it. They lowered the phylactery back down to rest on the altar.

Alaham stepped to the edge of the dais and raised his hands.

"Let it begin!"

The boneworks shuddered. Cascades of dust fell from the gears as they all began to spin. Huge sections of the bone machine began swinging into new positions, rotating, unfolding. The hallways of the maze, suspended within the machine, all began to move, spinning and raising, lowering, moving into new positions.

"They're forming runes," Ruby whispered next to him. Durham looked over to find that she'd crept up to the side of the cage once Alaham's back had turned. "That's how the bastard's going to do it. Form Hermit runes large enough to absorb the energies"

"Is it really as easy as that?" Durham asked. "Won't someone have thought of that before?"

"No, the ritual will still absolutely shatter him but runes that size will hold the energy long enough that he'll have switched bodies before it happens."

The chanting below was rising in crescendo and Alaham's own voice was adding to it, rolling out through the cave as the halls began locking into their new positions. One of the hallways was moving into position directly in front of them, fifty yards out, rotating so that the hollow end of it was pointing directly at the dais. Within it stood more robed figures, between them another vase. The new phylactery. It was ornate, short, squat and ugly. Durham frowned. There was something oddly familiar about it.

The chanting and drumming was at near deafening levels now and arcs of purple light had begun flickering along the runes above. At the edge of the dais, Alaham collapsed, falling to the floor, breaking apart into a pile of rags and bones, spinning and clattering. Durham felt something move past him, something intangible and evil. The phylactery on the altar shimmered with the same energies that played over the runes. It began to shake and vibrate, skittering around on the altar top as if it were alive. Durham supposed that it was, in a way. The vibrations grew stronger and stronger until the vase shattered explosively, sending shard of pottery flying across the dais. One of them sliced across Durham's cheek and he felt it go hot and wet. Ruby staggered back a step with a small cry and Durham saw a blossom of red on her shoulder. Another shard was embedded in the back of the journal she held in front of her, the thick pages possibly having saved her life.

A shriveled black mass of wet tissue was all that remained on the altar. The necromancer's heart. The essence of the lich. It pulsated with the slow rhythm of a heartbeat. It split open with a splatter, exposing its rotted brown interior and a wave of nausea hit Durham as the soul of the lich king rose free in a black swirl of bloated flies. The swarm hung in the air over the altar, waves of stench rolling away from it, then began moving slowly through the air towards the second phylactery. Four of the withermen advanced on Durham's cage and he knew that the time had come.

Durham crouched and clenched his fists. He knew it was futile but he was determined to put up as much of a fight as he could. He had no intention of just standing around while someone ripped his heart from his chest. The withermen reached the cage and stopped, seemingly puzzled. The cage hadn't opened for them. The cloud of flies had stopped midway along the walkway in an angry buzzing swarm.

Alaham's voice rang out as a hideous buzzing noise, as if the flies themselves called out in a chorus of rage.

"SOMEONE SHAT IN MY PHYLACTERY."

Realization dawned on Durham like a sunrise. He recognized the pot now. It was the same one he'd found—and used—in Alaham's chambers far below.

"Aye! And we got another surprise or two for ya!" cried a distinctly dwarven voice. The figures around the soiled phlyactery cast off their robes, revealing dwarves sitting atop each other's shoulders. Nibbly hopped down from Rasp's shoulders and nonchalantly gave the phylactery a kick, sending it off the end of the hallway. It spun through the air as it fell, disappearing with a crash into the clustered masses of skeletons below.

The cavern reverberated with Alaham's buzzing roar of rage.

The dwarves in the hallway stepped aside, revealing the ballista and a grinning Leery. "Duck!" she yelled and stomped on the release lever. Durham hit the floor of his cage as the bolts flew. It was one of the chain bolts the dwarves had used at the crypt entrance—four bolts with a lattice of chain between them. It hit the cage above Durham's head, the chains catching against the ribs, swinging the bolts in with shattering force. Broken bits of bone rained down on him and the great grinning skull crashed down onto the floor next to him as the remnants of the ribs were thrown and scattered across the dais.

He was free.

Most of the withermen were still in their ritual pose, still kneeling, still chanting. Durham had the notion that no matter what happened on the dais that they couldn't stop—once the ritual had begun they needed to keep the chant going, keep the magical energies in control. That still left the four surrounding him, the four who had come for his heart. They advanced on him

There was a nice length of broken rib laying next to him, its broken end jagged and pointy. Just about the size of a city guard truncheon. Durham grabbed it and stood. He favored the withermen with his most charming smile.

His first swing shattered the knee of the one in front of him, sending it hopping backward. Then the back-swing, catching the one to his right a smart crack alongside the head. Durham's smile felt like it would split his face. The shriveled old men were necromancers. Close quarters fighting wasn't in their skill set. He swung the rib forward, feeling like the conductor of a bone-crack orchestra, thumping the third alongside his hood, sending it into a spinning stagger. The fourth had stopped his advance, raising spindly arms in what might might have been an attempt at a placating gesture. Durham brought the rib truncheon down hard, relishing the hollow thonk noise it made on the thing's forehead. It pawed briefly at the impact point then fell backwards like a rigid plank. The witherman with the broken knee was hobbling towards him, arms outstretched. His hood had fallen away, revealing his face, eyes glowing with fierce pinpoints of light, a ropy tangled mass of braided hair and a thick thatch of beard framing a snarl of teeth. The framed teeth looked a likely target to Durham and he aimed the pointy end of the truncheon and thrust. The witherman made a curious gargling noise clutching at the rib jammed down his throat. Durham raised his leg and shoved hard with his foot, planting it squarely in the thing's chest. It staggered backwards and disappeared off the edge of the dais. Durham knelt next to Ruby.

"I'm ok," she said. Her voice was weak. Her hand was clutched to her shoulder, the fabric of her robe dark and wet between her fingers. "Keep yourself alive."

"No. Here," he said. He ripped the sleeve from his tunic and made a fumbling try at getting it around her shoulder. She batted at him with her free hand.

"You're already missing enough clothing. I'll manage it. Go

do something more useful."

The hallway with the dwarves in it began moving forward, the great bone gears spinning it along its way. The movement seemed in discord with the rest of the machine's part in the ritual. Purple lightning crackled against the sides, sending chips and chunks raining down. The close end advanced over the stairs, skeletons and necromancers alike scrambling both up and down to get clear, some of them falling into the darkness, the skeletons with silent grins, the withermen with reedy screams. Ginny stood atop the hall, a tangle of tendon ropes clutched in her fists, yanking and tugging on them to redirect the supporting gears. Eight of the dwarves were advancing down the walkway, Thud at their head, maces in their hands. They looked like they weren't quite sure how to deal with a cloud of flies. The fly column billowed and swirled, the buzzing forming again into Alaham's voice.

"Do you think you've won? Do you really think that, after centuries of planning that I wouldn't have accounted for all contingencies? Prepare the alternate phylactery!"

Durham felt himself grabbed from behind by strong, wiry fingers. Some of the withermen, at least, had left the chant. They began dragging him backwards. An alternate phylactery?

Durham's mind raced. There had been other vases in the chamber pot room, hadn't there? He struggled enough to half turn and look ahead. He was being dragged by two of the withermen, a third and fourth to either side. They were taking him toward the lift that led to Alaham's rooms below.

The cloud of flies dispersed, separating out in all directions, up and out, amongst the bones. And the boneworks ground to a shuddering halt. The sudden absence of its noise was startling. The drumming and the chanting continued but the the ticking and whirring, so constant that it almost faded below perception, had ceased. The machine shuddered and gave a deep creaking groan as if hundreds of gears strained against each other, wanting to move.

Thud barely paused. "Make for the dais! Get offa this bridge!" The dwarves charged forward.

Behind them the boneworks began to move again. No longer spinning, no longer a machine. Huge bits of it began uncurling and unfolding, sections reaching out and connecting to each other in new ways. Dust fell from it like waterfalls as the bones ground together, taking a new, massive shape. Thousands of skeletons, clutching together to bind themselves into great limbs and a massive torso. A huge head formed at one end as the bones melded into their new places. The dwarves reached the dais, looking back over their shoulders as they ran. They formed up on the edge, in the space left by the withermen Durham had defeated. Gong crouched behind his shield at the center, Thud, Ginny and Mungo to his right, Clink, Goin, Cardamon and Leery to his left. Alaham filled the cave before them, a gargantuan wickerman of bones, crouching in the great emptiness. Each step forward it made crushed a half dozen skeletons beneath its feet. Others raced towards and clambered on, adding themselves to the massive bonetangle nightmare.

The withermen tossed Durham onto the lift and crowded around him. He got one last glimpse of the dwarves, could just hear Thud's call. "Brace lads," his voice rang. "Gonna be a bumpy one!" The lift began to descend, the dwarves replaced by leathery crazed faces looming over him. They raised him up onto their shoulders as the lift reached the cavern floor. Alaham towered above, great crashes echoing through the cavern as its massive arms began raining blows on the dais. Durham's back was to the ground and he was being carried feet first, his view now an upside-down look at where they'd been. Nonetheless he spotted something familiar at the base of the massive stalagmite that made up the dais. Durham whistled.

Squitters was bounding at full speed when he barreled into the withermen. It wasn't so much an attack as an amazingly enthusiastic, tail wagging attempt to get to Durham. The withermen were completely unprepared for it however and the lot of them went down in a tangle of scrawny limbs, Squitters scampering about happily on top of them. He had the skull Ruby had thrown for him clamped in his mouth. Durham scrambled to his feet and gave Squitters a quick pat on the head. Then he ran. He was headed in the same direction that the withermen had been carrying him but now was on his own two feet and accompanied by a friendly dog-thing rather than four unfriendly necromancer things determined to rip his heart out. Things were looking up. The skeletons surrounding him ignored him, continuing to stream toward the bone colossus. No orders had been given to them regarding Durham and he ran past them as if invisible. He spared a glance up. The massive thing that Alaham had become was still pounding at the dais, telling Durham that at least one of the dwarves was still alive up there. His stomach clenched at the thought of Ruby, laying out in the open, wounded. He ran faster. He hadn't the slightest idea of where he was going or what to do.

Alaham's first attack had been a swipe across the dwarven line, leaving them scattered and rolling across the stone. Thud and Ginny had managed to scramble behind the altar. Thud had seen Mungo dive into the hole beneath the throne. He could see Gong and Cardamon in a crumpled heap next to Ruby who was dragging herself along on one arm. He had no idea where she was trying to get to but Alaham didn't seem much interested in her. He'd seen Leery go sailing off into empty space but that was the sort of thing that often happened to Leery. She tended to survive so he wasn't much worried about her. He couldn't see any sign of Clink. There was a massive crash on the altar just above him and bits of shattered bone rained down. The altar was decent cover, sparse as that cover may be. No matter how many bones you bundled together and no matter how hard you swung them he didn't figure they were going to do much to a slab of stone. It seemed Alaham had come to the same conclusion. The bone colossus was moving forward, its forelimbs on the dais, trying to heave itself up. Bones split and splintered with the strain. He heard a distant yell and the chunk of the ballista firing. It seemed that at least some of the other dwarves were still in the hallway. Unfortunately he knew that they'd just fired the last cluster of bolts and whatever damage it may have done didn't seem to have been enough to even grab the monstrosity's attention. He did, however, still have the crossbow he'd commandeered from Mungo and he could see one weak link that he could still exploit—the dozen chanting withermen remaining on the dais. He took aim and fired. One of the withermen slumped forward with a sigh, its chanting silenced. He began cranking another bolt into place.

Next to him Ginny had her mace out. They both cringed as the next swing landed against the side of the altar, as if trying to dodge it. If the thing managed to climb up onto the dais the altar would no longer be much of an obstacle. Until then, however, it seemed enough to keep them alive. Ginny clambered to her feet, brandishing the mace. She let out a yell and charged one of the withermen as Thud fired his bolt at a third.

 ♣♣♣

Far below them Durham was progressing across the cave floor, looking for the pool of water that he'd fallen into earlier. It had been right next to the door to the sitting room which had, in turn, had the door to the hall where the closet with the vases had been. It was where the new phylactery had been kept. Perhaps it was where the replacement was kept as well. There were skeletons everywhere, watching him with their hollow eyes, making it difficult to move faster than a slow jog. They were shuffling en masse towards the massive bone thing that dominated the middle of the cavern, adding themselves to it, their rusted bits of armor clanking and rattling, bony feet scraping along the cavern floor. Durham had to shoulder his way through them, fearing that at any moment Alaham would notice him and send the command and he'd have hundreds of bony fingers clutching at him. None of the skeletons were of the neat and clean sort that he'd seen in an apothecary's office. They had varying amounts of dried fleshy bits still attached to them, wispy hair and beards, claw-like fingernails. Durham was trying not to focus on the rancid dried meat smell, figuring that stopping to vomit wasn't going to be of much help. Squitters gamboled back and forth through the sea of legs, occasionally pausing to tear a dangly bit of meat off of one of the skeletons to happily chew on. That was enough to finally make Durham stop to vomit. The macabre horde pressed on around him.

Thud was just sighting in on a fourth witherman when things took a turn for the worse. Skeletons began appearing at the edge of the dais. They'd climbed the walls of the stalagmite, dozens of them, crawling at last over the edge, standing and tottering forward from all sides.

"Fall back!" he yelled.

"Fall back to where?" Ginny asked. There was a note of panic in her voice. A note the equivalent of a major chord being played by a symphony orchestra. "They're everywhere!"

"Regroup on me!"

Gong began rolling toward them, apparently having decided it was more expedient than getting up and running. Cardamon, however, didn't move. Hopefully he was just napping. Ruby either hadn't heard or had her own plan—she was still crawling slowly across the floor in the opposite direction. Whatever status Alaham had commanded on her as a scribe still seemed to be in effect. The wave of skeletons reached her and ignored her, stepping over and around. No sign of Mungo. He'd disappeared into the hole under the throne, giving Thud the notion that it might be a way out.

Gong came to a stop against the side of the altar with a clang and an oof.

"Ooh, dizzy," he said. "How's things over here?"

Thud shrugged. "Three dwarves against an army of skellies, half dozen necros and a giant bone monster. Not bad, all things considered."

"Aye, good. Was almost worried." He scrambled to his knees and Thud handed him his mace. He fired his last crossbow bolt at a necromancer but couldn't see through the skeletons to determine if he'd hit. He heard a crash of bones behind him, a thud from the top of the altar and Rasp fell into their midst.

He made a noise vaguely akin to someone choking on an olive. "That big bony bastard packs a punch," he said, his voice wheezing. "Ballista was done for so I came over to see what ya was up to."

"Four dwarves!" Thud said. "Now we're talking! Form up!"

They stood, shoulder to shoulder, keeping the altar at their backs. Skeletons advanced from all sides and the great bone thing loomed over their heads, its shadow falling across them.

Mungo chose that moment to pop up from his hole. His beard was hanging from one cheek and he held a green mace aloft in his hand.

"Behold the Mace of MacGuffin!"

It was an awkward looking thing, head too big for the haft, twisting tendrils of green smoke wafting about it.

Mungo took two running steps and flung it at Alaham's massive form. The dwarves watched, mouths open, as it arced slowly over their heads. It fell woefully short and disappeared into empty space beyond the edge of the dais.

"…and Mungo," Thud said.

Any response from the other dwarves was completely obliterated by an earsplitting crack of noise from below. The entire cavern shook, stalactites raining down. The bone colossus fell backward, out of view, its great arms waving wildly. The skeletons faltered in their advance and Mungo sprinted towards the dwarves, or whatever passed for a sprint with foot long legs. He was holding the loose side of his beard up with one hand.

"What in the hells was that?" Thud asked.

"The mace," Mungo gasped. "Single application. Detonates."

"Did ye get im?" Gong asked. They popped their heads up over the side of the altar to look.

Alaham was already rising, the lower limbs that had been blown apart in the blast already reforming. The skeletons surrounding the dwarves started forward again.

The necromancer's chanting abruptly stopped and was replaced with one continuous low tone, all of their voices in chorus. Alaham's laugh filled the cave.

"You've lost," he said. "The ritual is complete. As soon as the fool's heart is placed in the phylactery I will be born anew!"

Thud patted Mungo on the back. "Well, it was a good effort, lad. Didn't happen to find any other explodey maces down there, eh?"

Mungo shook his head sadly.

The skeletons arrived and after that everything was swinging maces, crossbows and fists and splintering bones.

༺༺༺

The shock wave from the explosion had sent Durham sailing through the air. He landed, once again, in the icy pool of water he'd been looking for. He came up spluttering and then yelped as a six foot long stalactite crashed into the water next to him. He looked back in the direction of the dais, where the explosion had come from. Whatever had caused it had lain waste to the cavern floor at the foot of the dais's stalagmite. Pieces of skeletons were raining down across the entire cave and Alaham seemed to have had his legs blown off. It wasn't slowing him down much, however. Skeletons crawled across his surface like roaches, clumping back up, forming new limbs. The rune overhead was so bright it hurt to look at, crackling arcs of light rippling, their intensity leaving after-images in his eyes. There couldn't be much time left. He wondered how Squitters had fared through the explosion. More worrying were the half dozen withermen necromancers that were running in his direction. Someone, apparently, had finally noticed that he was on his own, beating heart still secure in his chest.

Durham splashed to his feet and ran through the doorway in the side of the cavern, promptly stepping on the cookie platter which slid out from under him sending him face first into the musty couch. He pushed off with his feet and half rolled, half fell over the top of the couch then did a graceful combination of running and staggering to the far door.

And there was the room, just to the right, just as he remembered. He noted with no small amount of amazement, that Miss Cluck was there. She'd collected straw from the floor and made herself a nest and was now clucking away happily, one beady eye fixed on him. The phylactery was next to her, tall and slender, crusted with jewels and with a mouth and neck wide enough for a heart. Durham picked it up and flung it against the wall, hard. It gave a loud clang and fell to the floor, undamaged.

The bastard had made it out of metal.

There was a noise behind him. Durham spun around in a panic. The withermen were there. He slammed the door shut, pushing his shoulder against it. It shook with blows from the other side as the withermen attempted to break through. Taps, really, more than blows. The scrawny old men were not well suited to door bashing. Durham frantically looked around the small room, hoping for something that could be used as a weapon. The phylactery, possibly. Miss Cluck had laid an egg which, amusing as it might be to throw at the necromancers, probably wasn't going to be of much help. He doubted he had the time or…resources, as it were, to poop in the replacement phylactery. He picked it up by the neck and stepped away from the door, holding it ready to start swinging at whatever came through.

ℓℓℓ

Ruby's arm and shoulder were numbness with a burning

edge of pain. Her good arm wasn't doing much better. Writing in a journal was poor preparation for dragging oneself across a rough stone floor or, for that matter, getting impaled by a ceramic shard. She tried not to think about what sort of grime might have been coating the outside or, worse, the inside of Alaham's phylactery. The front of her robe was torn and black with dirt and her fingertips were raw and bleeding. She'd felt at least three of her fingernails break off and suspected that the others had as well and just been more polite about it. Ruby was wire and leather, however, chewed by thousands of hours on the road into pure gristle. Her original idea had been to simply move out of the center of the dais, going by the instinctive notion that this would make her less of a target. Crawling across the ground to do so had seemed like a manageable plan at the time but, she had recently been informed by her wounded shoulder, she hadn't been thinking particularly clearly when she'd hatched that part of the plan. Perhaps shock from the unpleasantness of being recently pierced, her shoulder went on to suggest politely. Alaham hadn't killed her earlier when he'd had her completely captive and she was hoping her immunity still held. The skeletons seemed to have ignored her when they'd charged the dwarves but they were marionettes under old orders and there was no certainty that Alaham wouldn't have reconsidered her status since then. It was either stand up to keep mobile or stay put and avoid getting stepped on. Now she was near Alaham's throne. Between her and the throne lay the pile of twisted rags and scatter of bones that was what remained of the lich's original body. A shadow fell across her and she glanced up just in time to see Alaham's arm coming down, not attacking but reaching for purchase in the spot where she happened to be.

Sudden impending death often brings with it a moment of suspended time, one's mind having decided that if this is its last moment that it might as well try and make it last. It is a moment of pure clarity, the mind burning everything it has to move at double speed, running through all of its options. Ruby used her moment of clarity to appreciate Alaham's creation. There was a macabre beauty to it, elegant rows of teeth, skulls in sweeping ridges up its face, connected with patterned rows of straight bones. She wondered which of those hundreds of skulls Alaham had tucked himself into. Which eyes did he watch from as he came to take their lives? She rolled, every muscle wire coiled until just the right moment, the great grasping claw scraping across the stone where she'd been, each finger a cluster of a half dozen skeletons.

Like everything else, it was a puppet. She could see from where she was that the head was as hollow as she'd expected. Just a giant shell.

A thought occurred and she twisted her head around.

She laughed.

She'd seen what Alaham had overlooked.

She'd found it right where she'd expected as soon as she'd thought to look for it.

His discarded skull, his true skull, lay before her now where Alaham had abandoned it. It was on its side atop the pile of bones and rags, regarding her silently from hollow sockets. And atop it the crown. She reached out and gave it a tug with her hand, removing it from the skull. There was a brief cliche of crackling energy across its surface and then it went dark.

There was a pregnant moment as the massive amounts of necromantic energy that had been gathered paused for thoughtful reflection.

Then from all across the cavern came a wall of sound. A sound never heard before or since. The sound of tens of hundreds of thousands of bones collapsing onto a cave floor. Ruby would spend hours trying to do that sound justice in her journal but would never manage to come close to the sheer crackling thunder of that noise. She watched as the great beast of bone slid into chaos, huge masses of it breaking off and falling to the floor, achingly slowly, where they burst apart in great cavalcades of bone that looked like massive splashes of water. A group of bedraggled and bloody dwarves stood by the altar, looking about, mouths hanging open, utterly stupefied. Ruby grinned at them.

She was premature.

The last few withermen around the edge of the dais suddenly rose into the air, backs arching. The great black column of flies rose again from the wreckage below.

"The ritual is complete!" Alaham crowed. "You have failed! The heart has reached the phylactery!"

All across the cavern the withermen screeched as the great rune above crackled. The energy built up within it flared out into the cave, so bright Ruby could swear that she saw the dwarve's bones through their skin. Arcs of energy sizzled through the air, drawing a searing line to each of the withermen, bursting them apart into dust and scraps like a long string of damp firecrackers. Another massive shock of noise came that threw them all to the floor and then, for the first time in centuries, the cavern fell completely silent.

Thud was at a level of confusion that he wasn't particularly happy with but, due to the sudden lack of things attempting to kill him he decided that he could live with it for a moment. He saw Ginny's mouth move but his ears were ringing so loudly he couldn't make out a word of what she said. Somehow, against odds he wasn't even going to begin to try to calculate, they were still alive.

They'd won the battle but lost the war.

Alaham had resurrected.

Down there, somewhere, what had once been Durham was now the necromancer lich king. Thud walked slowly to the edge of the dais and looked down into the cavern. The cave floor was a great charnel sea of bone straight out of a poet's worst fever dreams. But there, at the far edge, movement.

Durham.

Alaham.

He walked toward them amongst the bones, his maniacal laughter echoing through the cave. Thud watched silently as the figure picked its way through the thousands of shattered skeletons. The other dwarves gathered around him, shoulders slumped. Ruby as well, propped up by Gong, ugly brown crown clenched in her hands.

Duralaham? Aladurham?

The thing was well on its way to looking the part. Its clothes were already ragged, its skin caked with dirt and blood, water dripping from it as it walked. For some reason that Thud couldn't quite fathom it was carrying a chicken under one arm. It was still laughing, a crazed sound that set Thud's teeth on edge. He clenched his fists, trying to fan his rage into enough will to fight again. He knew that they were hopelessly outclassed but at least they outnumbered the thing. For the moment. Could it just wave a hand and bring all of the skeletons back?

It reached the foot of the great stairs and started up, kicking bones clear as it came. They clattered as they fell, the sound echoing through the great silent chamber.

The dwarves backed up as a group as the lich-king reached the top of the stairs, keeping a healthy amount of space between them.

"Thud," it said, through its sinister grin.

"Alaham," he hissed back.

"Right here," it said, and held up an egg.

Thud blinked.

"Wot?"

"He's in this egg."

"He's…wot?"

Durham laughed again.

"Miss Cluck saved us. She laid this egg. I dropped it in the phlyactery." Durham held the egg up. "Ladies and gentlemen, may I introduce to you the new and mighty form of Alaham the Necromancer, Alaham the Lich, Alaham the King…" he paused and gestured grandly, holding the egg high. "Alaham the mighty egg."

"Ha!" Thud said, then tried again. "HA!"

And then he roared with laughter. The dwarves around him were laughing and crying. Gong dropped Ruby in the process but she was laughing hard enough that she didn't seem to mind.

Durham staggered and Thud rushed forward to grab him in a mighty hug, then regretted it instantly on account of the height difference and Durham's lack of pants.

Thud knelt next to Cardamon and gave his shoulder a shake.

"Nrg," Cardamon said.

"How alive are you?"

Cardamon opened one eye, squinting against the light.

"Well, you don't look like anything I'd wanna find in me afterlife so I'm guessing I'm alive enough." He tried to sit and winced, falling back. "Think me ribs may be subdivided a bit. And me arm." He lifted his head and glanced around. "Managed to win without me, eh? Musta been an easy fight."

"Now you knows why I got you on trap team 'stead o' vanguard, eh?" Thud said. "S'posed to take hits like that on yer shield."

"Next time someone swings a giant bone arm at me I'll keep that in mind." He closed his eyes. "This is the part where I go back to sleep so's I can wake up in a soft bed somewheres."

Leery chose that moment to appear at the edge of the dais, arriving via an elegant forward walkover. "Sorry I'm late," she said. "Had to jump back and forth between walls then hand over hand along a ledge then…"

"You're most able at the moment," Thud interrupted. "That walkway o'er there leads all the way out. Bring in the support teams. Tell 'em bring some stretchers too an' tell Doc to bring 'is field kit. I want you hurryin'. No flippin', rollin' or climbin' along the way, eh?"

She nodded and took off at a run.

Thud went over to Ruby. She was sitting against the altar, Mungo crouched next to her examining her wound through his loupe. His beard was completely gone now. Thud glanced around and saw it on the ground nearby. Miss Cluck seemed to have taken up residence on it.

"How is she?" he asked.

Mungo shrugged. "She has a fragment of phylactery in her shoulder but I can't objectively determine the particular level of…"

"How are you?" Thud tried again, addressing Ruby directly.

She winked at him. "Gonna have a new scar to scare the boys. I'll be haunting your dreams in no time. Could use some clean bandages though. Everyone here looks like they were dipped in a latrine."

Thud grinned. "On their way. You hurt, Mungo?"

"Negative."

"Ginny?"

"Cuts and scrapes. I'll live."

"Gong?"

"Just some fresh scratches in me breastplate."

"An' Durham? Don't think I'd forget ye, lad. I've thought you were a dead 'un two or three times this trip."

"Still have my heart so I think I came out ahead. And you?"

"Fine, fine, thanks for asking." He pulled out a bent and wrinkled cigar, struck a match and sent out a contented ring of smoke. "Gots lots o' questions, though. First one on me mind is why'd all them skeletons fall apart?"

"The crown," Ruby said. "It's what he was using to give them all life. As soon as I pulled it off of his head he lost them." She fixed him with a penetrating stare. "This is my serious face, Thud. We are going to have a long talk about that crown. In the meantime, don't touch it. Pick it up with a stick and drop it in a bag."

Thud nodded. "All right, I can live with that. Mungo, about that mace…"

"I hypothesized that using it would be of more intrinsic value than contract completion. I anticipated a more significant result, however."

"Well, seems maybe the contract don't exactly exist so good call. An' the boom was big enough. Slowed him down just long enough."

"Wait," Gong said. "What was that you said about the contract?"

"Seems it was a sham. Ploy by Alaham to get us to bring Durham here."

"So we ain't getting paid for this? And what'd he want with Durham? No offense meant,"

"None taken," Durham said.

"Needed him for that spell he was tryin' to do," Thud said. "Seems Durham here is the last of Alaham's line…" Thud paused thoughtfully. "Which makes you his heir, don't it?"

"I suppose," Durham said. "He seemed to think so, anyway." He waved his arm, indicating the great, dark, stinking cave full of bones. "All this can be mine."

"Yer missin' the bigger picture, lad," Thud said. "Alaham ruled Tanahael. That ruined city up top and all the land surrounding it is likely yours as well. You inherited an entire kingdom. Might be it's a bit fallen apart, looted, deserted and overgrown but it's still a kingdom however scruffy it might be."

"Ermmm…"

"Better than that knighthood you was wantin', eh? Let that sink in your nog a bit and we'll talk about that more later too.

Tell me about that egg."

Durham gave a slight shake of his head, clearing away the thought of a kingdom. "I remembered you saying that any living bit would do for a phylactery. I don't know that there's much life inside an egg but I guess it was alive enough to count. I didn't have much else in the way of options. Surprised it worked, actually. Glad it did. I'd have hated for my last living act to have been dramatically dropping a useless egg in a vase." He held the egg up. Everyone was silent. "Should I break it?"

"Well, let's not be hasty. Satisfying as it might be to watch Alaham'n'eggs go sliding down a wall I'm feared that might just release him again. Figure he ain't got lips in there so he's probably not much in the way of reciting spells or anything. 'Til he hatches at least. Keep it safe, we'll do more figgerin' on that later also."

A procession of dwarves appeared from the hallway and started across the bridge. The Dungeoneers were back to their usual crisp efficiency. Cardamon and Ruby were loaded onto stretchers and bustled off with Doc trotting along beside them. Nibbly began directing the members of the looting team around the cave. Gryngo began disassembling the ballista. Thud clapped Durham on the shoulder.

"I'm heading back to camp and yer back on me shadow duty. First order is to find you some pants. Also, got a bottle o' spirits back there I'm gonna need some help with."

Durham's gastrointestinal track winced.

"Bring the chicken," Thud added.

♪♪♪

Walking back through the dungeon was an eye-opening experience for Durham. It bore little resemblance to what it had been when they'd come through the other way. The furnishings were gone, the walls stripped of their tapestries, the statue pedestals empty. The rugs had been rolled up and removed. The whole place was taking on the feel of an empty house. They ascended through the catacombs, crossed the graveyard and made their way back through the temple. The wagons were lined up in front of it, sagging with the weight of their loads. Left over trap barrels and empty coops were piled to the side, unloaded to make more room for the haul. It was early evening, the sun deep and orange over the edge of the ruins. The smell of roasting mole hung in the air.

"Want me to roast 'er up for ya?" Gammi asked, meeting

them at the edge of camp and looking pointedly at Miss Cluck.

"No, not this one," Durham said.

"Saved us all, this chicken," Thud said. "She's our official mascot now. Corporal Cluck. Gave her a promotion."

"Outranked by me own fowl," Gammi said, shaking his head. "I'll get one of the other ones cookin' for ya."

🐾🐾🐾

Dinner was lively. Thud ordered that they needed to empty all of the alcohol to make room on the wagons and the dwarves performed their duty with enthusiasm. Ruby had a pot of water boiling on the fire and was sipping at her tea but Durham knew for a fact that she'd been adding brandy to each cup. Mungo had salvaged his beard, now adorned with a few chicken feathers.

"Mission success!" he said as he walked past Durham and gave him a wink.

They spent hours around the fire that night, relating their various versions of what had transpired in the Crypt of Alaham. The story of the egg was a popular one and silence fell at the end of it when Durham held it up for everyone to see.

"I think," he said. "I have an idea of what to do with it that should solve all of the potential problems with it." There was an expectant silence from his audience. Durham stood, walked over and dropped the egg into Ruby's boiling tea water. Ruby looked slightly annoyed but the dwarves cheered. Later on Dadger and Gong produced a banjo and a drum. Ruby seemed annoyed by that as well.

ᘒᘒᘒ

Durham awoke to the green glow of bright sunlight through tent walls. He sat up. It felt like his brain was moving about two seconds behind his skull. The smell of coffee was enough to persuade him to stagger out of the tent. The dwarves had a blessedly shady canopy set up. There were only a few in the camp, a number more bustling about the wagons. Durham guessed that the others might be back underground, working, clearing and hauling.

"Behold the King of Tanahael," Ruby said. She patted the bench at her side.

Durham rolled his eyes. Thud held out a cup of coffee. Durham took it and sat.

Ruby held up a large, dusty book, the cover faded and

cracked with age.

"Like it or not it's all in here. They recovered this from Alaham's collection. Book of lineages."

"That book looks older than I am. How could it have me in it?" He took a sip of the coffee and wheezed. Thud was apparently a subscriber to the "hair of the dog" cure. The dwarf grinned at him and winked, raising his own mug in a silent toast.

"It is," Ruby said. "This book traces the lines of Tanahael up to a century or so ago. This one, however," she said, holding up a comparatively newer book, "is much more recent. And you're in it. Between the two it's pretty clear."

Durham was a little shocked to discover that his name had been put in a book without his knowing about it. He was a lot shocked at being king of something.

"I have no interest in being king of anything," Durham said. "No one knows. Can't we just keep this quiet?"

"I can see how kingin' about might put a damper on yer career guarding the sheep gate," Thud said. "On the other hand, big parcel of land with no one livin' on it and likely there's enough from your share in the dungeon haul to put a nice little house out here."

"Wouldn't me being king and Alaham's heir mean that all of the dungeon loot is mine anyway?"

Thud frowned. "Not sure you want ter play that card, son. If ya do…well, we'd leave you with a big pile of statues, rugs and books in the field out here, minus our expenses for clearing a dungeon in your kingdom which we'd take in the form of the small valuables. Then we'd send you our bill for services rendered. Since Alaham made the contract you inherit responsibility for that as well."

"I…uh…was just speculating."

"On the other hand," Thud went on, "I want ter do right by ya. We could sell the loot as planned, subtract our costs and fee, give you your fair share of the rest and I could bring out a Dwarven construction team to build a nice big manor house. You could sublet the land for farming, build yerself a nice little steady income and live a life of ease. You could even still be a gaurd if'n ya wanted, either back in Karthor or we could build you yer own sheep gate out here that you could stand next to."

"A manor house?"

"You saved the team. Barring any more idle speculation about who owns the dungeon haul you're in me good graces. Plenty of worked stone laying around out here so materials cost would be mighty low and I got plenty enough credit with the dwarves for a work crew. So them's your options as I see 'em. Seems a pretty clear choice of shaft to me but it's yer call to make."

"There's a little more to being a king than living in a big house," Ruby said. "Both Karthor and Iskae probably think they have some claim to this area even though they're not using it. Claiming it as your kingdom might annoy them enough to send a few men out to conquer you and take it back. Should you bring them evidence of the claim they'll likely counter-offer to declare it a fiefdom and assign it to you and your descendants. Then you'd be responsible for collecting taxes and raising troops if necessary. Complicated business, being king. More coffee?"

"Found a friend for ya," Thud said. He whistled.

Squitters came bounding from between the tents moments later. He ran to Durham and began bouncing his front legs up and down, making ghostly grunting noises. Durham reached out and scratched his bony head.

"How is he still alive?" Durham said. "Err…animated?"

"I can only guess that there's still a trickle of power in that egg," Ruby said. "Just enough for Alaham's first construct to keep going."

"'Spect he don't eat much so there's that," Thud said. "Thinkin' he comes with the kingdom."

Gryngo and Giblets came strolling up. Squitters barked enthusiastically at them. "Beggin' me pardons but everything's all set, Thud" Gryngo said.

"Hope yer don't mind a lake in the middle of yer kingdom," Thud said to Durham.

"Where would a lake come from?"

"Lakes don't really show up so much as they take the place of somethin' else that went missin'. Least that's the case here."

"Cave's buggered," Giblets said. "Ceilin's cracked as grandmudder teefs. One column holdin' the whole thing. Big column, yeh, but solo."

"We got it rigged up to bring it down," Gryngo said. "Better now than as a surprise later."

"Not to mention it bein' the biggest mass grave I ever heard of," Thud added. "Only right. Gonna leave one helluva hole. River that made the cave's gonna fill it in no time. And you get to name it, what with it being your kingdom and your lake. Tanahael Lake? Alaham Lake?"

"Lake Dungeoneer," Durham said.

Thud's face lit up and he gave Durham a silent nod.

"The crown," Ruby said, "Does not come with the kingdom."

Thud arched an eyebrow "So tell me 'bout this crown."

Ruby sipped at her tea, considering.

"Based on what Alaham was able to do with it, this can only be the Crown of the Bonebin, which makes it one of the most dangerous item in existence."

Thud nodded. "Kinda suspected as such. I reckon you already got a notion of what you want me to do with it."

"My notion is that you don't do anything at all with it. It needs to be taken directly to the Widow and handed over."

"What widow's that?" Thud asked.

"She's one of the Hermits of Grimm. She's the one that directed the gray Hermits in the making of the artifacts. She needs to know that the crown was removed from where it had been hidden and it needs to be back in the Hermit's care. The fact that Alaham had it may have deeper implications on the safety of all of the other bone artifacts. Trust me, Thud, when I say that any one of them in the wrong hands could bring another war, larger than the Daemonwars. The crown needs to be taken straight to the Godspires and delivered to the Widow in the monastery of Grimm."

Thud sucked thoughtfully on his cigar. "I imagine she'd be

pretty happy to have that back, eh? Might even bestow some sot of reward…"

"The crown is going back to her even if we have to pay her to take it," Ruby said. "But yes, I imagine that having a Hermit grateful to you will have some sort of substantial benefit."

"Well, alright then," Thud said. "We'll make for the Godspires. We'll have a little chat with Farmer Radish 'bout who he chooses to associate with then we'll stop by Karthor along the way and Durham can claim either his kingdom or his guard post. Might even turn out this Widow lady has some other artifacts she needs recoverin', eh?"

"Who was her husband?" Durham asked.

Ruby looked somber. "The man they raised as the Avatar of Grimm. Bonebin. His name before that is known only to the Widow. He was laid to rest with the rest of them, to wait. They both knew going in that it would be the end result. He sacrificed himself and his own wife had to perform the ritual that did it to him. The elves wrote a song about it."

"'Course they did," Thud said with a snort.

$$ɞɞɞ$$

The wagons were loaded, the camp packed and the oxbears harnessed. Durham had made himself a spot in the back of the lead wagon on a roll of musty carpets. Corporal Cluck was at his feet, chewing at a louse. Squitters next to her, looking like he wanted to chew on Corporal Cluck. Ruby sat on Durham's left, writing steadily in her journal. Durham imagined she had a lot to record. Thud turned to her from the front bench.

"Either of you want to say a few words to lay them folks to rest?"

Ruby stood and looked out over the ruins of Tanahael. She thought for a moment.

"You were at rest until torn from your slumber. Be at peace again." She sat back down.

"…and know that your kingdom will live again," added Durham. Thud gave him a proud smile and a satisfied nod then waved his hand in the air. Gryngo, a few hundred yards away, waved back. He stooped to the ground briefly then came toward them at a run. There was a long, anticipatory wait; long enough for Gryngo to reach them and swing up into his seat on the last wagon.

"Hot spot," he said.

The ground leapt beneath them. The oxbears had just

enough time to give a few unhappy growls before a sound like a distant roll of thunder reached them. After about ten anticlimactic seconds Durham saw the center of the ruins slowly fold together then sink down into the ground. The broken pillars and buildings around them followed suite, tipping toward the center and then sliding down, expanding out in a ring, the ground tumbling with shocking speed. Durham caught a glimpse of a great dark hole appearing in the center of the collapse before a massive billowing cloud of dust rose, obscuring the view of the last remnants of the city of Tanahael. A massive crater had taken its place, three quarters of a mile across and a quarter mile deep. The dwarves watched in silence as the cloud of dust lifted and was caught by the breeze, stretching out across the horizon, turning the afternoon sun into a smoky ball of sullen red.

Squitters barked.

"That's going to confuse the hell out of the next adventurers that come along to explore Tanahael," Nibbly said from the seat next to Thud.

Thud chuckled. He produced the boiled egg that was Alaham from inside his vest. Gammi had painted a friendly looking skull on the side of the egg to make sure that he didn't mix it up with the eggs that didn't have boiled necromancer lich kings inside of them. He set the egg upright in a knothole atop the wagon's forewall, with the skull facing forward.

"Whaddaya say, Hamenegg?" Thud said. "Let's go have an adventure."

Afterword

I'm going to make an assumption here, so bear with me for just a moment. That assumption is that you reached this afterword by means of finishing the story rather than, say, jumping here midway through chapter two. As such, I'm going to make the further assumption that you have an interest in hearing more of the exploits of the Dungeoneers. Well, have I got news for you! But not here. You can subscribe to Dungeoneers news at my website. Don't worry — any emails I send will be along the lines of "New Book Coming Out!" rather than "Ten Dwarven Beard-Care Tips. You Won't Believe Number 8!". If you'd like the news plus a bit extra you can also track me down on Twitter. Hope to see you there!

I'd like to thank my beta readers — a role people are more happy to sign up for than to actually do. Hopefully they'll forgive me for any of their advice that ended up ignored and gloat about the mess that the book would have been without them.

Made in the USA
Las Vegas, NV
15 August 2021

28234992R00184